D0810160

MRS PEPPERPOT
OMNIBUS

Alf Prøysen

MRS PEPPERPOT OMNIBUS

LEOPARD

This edition published in 1995 by Leopard Books,
an imprint of Random House, 20 Vauxhall Bridge Road, London SW1V 2SA

The following stories were first published in an omnibus edition
by Hutchinson & Co. Ltd. in 1966
Copyright © Alf Prøysen 1966
'Little Old Mrs. Pepperpot'; 'Mrs. Pepperpot and the Mechanical Doll'; 'Mr. Pepperpot
Buys Macaroni'; 'Queen of the Crows'; 'Mrs Pepperpot at the Bazaar'; 'Mr. Puffblow's Hat;
'Miriam-from-America'; 'Jumping Jack and his Friends';'The Potato with Big Ideas'; 'The
Mice and the Christmas Tree'; 'Never Take No for an Answer'; 'Mr. Learn-a-lot and the
Singing Midges'; 'Mrs Pepperpot Tries to Please her Husband'; 'Mrs. Pepperpot Minds the
Baby'; 'Mrs. Pepperpot's Penny Watchman'; 'The Bad Luck Story'; 'Mrs. Pepperpot and the
Moose'; 'Mrs. Pepperpot Finds a Hidden Treasure'; 'Mr. Big Toe's Journey'; 'A Concertina
Concert'; 'A Birthday Party in Topsy Turvy Town'; 'Father Christmas and the Carpenter";
"Mrs. Pepperpot to the Rescue';'Mrs. Pepperpot on the Warpath'; 'The Nature Lesson';
'The Shoemaker's Doll'; 'Mrs. Pepperpot is taken for a Witch'; 'The Little Mouse who was
Very Clever'; 'Mrs. Pepperpot's Birthday';'The Dancing Bees'; 'How the King Learned to
Eat Porridge'; 'Mrs. Pepperpot Turns Fortune-Teller'.
The following stories were first published by Hutchinson Junior Books Ltd. in 1968
Copyright © Alf Prøysen 1968
'Mrs. Pepperpot in the Magic Wood'; 'Mrs. Pepperpot and the Puppet Show'; 'Midsummer
Eve with the Ogres'; 'Mrs Pepperpot and the Baby Crow'; 'Mrs. Pepperpot Learns to Swim';
'Mrs. Pepperpot Gives a Party'; 'Sir Mark the Valiant'; 'Mrs. Pepperpot Turns Detective';
'Mrs. Pepperpot and the Brooch Hunt'.
The following stories were first published by Hutchinson Junior Books Ltd. in 1971
Copyright © Alf Prøysen 1971
'Mrs. Pepperpot's Outing'; 'Mrs. Pepperpot has a Visitor from America';'Gapy Gob Gets a
Letter from the King'; 'Mrs. Pepperpot and the Budgerigar'.
The following stories were first published by Hutchinson Junior Books Ltd. in 1973
Copyright © Alf Prøysen 1973
'The New Year's Eve Adventure'; 'Fate and Mrs. Pepperpot'; 'Mrs. Pepperpot Helps Arne';
'Spring Cleaning'; 'Easter Chicks'; 'The Cuckoo'; 'Midsummer Romance'; 'Mrs. Pepperpot
and the Pedlar'; 'The Moose Hunt'; 'Mr. Pepperpot and the Weather'; 'Mrs Pepperpot in
Hospital'; 'Mrs. Pepperpot's Christmas'.
ISBN 0 7529 0131 1
Printed and bound in Great Britain by Mackays of Chatham

Little old Mrs. Pepperpot

THERE was once an old woman who went to bed at night as old women usually do, and in the morning she woke up as old women usually do. But on this particular morning she found herself shrunk to the size of a pepperpot, and old women don't usually do that. The odd thing was, her name really was Mrs. Pepperpot.

'Well, as I'm now the size of a pepperpot, I shall have to make the best of it,' she said to herself, for she had no one else to talk to; her husband was out in the fields and all her children were grown up and gone away.

Now she happened to have a great deal to do that day. First of all she had to clean the house, then there was all the washing which was lying in soak and waiting to be done, and lastly she had to make pancakes for supper.

'I must get out of bed somehow,' she thought, and, taking hold of a corner of the eiderdown, she started rolling herself up in it. She rolled and rolled until the eiderdown was like a huge sausage, which fell softly on the floor. Mrs. Pepperpot crawled out and she hadn't hurt herself a bit.

The first job was to clean the house, but that was quite easy; she just sat down in front of a mouse-hole and squeaked till the mouse came out.

'Clean the house from top to bottom,' she said, 'or I'll tell the cat about you.' So the mouse cleaned the house from top to bottom.

Mrs. Pepperpot called the cat: 'Puss! Puss! Lick out all the plates and dishes or I'll tell the dog about you.' And the cat licked all the plates and dishes clean.

Then the old woman called the dog. 'Listen, dog; you make the bed and open the window and I'll give you a bone as a reward.' So the dog did as he was told, and when he had finished he sat down on the front door-step and waved his tail so hard he made the step shine like a mirror.

'You'll have to get the bone yourself,' said Mrs. Pepperpot, 'I haven't time to wait on people.' She pointed to the window-sill where a large bone lay.

After this she wanted to start her washing. She had put it to soak in the brook, but the brook was almost dry. So she sat down and started muttering in a discontented sort of way:

'I have lived a long time, but in all my born days I never saw the brook so dry. If we don't have a shower soon, I expect everyone will die of thirst.' Over and over again she said it, all the time looking up at the sky.

At last the raincloud in the sky got so angry that it decided to drown the old woman altogether. But she crawled under a monk's-hood flower, where she stayed snug and warm while the rain poured down and rinsed her clothes clean in the brook.

Now the old woman started muttering again: 'I have lived a long time, but in all my born days I have never known such a feeble South Wind as we have had lately. I'm sure if the South Wind started blowing this minute it couldn't lift me off the ground, even though I am no bigger than a pepperpot.'

The South Wind heard this and instantly came tearing along, but Mrs. Pepperpot hid in an empty badger set, and from there she watched the South Wind blow all the clothes right up on to her clothes-line.

Again she started muttering: 'I have lived a long time, but in all my born days I have never seen the sun give so little heat in the middle of the summer. It seems to have lost all its power, that's a fact.'

When the sun heard this it turned scarlet with rage and sent down fiery rays to give the old woman sunstroke. But by this time she was safely back in her house, and was sailing about the sink in a saucer. Meanwhile the furious sun dried all the clothes on the line.

'Now for cooking the supper,' said Mrs. Pepperpot; 'my husband will be back in an hour and, by hook or by crook, thirty pancakes must be ready on the table.'

She had mixed the dough for the pancakes in a bowl the day before. Now she sat down beside the bowl and said: 'I have always been fond of you, bowl, and I've told all the neighbours that there's not a bowl like you anywhere. I am sure, if you really wanted to, you could walk straight over to the cooking-stove and turn it on.'

And the bowl went straight over to the stove and turned it on.

Then Mrs. Pepperpot said: 'I'll never forget the day I bought my frying-pan. There were lots of pans in the shop, but I said: "If I can't have that pan hanging right over the shop assistant's head, I won't buy any pan at all. For that is the best pan in the whole world, and I'm sure if I were ever in trouble that pan could jump on to the stove by itself." '

And there and then the frying-pan jumped on to the stove. And when it was hot enough, the bowl tilted itself to let the dough run on to the pan.

Then the old woman said: 'I once read a fairy-tale about a pancake which could roll along the road. It was the stupidest story that ever I read. But I'm sure the pancake on the pan could easily turn a somersault in the air if it really wanted to.'

At this the pancake took a great leap from sheer pride and turned a somersault as Mrs. Pepperpot had said. Not only one pancake, but *all* the pancakes did this, and the bowl went on tilting and the pan went on frying until, before the hour was up, there were thirty pancakes on the dish.

Then Mr. Pepperpot came home. And, just as he opened the door, Mrs. Pepperpot turned back to her usual size. So they sat down and ate their supper.

And the old woman said nothing about having been as small as a pepperpot, because old women don't usually talk about such things.

Mrs. Pepperpot and the mechanical doll

IT WAS two days before Christmas. Mrs. Pepperpot hummed and sang as she trotted round her kitchen, she was so pleased to be finished with all her Christmas preparations. The pig had been killed, the sausages made, and now all she had to do was to brew herself a cup of coffee and sit down for a little rest.

'How lovely that Christmas is here,' she said, 'then everybody's happy—especially the children—that's the best of all; to see them happy and well.'

The old woman was almost like a child herself because of this knack she had of suddenly shrinking to the size of a pepperpot.

She was thinking about all this while she was making her coffee, and she had just poured it into the cup when there was a knock at the door.

'Come in,' she said, and in came a little girl who was oh! so pale and thin.

'Poor child! Wherever do you live—I'm sure I've never seen you before,' said Mrs. Pepperpot.

'I'm Hannah. I live in the little cottage at the edge of

the forest,' said the child, 'and I'm just going round to all the houses to ask if anybody has any old Christmas decorations left over from last year—glitter or paper-chains or glass balls or anything, you know. Have *you* got anything you don't need?'

'I expect so, Hannah,' answered Mrs. Pepperpot, and went up into the attic to fetch the cardboard box with all the decorations. She gave it to the little girl.

'How lovely! Can I really have all that?'

'You can,' said Mrs. Pepperpot, 'and you shall have something else as well. Tomorrow I will bring you a big doll.'

'I don't believe that,' said Hannah.

'Why not?'

'You haven't *got* a doll.'

'That's simple; I'll buy one,' said Mrs. Pepperpot. 'I'll bring it over tomorrow afternoon, but I must be home by six o'clock because it's Christmas Eve.'

'How wonderful if you can come tomorrow afternoon—I shall be all alone. Father and Mother both go out to work, you see, and they don't get back until the church bells have rung.'

So the little girl went home, and Mrs. Pepperpot went down to the toy-shop and bought a big doll. But when she woke up next morning there she was, once more, no bigger than a pepperpot.

'How provoking!' she said to herself. 'On this day of all days, when I have to take the doll to Hannah. Never mind! I expect I'll manage.'

After she had dressed she tried to pick up the doll, but it was much too heavy for her to lift.

'I'll have to go without it,' she thought, and opened the door to set off.

But oh dear! it had been snowing hard all night, and the little old woman soon sank deep in the snowdrifts. The cat was sitting in front of the house; when she saw something moving in the snow she thought it was a mouse and jumped on it.

'Hi, stop!' shouted Mrs. Pepperpot. 'Keep your claws to yourself! Can't you see it's just me shrunk again?'

'I beg your pardon,' said the cat, and started walking away.

'Wait a minute,' said Mrs. Pepperpot, 'to make up for your mistake you can give me a ride down to the main road.' The cat was quite willing, so she lay down and let the little old woman climb on her back. When they got to the main road the cat stopped. 'Can you hear anything?' asked Mrs. Pepperpot.

'Yes, I think it's the snow-plough,' said the cat, 'so we'll have to get out of the way, or we'll be buried in snow.'

'I don't want to get out of the way,' said Mrs. Pepper-pot, and she sat down in the middle of the road and waited till the snow-plough was right in front of her; then she jumped up and landed smack on the front tip of the plough.

There she sat, clinging on for dear life and enjoying herself hugely. 'Look at me, the little old woman, driving the snow-plough!' she laughed.

When the snow-plough had almost reached the door of Hannah's little cottage, she climbed on to the edge nearest the side of the road and, before you could say Jack Robinson, she had landed safely on the great mound of snow thrown up by the plough. From there she could walk right across Hannah's hedge and slide down the other side. She was shaking the snow off her clothes on the doorstep when Hannah came out and picked her up.

'Are you one of those mechanical dolls that you wind up?' asked Hannah.

'No,' said Mrs. Pepperpot, 'I am a woman who can wind myself up, thank you very much. Help me brush off all the snow and then let's go inside.'

'Are you perhaps the old woman who shrinks to the size of a pepperpot?'

'Of course I am, silly.'

'Where's the doll you were going to bring me?' asked Hannah when they got inside.

'I've got it at home. You'll have to go back with me and fetch it. It's too heavy for me.'

'Shouldn't you have something to eat, now that you've come to see me? Would you like a biscuit?' And the little girl held out a biscuit in the shape of a ring.

'Thank you very much,' said Mrs. Pepperpot and popped her head through the biscuit ring.

Oh, how the little girl laughed! 'I quite forgot you were so small,' she said; 'let me break it into little pieces so that you can eat it.' Then she fetched a thimble and filled it with fruit juice. 'Have a drink,' she said.

'Thank you,' said Mrs. Pepperpot.

After that they played a lot of good games; ride-a-cock-horse with Mrs. Pepperpot sitting on Hannah's knee, and hide-and-seek. But the little girl had an awful time trying to find Mrs. Pepperpot—she hid in such awkward places. When they had finished playing Hannah put on her coat and with Mrs. Pepperpot in her pocket she went off to fetch her beautiful big doll.

'Oh, thank you!' she exclaimed when she saw it. 'But do you know,' she added, 'I would really rather have *you* to play with all the time.'

'You can come and see me again if you like,' said Mrs. Pepperpot, 'I am often as small as a pepperpot, and then it's nice to have a little help around the house. And, of course, we can play games as well.'

22

So now the little girl often spends her time with Mrs. Pepperpot. She looks ever so much better, and they often talk about the day Mrs. Pepperpot arrived on the snow-plough, and about the doll she gave Hannah.

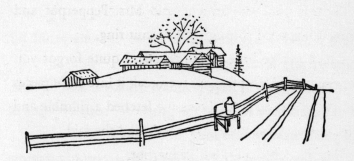

Mr. Pepperpot buys macaroni

'It's a very long time since we've had macaroni for supper,' said Mr. Pepperpot one day.

'Then you shall have it today, my love,' said his wife. 'But I shall have to go to the grocer for some. So first of all you'll have to find me.'

'Find you?' said Mr. Pepperpot. 'What sort of nonsense is that?' But when he looked round for her he couldn't see her anywhere. 'Don't be silly, wife,' he said; 'if you're hiding in the cupboard you must come out this minute. We're too big to play hide-and-seek.'

'*I'm* not too big, I'm just the right size for "hunt-the-pepperpot",' laughed Mrs. Pepperpot. 'Find me if you can!'

'I'm not going to charge round my own bedroom looking for my wife,' he said crossly.

'Now, now! I'll help you; I'll tell you when you're warm. Just now you're very cold.' For Mr. Pepperpot was peering out of the window, thinking she might have jumped out. As he searched round the room she called out 'Warm!', 'Colder!', 'Getting hotter!' until he was quite dizzy.

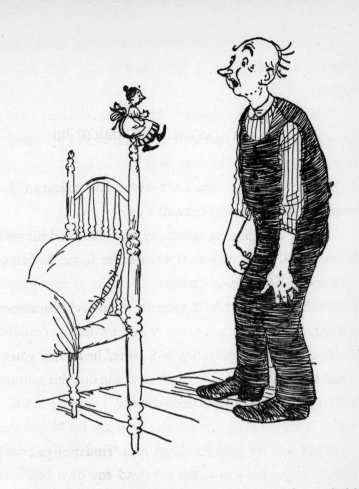

At last she shouted, 'You'll burn the top of your bald head if you don't look up!' And there she was, sitting on the bedpost, swinging her legs and laughing at him.

Her husband pulled a very long face when he saw her. 'This is a bad business—a very bad business,' he said, stroking her cheek with his little finger.

'I don't think it's a bad business,' said Mrs. Pepperpot.

'I shall have a terrible time. The whole town will laugh when they see I have a wife the size of a pepperpot.'

'Who cares?' she answered. 'That doesn't matter a bit. Now put me down on the floor so that I can get ready to go to the grocer and buy your macaroni.'

But her husband wouldn't hear of her going; he would go to the grocer himself.

'That'll be a lot of use!' she said. 'When you get home you'll have forgotten to buy the macaroni. I'm sure even if I wrote "macaroni" right across your forehead you'd bring back cinnamon and salt herrings instead.'

'But how are you going to walk all that way with those tiny legs?'

'Put me in your coat pocket; then I won't need to walk.'

There was no help for it, so Mr. Pepperpot put his wife in his pocket and set off for the shop.

Soon she started talking: "My goodness me, what a lot of strange things you have in your pocket—screws and nails, tobacco and matches—there's even a fish-hook! You'll have to take that out at once; I might get it caught in my skirt.'

'Don't talk so loud,' said her husband as he took out the fish-hook. 'We're going into the shop now.'

It was an old-fashioned village store where they sold everything from prunes to coffee cups. The grocer was particularly proud of the coffee cups and held one up for Mr. Pepperpot to see. This made his wife curious and she popped her head out of his pocket.

'You stay where you are!' whispered Mr. Pepperpot.

'I beg your pardon, did you say anything?' asked the grocer.

'No, no, I was just humming a little tune,' said Mr. Pepperpot. 'Tra-la-la!'

'What colour are the cups?' whispered his wife. And her husband sang:

> 'The cups are blue
> With gold edge too,
> But they cost too much
> So that won't do!'

After that Mrs. Pepperpot kept quiet—but not for long. When her husband pulled out his tobacco tin she couldn't resist hanging on to the lid. Neither her husband nor anyone else in the shop noticed her slipping on to the counter and hiding behind a flour-bag. From there she darted silently across to the scales, crawled under them, past a pair of kippers wrapped in newspaper, and found herself next to the coffee cups.

'Aren't they pretty!' she whispered, and took a step backwards to get a better view. Whoops! She fell right into the macaroni drawer which had been left open. She hastily covered herself up with macaroni, but the grocer heard the scratching noise and quickly banged the drawer shut. You see, it did sometimes happen that mice got in the drawers, and that's not the sort of thing you want people to know about, so the grocer pretended nothing had happened and went on serving.

There was Mrs. Pepperpot all in the dark; she could hear the grocer serving her husband now. 'That's good,' she thought. 'When he orders macaroni I'll get my chance to slip into the bag with it.'

But it was just as she had feared; her husband forgot what he had come to buy. Mrs. Pepperpot shouted at the top of her voice, 'MACARONI!', but it was impossible to get him to hear.

'A quarter of a pound of coffee, please,' said her husband.

'Anything else?' asked the grocer.

'MACARONI!' shouted Mrs. Pepperpot.

'Two pounds of sugar,' said her husband.

'Anything more?'

'MACARONI!' shouted Mrs. Pepperpot.

But at last her husband remembered the macaroni of his own accord. The grocer hurriedly filled a bag. He thought he felt something move, but he didn't say a word.

'That's all, thank you,' said Mr. Pepperpot. When he got outside the door he was just about to make sure his

wife was still in his pocket when a van drew up and offered to give him a lift all the way home. Once there he took off his knapsack with all the shopping in it and put his hand in his pocket to lift out his wife.

The pocket was empty.

Now he was really frightened. First he thought she was teasing him, but when he had called three times and still no wife appeared, he put on his hat again and hurried back to the shop.

The grocer saw him coming. 'He's probably going to complain about the mouse in the macaroni,' he thought.

'Have you forgotten anything, Mr. Pepperpot?' he asked, and smiled as pleasantly as he could.

Mr. Pepperpot was looking all round. 'Yes,' he said.

'I would be very grateful, Mr. Pepperpot, if you would keep it to yourself about the mouse being in the macaroni. I'll let you have these fine blue coffee cups if you'll say no more about it.'

'Mouse?' Mr. Pepperpot looked puzzled.

'Shh!' said the grocer, and hurriedly started wrapping up the cups.

Then Mr. Pepperpot realized that the grocer had mistaken his wife for a mouse. So he took the cups and rushed home as fast as he could. By the time he got there he was in a sweat of fear that his wife might have been squeezed to death in the macaroni bag.

'Oh, my dear wife,' he muttered to himself. 'My poor darling wife. I'll never again be ashamed of you being the size of a pepperpot—as long as you're still alive!'

When he opened the door she was standing by the cooking-stove, dishing up the macaroni—as large as life; in fact, as large as you or I.

Queen of the Crows

DID you know that the woman who was as small as a pepperpot was queen of all the crows in the forest?

No, of course you didn't, because it was a secret between Mrs. Pepperpot and me until now. But now I'm going to tell you how it happened.

Outside the old woman's house there was a wooden fence and on it used to sit a large crow.

'I can't understand why that crow has to sit there staring in at the kitchen window all the time,' said Mr. Pepperpot.

'I can't imagine,' said Mrs. Pepperpot. 'Shoo! Get along with you!'

But the crow didn't move from the fence.

Then one day Mrs. Pepperpot had her shrinking turn again (I can't remember now what she was supposed to be doing that day, but she was very busy), and by the time she had clambered over the doorstep she was quite out of breath.

'Oh dear, it's certainly hard to be so small,' she puffed.

Suddenly there was a sound of flapping wings and the

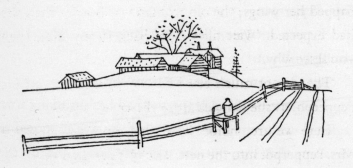

crow swooped down, picked up Mrs. Pepperpot by her skirt and flew up over the highest fir trees in the forest with her.

'What's the idea, may I ask? You wait till I'm back to my proper size and I'll beat you with my birch rod and chase you off for good!'

'Caw-caw! You're small enough now, at any rate,' said the crow; 'I've waited a long time for this. I saw you turn small once before, you see, so I thought it might happen again. And here we are, but only just in time. Today is the Crows' Festival and *I'm* to be Queen of the Crows!'

'If you're to be Queen of the Crows, you surely don't need to take an old woman like me along?'

'That's just where you're wrong,' said the crow, and flapped her wings; the old woman was heavier than she had expected. 'Wait till we get back to my nest, then you'll see why.'

'There's not much else I *can* do,' thought poor Mrs. Pepperpot as she dangled from the crow's claws.

'Here we are; home!' said the crow, and dropped Mrs. Pepperpot into the nest. 'Lucky it's empty.'

'It certainly is; I fell right on a spiky twig and grazed my shinbone.'

'Poor little thing!' said the crow. 'But look, I've made you a lovely bed of feathers and down. You'll find the

35

down very snug and warm, and the feathers are just the thing when night falls and the wind begins to blow.'

'What do I want with feathers and down?'

'I want you to lie down and go to sleep,' said the crow. 'But first you must lend me your clothes. So please take off your head-scarf now, and your blouse and your skirt.

'The scarf I want you to tie round my neck, the skirt goes on one wing and the blouse on the other. Then I shall fly to the clearing in the forest where all the crows are meeting for the Festival. The finest-looking crow will be chosen queen, and that's going to be me! When I win I'll think of you. Caw-caw!'

'Well, if you think you'll be any better looking in my old clothes, you're welcome,' said Mrs. Pepperpot as she dressed up the crow.

'Hurry, hurry!' said the crow. 'There's another crow living over there in that fir tree on the hill. She'll be dropping in here on her way; we were going to the Festival together. But now that I'm all dressed up I'd rather go alone. Caw-caw-caw!' And off she flew.

Mrs. Pepperpot sat shivering in her petticoat, but then she thought of burrowing deep under the feathers and down as the crow had told her to do, and she found she was soon warm and cosy.

Suddenly the whole branch started swaying, and on the end perched a huge crow.

'Mary Crow, are you at home?' croaked the crow, sidling up and poking her big beak over the edge of the nest.

'Mary Crow has gone to the Festival,' said Mrs. Pepperpot.

'Then who are you, who are you?' asked the crow.

'I'm just an old woman shivering with cold, because Mary Crow has borrowed my clothes.'

'Caw-caw! Oh blow! She'll be the finest-looking crow at the Festival,' shrieked the crow as she threw herself into the air from the branch. 'But I'll have the scarf off her!'

Mrs. Pepperpot lay down to sleep again. Suddenly she rolled right over into the corner of the nest, the branch was shaking so much.

'That'll be another crow,' she thought, and quite right, it was; the biggest crow she had ever seen was swinging on the tip of the branch.

'Mary Crow, Mary Crow, have you seen Betty Crow?'

'I've seen both Mary Crow *and* Betty Crow,' said Mrs. Pepperpot.

'Who are you, who are you?' squawked the crow.

'I'm just an old woman shivering with cold because Mary Crow has borrowed my clothes.'

'Caw-caw! What a bore! Now Mary Crow will be the best-looking crow.'

'I'm not so sure about that,' said the old woman, 'because Betty Crow flew after Mary Crow and was going to have the scarf off her.'

'I'll take the skirt, I'll take the skirt!' croaked the biggest crow, and took off from the branch with such a bound that Mrs. Pepperpot had to hold on tight not to get thrown out of the nest.

In the clearing in the forest there were lots and lots of crows. They sat round in a circle and, one by one, they hopped into the middle to show themselves. Some of the crows could hop on one leg without touching the ground with their wings. Others had different kinds of tricks, and the crows sitting round had to choose the best one to be their queen.

At last there were only three crows left. They sat well away from each other, polishing their feathers and looking very fierce indeed. One had a scarf, the second had a skirt and the third had a blouse. So you can guess which crows *they* were. One of them was to be chosen queen.

'The crow with the scarf round her neck is the best,' said some of the crows, 'she looks most like a human being.'

'No, no; the crow with the skirt looks best!'

'Not at all! The crow with the blouse looks **most** dignified, and a queen should be dignified.'

Suddenly something fell with a bump to the ground; the jay had arrived right in the middle of the Festival with a strange-looking bird in its beak.

'Caw-caw! The jay has no business to be here!' croaked all the crows.

'I won't stay a minute,' said the jay. 'I've just brought you your queen!' and he flew off.

All the crows stared at the strange little raggedy bird in the middle of the ring. They could see it was covered in crow's feathers and down, but raggedy crows could not be allowed at the Festival.

'It's against the law!' said the biggest crow.

'Let's peck it, let's peck it!' said Mary Crow.

'Yes, let's hack it to pieces!' said Betty Crow.

'Yes, yes!' croaked all the crows. 'We can't have raggedy birds here!'

'Wait a minute!' said the raggedy bird, and climbed on to a tree-stump. 'I'll sing you a song.' And before they could stop it, it started singing 'Who Killed Cock Robin?' And it knew all the verses. The crows were delighted; they clapped and flapped their wings till the raggedy bird lost nearly all its feathers.

'D'you know any more? D'you know any more?' they croaked.

'I can dance the polka,' said the raggedy bird, and danced round the circle till they were all out of breath.

'You shall be our Queen!' they all shouted. 'Four Court Crows will carry you wherever you wish to go.'

'How wonderful!' laughed the Queen of the Crows. 'Then they must carry me to the house over there by the edge of the forest.'

'What would Your Majesty like to wear?'

'I would like to wear a skirt, a blouse and a head-scarf,' said the Queen.

Much later that night there was a knock at the cottage door. Mr. Pepperpot opened it, and there stood his wife.

'You're very late, wife,' he said. 'Where have you been?'

'I've been to a Festival,' she answered.

'But why are you covered in feathers?'

'You just go to bed and don't trouble yourself,' said Mrs. Pepperpot. She went over and stuck a feather in the corner of the window.

'Why do you do that?' asked her husband.

'For no reason at all.'

But she really did it because she had been chosen Queen of the Crows.

Mrs. Pepperpot at the bazaar

ONE day Mrs. Pepperpot was alone in her kitchen. At least, she was not *quite* alone, because Hannah, the little girl who had had the doll for Christmas, was there as well. She was busy scraping out a bowl and licking the spoon, for the old woman had been making gingerbread shapes.

There was a knock at the door. Mrs. Pepperpot said, 'Come in.' And in walked three very smart ladies.

'Good afternoon,' said the smart ladies. 'We are collecting prizes for the lottery at the school bazaar this evening. Do you think you have some little thing we could have? The money from the bazaar is for the boys' brass band—they need new instruments.'

'Oh, I'd like to help with that,' said Mrs. Pepperpot, for she dearly loved brass bands. 'Would a plate of gingerbread be any use?'

'Of course,' said the smart ladies, but they laughed behind her back. 'We could take it with us now if you have it ready,' they said. But Mrs. Pepperpot wanted to go to the bazaar herself, so she said she would bring the gingerbread.

So the three smart ladies went away and Mrs. Pepperpot was very proud and pleased that she was going to a bazaar.

Hannah was still scraping away at the bowl and licking the sweet mixture from the spoon.

'May I come with you?' she asked.

'Certainly, if your father and mother will let you.'

'I'm sure they will,' said the child, 'because Father has to work at the factory and Mother is at her sewing all day.'

'Be here at six o'clock then,' said Mrs. Pepperpot, and started making another batch of gingerbread shapes.

But when Hannah came back at six the old woman was not there. All the doors were open, so she went from room to room, calling her. When she got back to the kitchen she heard an odd noise coming from the table. The mixing bowl was upside down, so she lifted it carefully. And there underneath sat her friend who was now again as small as a pepperpot.

'Isn't this a nuisance?' said Mrs. Pepperpot. 'I was just cleaning out the bowl after putting the gingerbread in the oven when I suddenly started shrinking. Then the bowl turned over on me. Quick! Get the cakes out of the oven before they burn!'

43

But it was too late; the gingerbread was burnt to a cinder.

Mrs. Pepperpot sat down and cried, she was so disappointed. But she soon gave that up and started thinking instead. Suddenly she laughed out loud and said:

'Hannah! Put me under the tap and give me a good wash. We're going to the bazaar, you and I!'

'But you can't go to the bazaar like that!' said Hannah.

'Oh yes, I can,' said Mrs. Pepperpot, 'as long as you do what I say.'

Hannah promised, but Mrs. Pepperpot gave her some very queer orders. First she was to fetch a silk ribbon and tie it round the old woman so that it looked like a skirt. Then she was to fetch some tinsel from the Christmas decorations. This she had to wind round and round to make a silver bodice. And lastly she had to make a bonnet of gold foil.

'Now you must wrap me carefully in cellophane and put me in a cardboard box,' said Mrs. Pepperpot.

'Why?' asked Hannah.

'When I've promised them a prize for the bazaar they must have it,' said Mrs. Pepperpot, 'so I'm giving them myself. Just put me down on one of the tables and say you've brought a mechanical doll. Tell them you keep the key in your pocket and then pretend to wind me up so that people can see how clever I am.'

Hannah did as she was told, and when she got to the

bazaar and put the wonderful doll on the table, many people clapped their hands and crowded round to see.

'What a pretty doll!' they said. 'And what a lovely dress!'

'Look at her gold bonnet!'

Mrs. Pepperpot lay absolutely still in her cardboard box, but when she heard how everybody praised her, she winked at Hannah with one eye, and Hannah knew what she wanted. She lifted Mrs. Pepperpot very carefully out of the box and pretended to wind her up at the back with a key.

Everyone was watching her. But when Mrs. Pepperpot began walking across the table, picking her way through the prizes, there was great excitement.

'Look, the doll can walk!'

And when Mrs. Pepperpot began to dance they started shouting and yelling with delight, 'The doll is dancing!'

The three smart ladies who had been to see Mrs. Pepperpot earlier in the day sat in special seats and looked very grand. One of them had given six expensive coffee cups, the second an elegant table mat and the third a beautiful iced layer cake.

Mrs. Pepperpot decided to go over and speak to them, for she was afraid they had recognized her and thought it queer that she hadn't brought the gingerbread.

The three smart ladies were very pleased when the doll came walking across the table to them.

'Come to me!' said the one who had given the coffee cups, and stretched her hand out towards Mrs. Pepperpot, who walked on to it obediently.

'Let me hold her a little,' said the lady with the elegant table mat, and Mrs. Pepperpot went over to her hand.

'Now it's my turn,' said the lady with the iced cake.

'I'm sure they know it's me,' thought Mrs. Pepperpot, 'that's why they stare at me so hard and hold me on their hands.'

But then the lady with the cake said, 'Well, I must say, this is a much better prize than the gingerbread that the odd old woman offered us today.'

Now she should never have said that; Mrs. Pepperpot leaped straight out of her hand and landed PLOP! right in the middle of the beautiful iced layer cake. Then she got up and waded right through it. The cake lady screamed, but people were shouting with laughter by now.

'Take that doll away!' shrieked the second lady, but *squish, squash!* went Mrs. Pepperpot's sticky feet, right across her lovely table mat.

'Get that dreadful doll away!' cried the third lady. But it was too late; Mrs. Pepperpot was on the tray with

the expensive coffee cups, and began to dance a jig. Cups and saucers flew about and broke in little pieces.

What a-to-do! The conductor of the brass band had quite a job to quieten them all down. He announced that the winning numbers of the lottery would be given out.

'First prize will be the wonderful mechanical doll,' he said.

When Hannah heard that she was very frightened. What would happen if somebody won Mrs. Pepperpot, so that she couldn't go home to her husband? She tugged at Mrs. Pepperpot's skirt and whispered, 'Shall I put you in my pocket and creep away?'

'No,' said Mrs. Pepperpot.

'But think how awful it would be if someone won you and took you home.'

'What must be must be!' said Mrs. Pepperpot.

The conductor called out the winning number, '311!' Everyone looked at their tickets, but no one had number 311.

'That's a good thing!' sighed Hannah with relief. There would have to be another draw. But just then she remembered she had a ticket in her hand; it was number 311!

'Wait!' she cried, and showed her ticket. The conductor looked at it and saw it was the right one.

So Hannah was allowed to take Mrs. Pepperpot home.

Next day the old woman was her proper size again and Hannah only a little girl, and Mrs. Pepperpot said, 'You're my little girl, aren't you?'

'Yes,' said Hannah, 'and you're my very own Mrs. Pepperpot, because I won you at the bazaar yesterday.'

And that was the end of Mrs. Pepperpot's adventures for a very long time.

Mr. Puffblow's hat

THERE was once a man called Mr. Puffblow who had an enormous hat. Mr. Puffblow was a very severe sort of man, and when he walked down the street he used to get very angry indeed if any of the children stared at his hat. And if they as much as stopped and looked at the house where he lived he would rush out and chase them off, because he thought they wanted to steal his apples.

Nobody dared go against Mr. Puffblow. 'Ssh!' mothers would say to their children playing in the street. 'You'd better be quiet—Mr. Puffblow is coming this way!'

Every day at precisely half past eleven Mr. Puffblow walked down the street to fetch his pint of milk from the dairy. So, until *that* was over, everybody stayed indoors.

One day the West Wind came tearing through the town, and I don't think there is anything like the West Wind for upsetting things in the autumn; the mischief it gets up to is nobody's business.

Now suddenly the West Wind caught sight of Mr.

Puffblow walking down the street with his enormous hat on.

'Wheee!' said the West Wind. 'That's just the hat for me!'

So, with a puff and a blow, it tipped Mr. Puffblow's hat off his head.

The hat bowled along the pavement. Mr. Puffblow ran after it. But just as he was about to catch it, the West Wind pounced and blew it further away. This game went on for a long time until at last the West Wind carried the hat high up into the air, right over the rooftops of the town to the wood beyond.

'I'm tired of playing with you now,' said the West

Wind to the hat. 'I'm going to drop you in this brook and leave you to sink or swim. Good luck!'

The hat turned two more somersaults in the air, then plopped into the brook and floated away like a little round ship.

It so happened that a tiny fieldmouse had been out in the wood that day gathering nuts, and he had fallen into the brook. He could swim all right, but the current was so strong he was almost drowned struggling against it.

When he saw the hat sailing past he caught hold of the brim with his paws and clambered up to the top of the crown.

'This would make a very good ship,' thought the

fieldmouse. 'I wish some of the other mice could see me now.' And he gave a loud squeak.

Sure enough, another fieldmouse heard him, and when he saw the fine-looking ship he called the other mice, and in the end there were eight little fieldmice sailing along on the hat. The one who got on first was the captain, the second was his mate and the rest were the crew.

You have no idea what fun those fieldmice had with Mr. Puffblow's hat that autumn! Every day they went for a sail, and when winter came and it got too cold, they dragged the hat on to dry land and used it for a house. All through the winter they sat inside it, snug and warm, telling each other mouse fairy-tales and singing mouse carols at Christmas.

And when spring came they started sailing again.

Then one day there was a great noise and to-do in the wood. A whole crowd of children from the town were out for a picnic. There was a man with them and they were all laughing and shouting and having a fine time together. The man carried the smallest one on his shoulders while the others were clinging to his coat-tails. They picked flowers for him and showed him all the nicest things they could find in the wood on a spring day.

Suddenly they stopped by the brook. 'Look over there!' cried one of the children. 'Look at that big hat on the other bank!'

The mice had just dragged the hat out of the brook because they were going home to supper.

When the man saw the hat he laughed and laughed. Because, you see, he knew it.

Can you guess who he was? Mr. Puffblow! But a very much nicer Mr. Puffblow now, and do you know why? Well, when he used to wear that enormous hat on his head he was always afraid the children would laugh at him. But from the moment he lost the hat he became quite different; he was no longer afraid.

'There's your old hat, Mr. Puffblow!' shouted the children with glee. 'Don't you want to wear it again?'

'Certainly not!' said Mr. Puffblow. 'Come along now, children, let's pick anemones.'

So they did.

And the fieldmice are using Mr. Puffblow's hat for a ship to this day.

Miriam-from-America

THERE was once a doll who was so beautifully smart that she had to sit all day, every day, on top of a chest of drawers. She couldn't *do* anything, not even shut her eyes or stand on her feet, and her fine silk dress was sewn on to her body, so she couldn't be undressed. But there was no doubt about it; she was the grandest of all the dolls just because she sat on top of the chest of drawers.

The little girl who owned the doll never allowed her school friends to touch her. When they asked why they mustn't touch her, the little girl said:

'Don't you know that this doll is called Miriam and comes from America? What's more, she's crossed the Atlantic in a ship, and even *I*'m not allowed to touch her till I'm a big girl.'

When her friends heard this their eyes grew round with astonishment and, putting their hands behind their backs, they stood and stared at Miriam-from-America.

One day the window near the chest of drawers stood

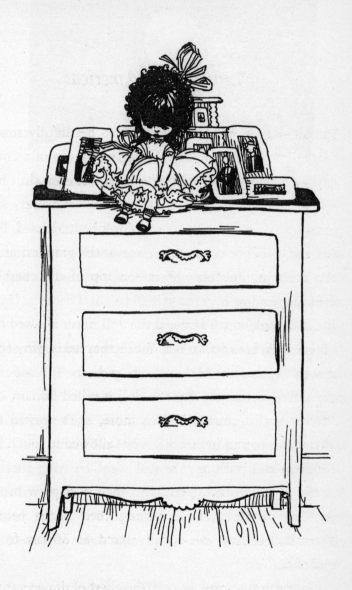

open, and someone opened the door as well so that there
was a draught. This blew Miriam off the chest straight
out of the window into the garden below. There she lay,
quite still, looking up at the sky.

It grew darker and darker, until it was late night and
the stars began to twinkle. All at once, the full moon
came sailing across the sky.

'What is that strange-looking thing in the garden?'
said the moon, and turned his light on Miriam.

Miriam said nothing; she just went on lying there.
But the wind whistled in the tree tops and answered for
her: 'That is Miriam-from-America. She is the most
elegant doll because she usually sits right on top of a
chest of drawers.'

'Can't she speak for herself?' asked the moon.

'I don't think so,' said the wind. 'Can you talk, Miriam?'

Miriam said nothing.

'Try and talk to us—just a little,' said the moon.

Miriam still didn't move, but the moon saw she wanted to say something, so he waited.

'Over the sea and under the sky!' Miriam said suddenly.

'Why do you say "over the sea and under the sky"?' asked the moon.

'Because I have sailed over the sea,' said Miriam, 'and I thought that was great fun. And now I'm lying under the sky and that is even more fun.'

'But I suppose sitting on a chest of drawers being the most elegant, the most beautiful, doll is more fun still?' said the wind.

'It's the dullest thing in the world!' said Miriam. 'Couldn't you two help me so that I don't have to be so elegant, so smart, any more?'

'That's easy,' said the wind, and blew Miriam straight into a big puddle. Miriam laughed; it was lovely to splash about in water. She had never tried that before.

'I must help too,' said the moon, and he threw a beam of light on the kennel where the dog Rover lay asleep. He woke up at once and saw Miriam lying in the puddle. So he took her smart silk dress between his

teeth and ran down the road with her. Miriam was jolted up and down, but she didn't mind a bit because she knew Rover well; she had often seen him from her chest of drawers when he lay curled up by the fire. And now here she was, having a lovely game with him!

The moon followed them down the street, and so did the wind, turning somersaults all the way. At last they came back to the house where Miriam lived. But how was she to get indoors again? The window was still open but Miriam couldn't possibly climb up to it.

'We shall have to ask the crow to carry her up in his beak,' said the moon. So they did. The crow was very ready to help. He flew through the window with Miriam and set her down on the chest of drawers.

Well, you can imagine the fuss there was next day when the little girl's mother saw what a mess Miriam was in! But the little girl was very pleased, because from now on she could play with Miriam as much as she liked. She took her for rides in the doll's pram, and every time the wind blew Miriam waved her hand—just a little bit. This was supposed to mean:

'Thank you, wind, for helping me get away from the chest of drawers!'

Jumping Jack and his friends

THE things I am going to tell you about in this story only happened last night. They happened after everyone had gone to bed; not only the little children and the big children, but the grown-ups as well.

In a shed—an ordinary kind of garden shed which people use for bicycles and shovels and rakes and spades —lived a family of toys.

There was a tricycle, a skipping rope hanging on a nail and two hop-scotch stones stuck in a crack in the floor. Almost hidden, stood a little red wheelbarrow which the children used in the sand pit, and in it lay a ball and a jumping jack. This jumping jack was so smart he had his name painted across his back in big letters: JUMPING JACK.

The toys had been in the shed all winter. They had seen the snowdrifts when the grown-ups came for shovels to clear the paths, and they had heard the wind howl and sigh. But just lately the toys had heard a new noise—a slow *drip . . . drip . . .* from the roof. Then it had turned into *drippy-drippy-drop* and at last a very quick *drip,*

drip, drip, drip, and they knew that all the snow had melted from the roof.

'Are we going out now?' asked Jumping Jack, who had never seen winter before.

'Not for a long time yet,' answered the Wheelbarrow.

One day a little boy came for the Tricycle. He got on it and pedalled out into the spring sunshine, ringing his bell loudly.

'Will it be our turn next?' asked Jumping Jack.

'Not yet,' said the Wheelbarrow.

Then a little girl, whose name was Cathy, came into the shed. 'Look, there's my ball!' she shouted, and hugged the Ball tightly. But it sagged and made a hissing noise because it had a split in its rubber tummy.

'Oh, you horrid Ball!' Cathy cried, and threw it back in the Wheelbarrow. Instead she took the Skipping Rope and ran out with it into the sunshine. She jumped and skipped so hard her hair stood out like a halo round her head.

'Why didn't she take the Ball with her?' asked Jumping Jack. But the Wheelbarrow only said 'Hmm.' It didn't want to be unkind to the poor Ball.

Nothing more was said. But a few days later they could hear a bouncing noise outside the shed; *bump-bump* it went against the wall, and the Wheelbarrow knew what that meant. So did the Old Ball; it lay there sighing through its crack all day long.

The Wheelbarrow thought about this for a long time —several days and nights. Then last night, after everyone had gone to bed, as I said, it gave a wooden creak and said to the Old Ball:

'I think it's a shame you're never to go out in the sunshine again. And I'm sorry to have to be the one to tell you, but you do understand, don't you, that Cathy has got a new ball and she's forgotten about you?'

'Yes,' sighed the Old Ball.

'I don't think Peter has forgotten *me*,' said Jumping Jack; 'he made such a fuss of me last summer. Anyway, it was just a mistake my being put out here in the shed. It was the charlady who carried all the summer toys out here when the snow came, and she didn't notice I'd got mixed up with them. I've been jumping mad ever since!'

'There's no need to get hoity-toity and stick your nose in the air even if you were only made last summer. You never know how long you will last. I've seen many jumping jacks in my time. They're fine as long as the strings don't break and both arms and legs are working. But sooner or later something gets broken and that's the end of that. . . . Well, not always, of course!' he added quickly when he saw that Jumping Jack looked quite frightened and ready to cry.

'I'm not at all perfect myself,' the Wheelbarrow went on. 'There's a weakness in one of my arms. The carpenter, who made me, put a thick layer of paint over the crack, so that it wouldn't show. But I've often been afraid when Peter filled me up with sand. Last year, I almost broke several times, so I don't think he'll use me again when summer comes along.'

'What a shame!' wheezed the Old Ball. He was sorry for the Wheelbarrow, but pleased at the same time that he wouldn't be left all alone in the dark shed.

'Then it's just me who is going out in the sunshine,' said Jumping Jack in a cheeky sort of way.

'You ought to be ashamed of yourself!' said the Wheelbarrow. 'We're all in the same boat—or rather, you and the Old Ball are in the same barrow, and that barrow happens to be me. And now I'm going to tell you what we're going to do—we three.'

'Do? What can we three do?' asked Jumping Jack.

'Listen. A long time ago there was an old wheelbarrow in here which told me that a night would come
when all old broken or unwanted toys would come to
life and go off and find new homes for themselves. I've
been waiting for that night ever since, and now tonight
I really think it's come, for I feel a sort of twitching and
tingling in my wheel as if it wants to run. Yes, I'm sure
we must be off!'

'But I don't want to go with you!' shouted Jumping
Jack, 'I want to stay with Peter. I want to go back to the
nursery with all the other toys; I don't want to go to a
new home!'

But before he could say any more the Wheelbarrow

lifted his arms and rolled out of the shed with the Old
Ball and Jumping Jack. The wheel creaked, the Old Ball
sighed and Jumping Jack's arms and legs were tossing to
and fro, so that it looked as if he was trying to get out,
which, of course, was what he *wanted* to do. But the
Wheelbarrow just went steadily on, balancing on one
wheel.

Soon they met other toys; first a tricycle with crooked

handlebars which lurched from one side of the road to the other and nearly ran over them.

'Good evening,' said the Wheelbarrow.

'I think you should say "Good night" when it's so late,' said the Tricycle. 'I don't know why, but I had such an awful itch in my pedals, I just had to come out on to the road. And now I don't know where I'm going. . . .' And he was off, lurching from side to side.

After a while they met a doll with only one arm.

'Good night!' said the Wheelbarrow, for he was not going to make the same mistake twice.

'Good night!' said the Doll as she danced and pranced in her pink knitted slippers.

'Where are you going?' the Wheelbarrow called after her.

'I don't know. And I don't know where I come from. I just know I have to keep on and on!'

'Why couldn't she have come with us?' asked Jumping Jack, when she had disappeared.

'Stupid!' said the Barrow. 'Don't you understand that the whole idea is that each toy should go to a different home? If one child gets a whole lot of old broken toys the same thing will happen again—some of them will be thrown away. No, each child is to have *one* toy.' And they rolled on.

They met many queer toys.

A skipping rope came waving along the road, and after it a humming-top, tripping and bumping over the stones in the road. A very small toy train came chuffing along at full speed. It headed straight for the ditch and disappeared under the water. But a moment later— *bubble-bubble, bubble-bubble, whoosh!*—up it came on the other side and ran straight into a wooden hoop which was bowling in the opposite direction. The hoop fell over, the train fell over, but that didn't worry them; they were up and off again before you could count three. A teddy-bear with a split down the back came plodding by. All he needed was a bit more sawdust stuffing and a few stitches, and some little girl would be glad to have him and mend his back.

After a time the Old Ball started rolling about in the barrow in a restless sort of way: 'I say, Wheelbarrow, can you stop a minute? There's a little cottage up there by the wood; something tells me I have to get off here.'

The Wheelbarrow stopped to let the Old Ball roll off, and it bounced up on the cottage window to look in. Sure enough there was a little girl asleep in bed clutching an old rag doll.

'This must be the place all right,' said the Old Ball. 'Thanks for bringing me along and for being so kind to me. I'll just stay here on the doorstep, then she's sure to find me in the morning. Goodbye!'

The Wheelbarrow and Jumping Jack said goodbye and rolled on until the Barrow suddenly said, 'I can feel a sort of pull inside me; I think we have to turn up this little path through the wood.'

So they did. There was still a bit of snow here and there, making the wheel go *crunch, crunch.*

At last they came to a clearing with an even smaller

cottage than the one where the Old Ball had stopped. The snow lay in drifts against the windows, so the Wheelbarrow took a run at one of them and managed to get high enough to look in. And there was a little boy asleep. By the stove stood a box with a string tied to it. That was all *he* had in the way of a wheelbarrow.

'There, I *thought* so!' said the Wheelbarrow. 'This is the place for me. But what about you, Jack? Haven't *you* felt anything yet? Haven't you had an itch in those long arms and legs of yours as if somebody was pulling your string?'

'No, I haven't!' said Jumping Jack very crossly. 'I'm

not broken, that's why. It's only the broken and cast-off toys who have to find new homes; I have Peter to love me at home, and I don't know why you brought me along—especially when I shouted to you to let me off, you stupid old bundle of sticks!'

'It wasn't my fault. Just when you wanted to get out, something told me to start off and take you with me, so I did.'

Then suddenly the Barrow *knew* why he had brought Jack along. 'Don't you understand? You had to see for yourself what happens tonight, so that you can go home and tell all the other toys. You must tell them they needn't worry even if they do get broken. There are lots of children who will have them and mend them too, so that they're as good as new.'

And all at once Jumping Jack could see it too. 'You're quite right,' he said.

And then he found, to his surprise, that he could move. What fun it was to stretch his legs and arms without being jerked by the string! He hopped first on one leg, then the other, and then he turned complete somersaults. Then he thanked the Wheelbarrow for his trip and said goodbye.

After that, with his string floating straight out behind him like a tail, he ran and ran till he reached the little shed in the garden at home.

And now Jumping Jack has been waiting all day for it to grow dark; for not until the children are in bed and asleep can he go out and give his message to all the broken and unwanted toys.

* * * * *

So if you wake up tomorrow morning and find that your old doll seems to be smiling just a little, or that your chipped trumpet sounds better than it has for a long time, that will be because Jumping Jack has told them about the trip he made with his friends the Wheel-barrow and the Old Ball last night.

The potato with big ideas

THERE was once a potato which lay waiting for someone to come and dig it up. The other potatoes were just

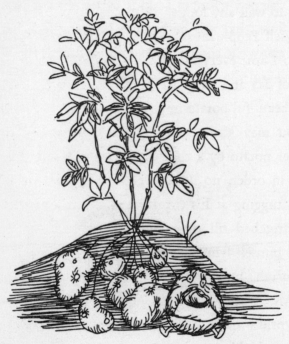

quietly growing larger and larger, but this particular potato had ideas; he was stuck-up. And he was bored with waiting.

'Hi, everybody!' the stuck-up potato said. 'I'm not

going to wait any longer. I'll try to get out of this hole by myself. People must be longing to see what a beautiful potato I am; everything that is beautiful must see the light of day and enjoy the sunshine. Here I come! The most beautiful potato in all the world!'

You may know that all potatoes are tied to the mother potato by a thin thread (so that she can keep them in order, no doubt). Now that stuck-up potato began tugging at his thread, and the thread stretched and stretched till one fine day the stuck-up potato found himself lying on the ground above.

'Hurrah, hurrah! Here I am at last! Good morning, Mr. Weed! Good morning, Mrs. Worm! I am the world's most beautiful potato. And if you, Mr. Sun, would like to shine on me for a moment, you can.'

'With the greatest of pleasure,' answered the sun, 'but it won't be good for you, you know.'

'Who cares? You just shine away and let me enjoy a nice hot sun-bath.'

So the sun shone on that stuck-up potato and turned him blue, green, red and purple all over. This made the potato more pleased with himself than ever:

'When the boys come past and see me lying here they will say: "My goodness! What a fine potato! We must take that home to Mother for dinner." And one of them will put me carefully in his pocket. When his mother sees me she will say: "Goodness gracious! What a wonderful potato; it's much too good for me. I will give it to the parson." And when the parson sees me he will say: "Goodness gracious! My, oh my! What a marvellous potato; I'll give it to the bishop." And when the bishop sees me he will say: "Goodness gracious! My, oh my! And bless my soul! But what an exquisite potato. I must send it straight to the Pope in Rome." Then I will be wrapped in silver paper and sent to the Pope. And when the Pope sees me he will put on his finest clothes and sit on his best silver throne and put me on a gold plate and eat me, while all the church bells ring to tell the world that now the Pope is eating the most beautiful potato from Puddlington-on-the-Marsh.'

But just as the potato was having this lovely dream, the farmer and his wife and their little boy came out into the field to start lifting the potatoes.

They sang as they worked, and shouted to each other every time they found a really whacking big potato.

'Wait till they see *me*, then they'll have something to crow about!' thought the stuck-up potato.

Suddenly the little boy shouted: 'Look at this funny-looking potato! It's blue and red and green all over!'

'Throw it in the pig-bucket,' said his father; 'you can't eat that sort. It's been on top of the earth instead of underneath, where it should have been. But the pigs won't mind what colour it is.'

And so that stuck-up potato ended his days in the pig-trough instead of on a gold plate in the Pope's palace in Rome, which all goes to show that even if you have big ideas it's sometimes wiser to leave them alone.

The mice and the Christmas tree

Now you shall hear the story about a family of mice who lived behind the larder wall.

*   *   *   *   *

Every Christmas Eve, Mother Mouse and the children swept and dusted their whole house with their tails, and for a Christmas tree Father Mouse decorated an old boot with spider's web instead of tinsel. For Christmas presents, the children were each given a little nut, and Mother Mouse held up a piece of bacon fat for them all to sniff.

After that, they danced round and round the boot, and sang and played games till they were tired out. Then

Father Mouse would say: 'That's all for tonight! Time to go to bed!'

That is how it had been every Christmas and that is how it was to be this year. The little mice held each other by the tail and danced round the boot, while Granny Mouse enjoyed the fun from her rocking-chair, which wasn't a rocking-chair at all, but a small turnip.

But when Father Mouse said, 'That's all for tonight! Time to go to bed!' all the children dropped each other's tails and shouted: 'No! No!'

'What's that?' said Father Mouse. 'When I say it's time for bed, it's time for bed!'

'We don't want to go!' cried the children, and hid behind Granny's turnip rocking-chair.

'What's all this nonsense?' said Mother Mouse. 'Christmas is over now, so off you go, the lot of you!'

'No, no!' wailed the children, and climbed on to Granny's knee. She hugged them all lovingly. 'Why don't you want to go to bed, my little sugar lumps?'

'Because we want to go upstairs to the big drawing-

room and dance round a proper Christmas tree,' said the eldest Mouse child. 'You see, I've been peeping through a crack in the wall and I saw a huge Christmas tree with lots and lots of lights on it.'

'We want to see the Christmas tree and all the lights too!' shouted the other children.

'Oh, but the drawing-room can be a very dangerous place for mice,' said Granny.

'Not when all the people have gone to bed,' objected the eldest Mouse child.

'Oh, do let's go!' they all pleaded.

Mother and Father Mouse didn't know what to say, but they couldn't very well disappoint the children on Christmas Eve.

'Perhaps we could take them up there just for a minute or two,' suggested Mother Mouse.

'Very well,' said Father, 'but follow me closely.'

So they set off. They tiptoed past three tins of herring, two large jars of honey and a barrel of cider.

'We have to go very carefully here,' whispered Father Mouse, 'not to knock over any bottles. Are you all right, Granny?'

'Of course I'm all right,' said Granny, 'you just carry on. I haven't been up in the drawing-room since I was a little Mouse girl; it'll be fun to see it all again.'

'Mind the trap!' said the eldest Mouse child. 'It's behind that sack of potatoes.'

'I know that,' said Granny; 'it's been there since I was

a child. I'm not afraid of that!' And she took a flying leap right over the trap and scuttled after the others up the wall.

'What a lovely tree!' cried all the children when they peeped out of the hole by the drawing-room fireplace. 'But where are the lights? You said there'd be lots and lots of lights, didn't you? Didn't you?' The children shouted, crowding round the eldest one, who was quite sure there had been lights the day before.

They stood looking for a little while. Then suddenly a whole lot of coloured lights lit up the tree! Do you know what had happened? By accident, Granny had touched the electric switch by the fireplace.

'Oh, how lovely!' they all exclaimed, and Father and Mother and Granny thought it was very nice too. They walked right round the tree, looking at the decorations, the little paper baskets, the glass balls and the glittering tinsel garlands. But the children found something even more exciting: a mechanical lorry!

Of course, they couldn't wind it up themselves, but its young master had wound it up before he went to bed, to be ready for him to play with in the morning. So when the Mouse children clambered into it, it started off right away.

'Children, children! You mustn't make such a noise!' warned Mother Mouse.

But the children didn't listen; they were having a wonderful time going round and round and round in the lorry.

'As long as the cat doesn't come!' said Father Mouse anxiously.

He had hardly spoken before the cat walked silently through the open door.

Father, Mother and Granny Mouse all made a dash for the hole in the skirting but the children were trapped in the lorry, which just went on going round and round and round. They had never been so scared in all their Mouse lives.

The cat crouched under the tree, and every time the lorry passed she tried to tap it with her front paw. But it was going too fast and she missed.

Then the lorry started slowing down. 'I think we'd better make a jump for it and try to get up in the tree,' said the eldest Mouse. So when the lorry stopped they all gave a big jump and landed on the branches of the tree.

One hid in a paper basket, another behind a bulb (which nearly burned him), a third swung on a glass ball and the fourth rolled himself up in some cotton wool. But where was the eldest Mouse? Oh yes, he had climbed right to the top and was balancing next to the star and shouting at the cat:

> 'Silly, silly cat,
> You can't catch us!
> You're much too fat,
> Silly, silly cat!'

But the cat pretended not to hear or see the little mice. She sharpened her claws on the lorry. 'I'm not interested in catching mice tonight,' she said as if to herself, 'I've been waiting for a chance to play with this lorry all day.'

'Pooh! That's just a story!' said the eldest who was also the bravest. 'You'd catch us quick enough if we came down.'

'No, I wouldn't. Not on Christmas Eve!' said the cat. And she kept her word. When they did all come timidly down, she never moved, but just said: 'Hurry back to your hole, children. Christmas Eve is the one night when I'm kind to little mice. But woe betide you if I catch you tomorrow morning!'

The little mice pelted through that hole and never stopped running till they got to their home behind the larder wall. There were Father and Mother and Granny Mouse waiting in fear and trembling to know what had happened to them.

When Mother Mouse had heard their story she said, 'You must promise me, children, never to go up to the drawing-room again.'

'We promise! We promise!' they all shouted together.
Then she made them say after her *The Mouse Law*, which
they'd all been taught when they were tiny:

> 'We promise always to obey
> Our parents dear in every way,
> To wipe our feet upon the mat
> And never, never cheek the cat.
>
> Remember too the awful danger
> Of taking money from a stranger;
> We will not go off on our own
> Or give our mother cause to moan.
>
> Odd bits of cheese and bacon-scraps
> Are almost certain to be traps,
> So we must look for bigger things
> Like loaves and cakes and doughnut-rings;
>
> And if these rules we still obey
> We'll live to run another day.'

Never take no for an answer

You see the old woman spinning yarn? She was hard at work one day when a young mouse came out of the hole by the stove.

'Well, well, fancy seeing you,' said the old woman.

'Peep, peep!' said the little mouse. 'My ma sent me to ask what the yarn is for that you're spinning?'

'It's for a jersey for my husband; the one he has is so worn he can't use it any more,' answered the old woman.

'Peep, peep! I'd better go and tell that to my ma!' And the little mouse disappeared down the hole. The old woman went on spinning, but it wasn't long before she heard a scuffling by the stove and there sat the mouse once more.

'You back again?' she asked.

'Peep, peep! My ma said to ask you who is to have your husband's old jersey when he gets the new one?'

'I'm going to use that myself when I milk the cows, because my old milking jacket isn't fit to wear any more,' said the old woman.

'Peep, peep! I'd better go and tell that to my ma,' said the mouse, and he was gone. But in no time at all he was back again.

'What d'you want to know this time?' the old woman asked.

'Peep, peep! My ma wants to know who is to have your old milking jacket when you get your husband's old jersey and he gets the new one?'

'The dog is going to have it in his kennel, because his old rug is so thin it's no good any more.'

'Peep, peep! I'd better go and tell that to my ma,' said the little mouse, and darted away to his hole by the stove. But he had hardly popped in before he popped out again.

'That was quick!' said the woman. 'What is it now?'

'Peep, peep! My ma wants to know who is to have the dog's old rug when he gets your old milking jacket and you get your husband's old jersey and he gets the new one?' said the mouse all in one breath.

'You can have it, if you like,' said the old woman.

'Peep, peep! Thank you *very* much,' said the little mouse. 'Now there'll be an eiderdown for *our* bed as well!' And he was so pleased he sang this song:

'Oh me, oh my!
We'll soon be as snug
As a bug in a rug,
What do you think of that!
Come and see me any time
I'll make you up another rhyme,
But please don't bring the cat.'

Mr. Learn-a-lot and the singing midges

ONE warm summer night Mrs. Midge said to her daughters, 'We'll go and visit Mr. Learn-a-lot, the schoolmaster.'

'What do we want to do that for?' asked the young midges. There were three of them: Big Sister Midge, Middle Sister Midge and Wee Sister Midge.

'We're going to sing to him. You're all so good at singing now, it's a pleasure to listen to you, and Mr. Learn-a-lot is such a good judge of music.'

So they all flew off to Mr. Learn-a-lot's house and hovered outside his bedroom window. Mrs. Midge peered through the glass while her daughters all talked at once in high, squeaky voices:

'Is the window shut, Mama?'

'Won't he open it, Mama?'

'Can't we get in, Mama?'

'I expect he'll open the window when he goes to bed,' said Mrs. Midge.

'He's opening the window now, Mama!'

'Can we go in now, Mama?'

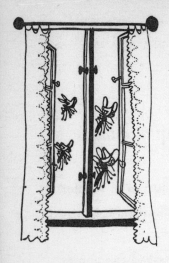

'What shall we sing for him, Mama?'

'Not so fast, children, there's no hurry. Let Mr. Learn-a-lot get nicely into bed first.'

'He's climbing into bed now, Mama! He's in bed, really he is, Mama! Wouldn't it be dreadful if he fell asleep before he heard our singing, Mama?' squeaked all the little midges. But Mrs. Midge was sure the schoolmaster would wake up again when they started singing.

'I think Big Sister Midge had better go in first,' she said.

'All right, but what am I to sing, Mama?'

'You can sing the song about "We midges have not got . . .",' said Mrs. Midge, and settled herself with her two younger daughters behind the curtain. 'And remember to fly in a circle over his head. If he likes your song he will sit up in bed. Now off you go!'

And Big Sister Midge flew round and round in a circle over Mr. Learn-a-lot's head and sang this song:

'We midges have not got a couple of beans
Yet in summer we all are as happy as queens,
For every night in a swoon of delight
We dance to the tune of our dizzy flight,
And all we need to keep in the pink
Is a tiny drop of your blood to drink.'

Three times she sang the same verse, and she was beginning to think Mr. Learn-a-lot didn't care for her song at all. But suddenly he sat bolt upright in bed.

'Come back! Come back, child!' whispered Mrs. Midge.

'Was I all right, Mama?'

'You were very good. Now we'll just wait till Mr. Learn-a-lot has fallen asleep again, then it'll be Middle Sister's turn. You can sing the song about "How doth the little busy me"—that is so very funny! There! Now I think it would be all right for you to start. But you mustn't leave off before Mr. Learn-a-lot has got right out of bed and is standing in the middle of the floor. Fly a little higher than your sister did. Off you go!'

And Middle Sister Midge sang as loudly as she could while she flew round and round the schoolmaster's head:

> 'How doth the little busy me
> Improve each shady hour
> By settling on your nose or knee
> As if upon a flower.'

She hadn't sung more than one verse before Mr. Learn-a-lot threw off the bedclothes and tumbled out of bed.

'Come back, come back!' whispered Mrs. Midge.

'Wasn't I good?' said Middle Sister as she arrived back all out of breath. 'And I wasn't a bit afraid of him!'

93

'That'll do; we midges are not in the habit of boasting,' said Mrs. Midge. 'Now it's Wee Sister's turn.'

'What shall I sing?' asked the smallest midge with the tiniest voice you ever heard.

'You can sing our evening song—you know—the one that goes:

> 'The day is done and all rejoice
> To hear again this still small voice.
> May the music of my wings
> Console you for my little stings.'

That's just the thing for tonight,' Mrs. Midge added thoughtfully.

'Oh yes, I know that one,' said Wee Sister; she was very pleased her mother had chosen one she knew.

'I expect it will be the last song tonight,' said Mrs. Midge, 'and don't worry if you don't get right through it. If Mr. Learn-a-lot suddenly claps his hands you must be sure to come back to me at once. Will you remember that?'

'Yes, Mama,' said Wee Sister, and off she flew.

Mr. Learn-a-lot was lying absolutely still. So Wee Sister began to sing—all on one top note:

'The day is done——'

Smack! Mr. Learn-a-lot clapped his hands together.

'Come back, come back!' called Mrs. Midge. But there was no sign of Wee Sister.

'Oh, my darling, sweet wee one, please come back to your mother!' wailed Mrs. Midge. No sound—no sound at all for a long time; then suddenly Wee Sister was sitting on the curtain beside them.

'Didn't you hear me calling?' asked Mrs. Midge very sternly.

'Oh yes, but you said I was to fly very, very quietly, and that clap of Mr. Learn-a-lot's sent me flying right into the darkest corner of the room.'

'Poor darling!' said Mrs. Midge. 'But you're safe back now. You've all been very good and very clever girls. And now I'd like to hear what you think of Mr. Learn-a-lot?'

Big Sister answered, 'He's nice; he likes the one who sings longest best!'

Middle Sister answered, 'He's very polite; he gets out of bed for the one who sings loudest!'

And Wee Sister said, 'I think he's very musical; he claps the one with the sweetest voice!'

'Yes, yes, that's all very true,' said Mrs. Midge; 'but now I will tell you something else about Mr. Learn-a-lot. He is not only a very learned gentleman, but he will provide us with the nicest, most enjoyable supper, and we needn't even wake him up. Shall we go?'

'Oh, that is a fine idea!' cried Big Sister, Middle Sister and Wee Sister Midge, for they always did just what their mother told them.

Poor Mr. Learn-a-lot!

Mrs. Pepperpot tries to please her husband

THINGS were not very lively at Mrs. Pepperpot's house. Mr. Pepperpot was in a bad mood—he had been in it for days—and Mrs. Pepperpot simply didn't know how to get him out of it. She put flowers on the table and cooked him his favourite dish, fried bacon with macaroni cheese. But it was all no use; Mr. Pepperpot just went on moping.

'I don't know what's the matter with him,' sighed Mrs. Pepperpot, 'perhaps he's pining for pancakes.' So she made him a big pile of pancakes.

When her husband came in for dinner his face lit up at the sight of them, but as soon as he'd sat down and picked up his knife and fork to start eating, his face fell again; he was as glum as before.

'Ah well!' he said, staring up at the ceiling, 'I suppose it's too much to expect.'

'I've had enough of this!' cried Mrs. Pepperpot. 'You tell me what's wrong, or I'll *shrink*, so I will!' (You remember that Mrs. Pepperpot had a habit of shrinking to the size of a pepperpot, though not usually, I'm

afraid, when she *wanted* to, but at the most inconvenient moments.) 'You have something on your mind, that's quite clear,' she went on. 'But you don't think of me, do you? Watching your face getting longer every day is no joke, I can tell you. Now even pancakes can't cheer you up.'

'Pancakes are all right,' nodded Mr. Pepperpot, 'but there's something else missing.'

'What could that be?' asked his wife.

'Couldn't we sometimes have a bit of bilberry jam with the pancakes, instead of just eating them plain?' And Mr. Pepperpot gave a great sigh.

At last she understood; it *was* a very long time since she had given him bilberry jam, and that was what the poor man had been missing.

'Well, if that's all you want, I'll go and pick some bilberries this very minute,' said Mrs. Pepperpot, and she snatched a bucket from a hook on the wall and rushed out of the door.

She walked rather fast because she was cross with her husband, and as she walked she talked to herself: 'I've got the silliest husband alive,' she muttered. 'I was a fool to marry him. In fact, there's only one bigger fool than me, and that's him. *Oh*, how stupid he is!'

In no time at all she reached the spot in the forest where the bilberries grew. She put her bucket under a bush and started picking into the cup she had in her apron pocket. Every time the cup was full she emptied it into the bucket. Cup after cup went in, until the bucket needed only one more cup to be quite full. But then, just as she had picked the last bilberry into the cup, lo and behold! She shrank to the size of a pepperpot.

'Now we're in a jam, that's certain, and I don't mean bilberry jam!' said the little old woman, who now had a tiny voice like a mouse. 'Still, I expect I can manage to get the cup as far as the bucket if I push and pull hard enough. After that we'll have to think again.'

So she crooked her arm through the handle and dragged the cup along. It was very hard at first, but then she came to an ant-path made of slippery pine-needles; here it was much easier, because the cup could slide along it. And all the time little ants and big ants kept scuttling to and fro beside her. She tried to talk to them.

'How d'you do, ants,' she said. 'Hard at work, I see. Yes, there's always plenty to do and that's a fact.' But the ants were far too busy to answer.

'Couldn't you stop for a minute and talk to me?' she asked. But they just hurried on. 'Well, I shall have to talk to myself; then I won't be disturbing anybody.' And she sat down with her back leaning against the cup.

As she sat there, she suddenly felt something breathe down her neck; she turned round, and saw a fox standing there waving his tail in a friendly sort of way.

'Hullo, Mr. Fox. Are you out for a stroll?' said Mrs. Pepperpot. 'Lucky you don't know my hens are . . . Oh dear! I nearly let my tongue run away with me!'

'Where did you say your hens were, Mrs. Pepperpot?' asked the fox in his silkiest voice.

'That would be telling, wouldn't it?' said Mrs. Pepperpot. 'But, as you see, I'm rather busy just now; I've got to get this cup of bilberries hauled over to the bucket somehow, so I haven't time to talk to you.'

'I'll carry the cup for you,' said the fox, as polite as could be. 'Then you can talk while we walk.'

'Thanks very much,' said Mrs. Pepperpot. 'As I was saying, my hens are . . . There now! I nearly said it again!'

The fox smiled encouragingly: 'Just go on talking, it doesn't matter what you say to *me*.'

'I'm not usually one to gossip, but somehow it seems so easy to talk about my hens being . . . Goodness, why don't I keep my mouth shut? Anyway, there's the bucket. So, if you would be so kind and set the cup down beside it I'll tell you where my hens are.'

'That's right, you tell me. Your hens will be quite safe with me.'

'They certainly will!' laughed Mrs. Pepperpot, 'for they're all away! They were broody, so I lent them to the neighbours to hatch out their eggs.'

Then the fox saw he had been tricked, and he was so ashamed he slunk away into the forest and hid himself.

'Ha, ha, ha! That was a fine trick you played on the fox!' said a voice quite close to Mrs. Pepperpot. She looked up and there stood a wolf towering over her.

'Well, if it isn't Mr. Wolf!' said Mrs. Pepperpot, swallowing hard to keep up her courage. 'The ve.. very person I need. You can help me tip this cup of bilberries into the bucket.'

II

'Oh no, you can't fool me like you did the fox,' said the wolf.

'I'm not trying to fool you at all,' said Mrs. Pepperpot; she had had a good idea and was no longer afraid. 'You'd better do as I say or I'll send for One-eye Threadless!'

The wolf laughed. 'I've heard many old wives' tales but I've never heard that one before!'

'It's not an old wives' tale,' said Mrs. Pepperpot indignantly, 'and I'm not just an old wife; I'm Mrs. Pepperpot who can shrink and grow again all in a flash. One-eye Threadless is my servant.'

'Ha, ha! I'd like to see that servant of yours!' laughed the wolf.

'Very well; stick your nose into my apron pocket here and you'll meet him,' said Mrs. Pepperpot. So the wolf put his nose in her apron pocket and pricked it very severely on a needle she kept there.

'Ow, ow!' he shouted and started running towards the forest. But Mrs. Pepperpot called him back at once: 'Come here! You haven't done your job yet; empty that cup into that bucket, and don't you dare spill a single berry, or I'll send for One-eye Threadless to prick you again!'

The wolf didn't dare disobey her, but as soon as he had emptied the cup into the bucket he ran like the fox to the forest to hide.

Mrs. Pepperpot had a good laugh as she watched him go, but then she heard something rustle near the bucket. This time it was the big brown bear himself.

'Dear me! What an honour!' said Mrs. Pepperpot in a shaky voice, and she curtsied so low she nearly disappeared in the bushes. 'Has the fine weather tempted Your Majesty out for a walk?'

'Yes,' growled the big brown bear and went on sniffing at the bucket.

'How very fortunate for me! As Your Majesty can see, I've picked a whole bucket of berries, but it's not very safe for a little old woman like myself to walk in the forest alone. Could I ask Your Majesty to carry the bucket out to the road for me?'

'I don't know about that,' said the bear. 'I like bilberries myself.'

'Yes, of course, but you're not like the rest of them,

Your Majesty; you wouldn't rob a poor little old woman like me!'

'Bilberries; that's what I want!' said the bear, and put his head down to start eating.

In a flash Mrs. Pepperpot had jumped on his neck and started tickling him behind his ears.

'What are you doing?' asked the bear.

'I'm just tickling your ears for you,' answered Mrs. Pepperpot. 'Doesn't it feel good?'

'Good? It's almost better than eating the berries!' said the bear.

'Well, if Your Majesty would be so kind as to carry the bucket, I could be tickling Your Majesty's ears all the way,' said the artful Mrs. Pepperpot.

'Oh, very well then,' grumbled the bear.

When they reached the road the bear put the bucket down very carefully on a flat stone.

'Many, many thanks, Your Majesty,' said Mrs. Pepperpot as she made another deep curtsey.

'Thank *you*,' said the bear, and shuffled off into the forest.

When the bear had gone Mrs. Pepperpot became her usual size again, so she picked up her bucket and hurried homeward.

'It's really not very difficult to look after yourself, even when you're only the size of a pepperpot,' she told herself. 'As long as you know how to tackle the people you meet. Cunning people must be tricked, cowardly ones must be frightened, and the big, strong ones must have their ears tickled.'

As for bad-tempered husbands, the only thing to do with *them* is to give them bilberry jam with their pancakes.

Mrs. Pepperpot minds the baby

Now I'll tell you what happened the day Mrs. Pepperpot was asked to mind the baby.

It was early in the morning. Mrs. Pepperpot had sent her husband off to work. In the usual way wives do, she had made the coffee and the sandwiches for his lunch, and had stood by the window and waved till he was out of sight. Then, just like other wives, she had gone back to bed to have a little extra shut-eye, leaving all her housework for later.

She had been sleeping a couple of hours when there was a knock at the door. She looked at the clock. 'Good heavens!' she cried, 'have I slept so long?' She pulled her clothes on very quickly and ran to open the door.

In the porch stood a lady with a little boy on her arm.

'Forgive me for knocking,' said the lady.

'You're welcome,' said Mrs. Pepperpot.

'You see,' said the lady, 'I'm staying with my aunt near here with my little boy, and today we simply *have* to go shopping in the town. I can't take Roger and there's no one in the house to look after him.'

'Oh, that's all right!' said Mrs. Pepperpot. 'I'll look after your little boy.' (To herself she thought: 'However will I manage with all that work and me oversleeping like that. Ah well, I shall have to do both at the same time.') Then she said out loud: 'Roger, come to Mrs. Pepperpot? That's right!' And she took the baby from the lady.

'You don't need to give him a meal,' said the lady. 'I've brought some apples he can have when he starts sucking his fingers.'

'Very well,' said Mrs. Pepperpot, and put the apples in a dish on the sideboard.

The lady said goodbye and Mrs. Pepperpot set the baby down on the rug in the sitting-room. Then she went out into the kitchen to fetch her broom to start sweeping up. At that very moment she *shrank*!

'Oh dear! Oh dear! Whatever shall I do?' she wailed, for of course now she was much smaller than the baby. She gave up any idea of cleaning the house; when her husband came home she would have to tell him that she had had a headache.

'I must go and see what that little fellow is doing,' she thought, as she climbed over the doorstep into the sitting-room. Not a moment too soon! For Roger had crawled right across the floor and was just about to pull the tablecloth off the table together with a pot of jam, a loaf of bread, and a big jug of coffee!

Mrs. Pepperpot lost no time. She knew it was too far for her to get to the table, so she pushed over a large silver cup which was standing on the floor, waiting to be polished. Her husband had won it in a skiing competition years ago when he was young.

The cup made a fine booming noise as it fell; the baby turned round and started crawling towards it.

'That's right,' said Mrs. Pepperpot, 'you play with that; at least you can't break it.'

But Roger wasn't after the silver cup. Gurgling: 'Ha' dolly! Ha' dolly!' he made a bee-line for Mrs. Pepperpot, and before she could get away, he had grabbed her by the waist! He jogged her up and down and every time Mrs. Pepperpot kicked and wriggled to get free, he laughed. ' 'Ickle, 'ickle!' he shouted, for she was tickling his hand with her feet.

'Let go! Let go!' yelled Mrs. Pepperpot. But Roger was used to his father shouting 'Let's go!' when he threw him up in the air and caught him again. So Roger shouted 'Leggo! Leggo!' and threw the little old woman up in the air with all the strength of his short arms. Mrs. Pepperpot went up and up—nearly to the ceiling! Luckily she landed on the sofa, but she bounced several times before she could stop.

'Talk of flying through the air with the greatest of ease!' she gasped. 'If that had happened to me in my normal size I'd most likely have broken every bone in my body. Ah well, I'd better see what my little friend is up to now.'

She soon found out. Roger had got hold of a match-box and was trying to strike a match. Luckily he was using the wrong side of the box, but Mrs. Pepperpot had to think very quickly indeed.

'Youngsters like to copy everything you do, so I'll take this nut and throw it at him. Then he'll throw it at me—I hope.'

She had found the nut in the sofa and now she was in such a hurry to throw it she forgot to aim properly. But it was a lucky shot and it hit Roger just behind the ear, making him turn round. 'What else can I throw?' wondered Mrs. Pepperpot, but there was no need, because the baby had seen her; he dropped the match-box and started crawling towards the sofa.

'Ha' dolly! Ha' dolly!' he gurgled delightedly. And now they started a very funny game of hide-and-seek—at least it was fun for Roger, but not quite so amusing for poor little old Mrs. Pepperpot who had to hide behind the cushions to get away from him. In the end she managed to climb on to the sideboard where she kept a precious geranium in a pot.

'Aha, you can't catch me now!' she said, feeling much safer.

But at that moment the baby decided to go back to the match-box. 'No, no, no!' shouted Mrs. Pepperpot. Roger took no notice. So, when she saw he was trying to strike another match, she put her back against the flowerpot and gave it a push so that it fell to the floor with a crash.

Roger immediately left the match-box for this new and interesting mess of earth and bits of broken flowerpot. He buried both his hands in it and started putting it in his mouth, gurgling, 'Nice din-din!'

'No, no, no!' shouted Mrs. Pepperpot once more. 'Oh, whatever shall I do?' Her eye caught the apples left by Roger's mother. They were right beside her on the dish. One after the other she rolled them over the edge of the dish on to the floor. Roger watched them roll, then he decided to chase them, forgetting his lovely meal of earth and broken flowerpot. Soon the apples were all over the floor and the baby was crawling happily from one to the other.

There was a knock on the door.

'Come in,' said Mrs. Pepperpot.

Roger's mother opened the door and came in, and there was Mrs. Pepperpot as large as life, carrying a dustpan full of earth and broken bits in one hand and her broom in the other.

'Has he been naughty?' asked the lady.

'As good as gold,' said Mrs. Pepperpot. 'We've had a high old time together, haven't we, Roger?' And she handed him back to his mother.

'I'll have to take you home now, precious,' said the lady.

But the little fellow began to cry. 'Ha' dolly! Ha' dolly!' he sobbed.

'Have *dolly?*' said his mother. 'But you didn't bring a dolly—you don't even have one at home.' She turned to Mrs. Pepperpot. 'I don't know what he means.'

'Oh, children say so many things grown-ups don't understand,' said Mrs. Pepperpot, and waved goodbye to Roger and his mother.

Then she set about cleaning up her house.

Mrs. Pepperpot's penny watchman

STRANGE things had been happening in Mrs. Pepperpot's house. It all began when a little girl came to the door selling penny raffle tickets for a tablecloth. Mrs. Pepperpot hunted high and low until she found a penny; it was a nice shiny one, because someone had been polishing it. But just as she was writing her name on the ticket, the penny dropped on the floor and rolled into a crack by the trapdoor to the cellar.

'Bang goes my fortune,' said Mrs. Pepperpot, as she watched it disappear. 'Now I won't be able to buy a raffle ticket after all. But I can't let you go without giving you anything; what about a nice home-made short-cake?' And she stood on a stool to reach the cake-tin.

It was empty. Mrs. Pepperpot turned the tin almost inside out, but there was no sign of any short-cake.

'I can't understand it,' she said. 'I baked two whole rounds of short-cake on Friday. Today it's only Monday, and the tin is empty. Very mysterious. But I've got something you might like even better, little girl.' So

saying, Mrs. Pepperpot opened the trapdoor to the cellar
and went down the steps to fetch the big jar of bramble
jelly she had left over from the summer.

But what a sight met her eyes!

'Goodness Gracious and Glory Be!' she exclaimed,
for the big jar of bramble jelly was lying smashed under
the shelf with the jelly gently oozing out over the floor.
From the sticky mess a little trail of mouse footprints
ran across to the chimney.

There was nothing for it—Mrs. Pepperpot had to go
up to the little girl and tell her she couldn't even have
bramble jelly. But the little girl said it didn't matter a bit
and politely curtsied before going on to the next house.

Mrs. Pepperpot took a mouse-trap and went down
the cellar steps again. She baited it with cheese and set
it very carefully on the floor. When it was done she
turned to go upstairs again, but the hem of her skirt
brushed against it, and SNAP! went the trap, with a
corner of her skirt caught in it. That was bad enough,
but then, if you please, she shrank again!

'Now I really *am* stuck!' she told herself, and she
certainly was; she couldn't move an inch. After she had
sat there a while she saw a young mouse peeping over
the edge of an empty flowerpot.

'You're quite safe to come out,' said Mrs. Pepperpot.
'I'm too well tethered to do you any harm at the
moment.'

But the little mouse darted off to an empty cardboard box and then two little mice popped their noses over the edge.

'One and one makes two,' said Mrs. Pepperpot. 'I learned that at school, and I wouldn't be a bit surprised if you fetched a third one—for one and two make three!'

She was right. The two little mice darted off together and stayed away quite a long time while she sat and waited. Suddenly she heard a tinny little sound. Ping! Ping! And a big mouse came walking towards her on his hind legs, banging a shiny gong with a little steel pin. The shiny gong was Mrs. Pepperpot's lost penny!

The big mouse bowed low. 'Queen of the House, I greet you!' The little mice were peeping out from behind him.

'Thank goodness for that!' said Mrs. Pepperpot. 'For a moment I thought you might be coming to gobble me up—you're so much bigger than I am!'

'We're not in the habit of gobbling up queens,' said the large mouse. 'I just wanted to tell you, you have a thief in your house.'

Mrs. Pepperpot snorted. 'Thief indeed! Of course I have; you and all the other mice are the thieves in my house. Whose penny is it you're using for a gong, may I ask?'

'Oh, is that what it is? A penny?' said the big mouse. 'Well, it rolled through a crack in the floor, you see, so I thought I could use it to scare away the thief and to show I'm the watchman in this house. You really do need a watchman, Queen of the House, to keep an eye on things for you.'

'What nonsense!' said Mrs. Pepperpot. She tried to stand up, but it was rather difficult with her dress caught in the trap and she herself so tiny.

'Take it easy, Queen of the House,' said the big mouse. 'Let my son here tell you what he has seen.'

Timidly, one of the little mice came forward and told how he had climbed up the chimney one day and peeped through a hole into the kitchen. There he had seen a terrible monster who was eating up all the cake in the tin.

Then the other little mouse chirped in to tell how he had been playing hide-and-seek behind a jam-jar on the shelf when the monster had put out a huge hand and taken the jar away. But he had been so scared when he saw the little mouse that he had dropped the jar on the floor, and all the bramble jelly came pouring out.

Suddenly they heard Tramp! Tramp! Tramp! up above; the sound of huge boots walking about.

'That's the monster!' said one of the little mice.

'Yes, that's him all right!' said the other little mouse.

'Is it, indeed!' said Mrs. Pepperpot. 'If only I could get out of this trap, I should very much like to go and have a look at this monster.'

'We'll help you,' said all the mice, and they set to work to free Mrs. Pepperpot from the trap in the way only mice know how; they gnawed through her skirt, leaving a piece stuck in the spring.

'Now you must hurry up to the kitchen to see the monster,' they said.

'But how am I to get there?' asked Mrs. Pepperpot.

'Up through the chimney on our special rope; we'll pull you up.'

And that's what they did. They hoisted Mrs. Pepperpot higher and higher inside the chimney, until she could see a chink of light.

'That's the crack into the kitchen,' the big mouse told her from below.

She called down to him: 'Thank you Mr. Watchman, thank you for your help, and keep a sharp look-out!'

Then she climbed through the hole in the wall. As soon as she set foot on the floor she grew to her normal size. Standing in front of the stove, she put her hands on her hips and said, 'So it's you, husband, is it, who's been eating all my short-cake and stealing the bramble jelly in the cellar?'

Mr. Pepperpot looked dumbfounded: 'How did you know that?' he said.

'Because I have a watchman now, I have paid him a penny,' said Mrs. Pepperpot.

The bad luck story

IF YOU take the road past Mrs. Pepperpot's house and turn to the right, then to the left and carry straight on, you will come to a cottage.

In this cottage lived an old woman they called 'Mrs. Calamity', because she believed in omens and always expected the worst to happen. Another curious thing about her was that she had the habit of stealing cuttings from pot-plants in other people's houses. Not that this in itself was very serious, only sometimes the flowers died after she had been cutting them about. But Mrs. Calamity had the idea that stolen plants thrive much better than any you got as a present, which is just one of those old wives' tales.

One day she visited little old Mrs. Pepperpot. She sat on the edge of a chair very politely and talked about this and that, but all the time she was looking round at all the plants in Mrs. Pepperpot's window-sill.

'That's right; have a good look,' thought Mrs. Pepperpot to herself. 'I know what you're after; you want to take cuttings of my best geranium. But we'll see about that, my fine lady!'

Unfortunately, there was a knock at the door just at that moment, and Mrs. Pepperpot had to leave her visitor alone while she went to answer it.

A man stood there. 'Anyone called Cuthbertson live here?' he asked.

'Cuthbertson? There's never been anyone of that name in this house, as far as I know,' said Mrs. Pepperpot. 'You'd better ask at the post-office. Excuse me, I'm busy just now.' And she turned to shut the door.

Too late! For at that moment Mrs. Pepperpot shrank again!

She stretched her little neck as much as she could to look over the doorstep into the sitting-room. Sure enough! There was Mrs. Calamity ferreting about in Mrs. Pepperpot's flowerpots.

'I have a feeling you're going to regret that, Madam Thief,' thought Mrs. Pepperpot as she swung herself over the step into the yard. There she found a little wagtail pecking about, looking for something to eat.

'Hullo, little wagtail,' she said. 'If you'll help *me*, then I'll help *you*. You can have all the crumbs you want if you'll just go over to the front doorstep and stand quite still, facing the door.'

32

'That's easily done,' said the wagtail, and hopped across the yard.

No doubt Mrs. Calamity was wondering what had happened to the lady of the house. She came to the door and looked out, holding her hand carefully over her apron pocket where she had hidden the geranium cutting.

Then she caught sight of the wagtail on the step. 'Oh Calamity!' she wailed. 'I've looked a wagtail straight in the face and now I shall have bad luck for a year.'

And, clutching her apron pocket, she hurried away from the house.

But over her head the wagtail was following her, flying with Mrs. Pepperpot on its back. As she clung with her arms round the bird's neck, she said: 'D'you know where we could find a black cat?'

'A black cat?' answered the wagtail. 'I should think I do! The horrible creature was lying in wait for me down by the bend in the road. She's probably still there. So don't ask me to land anywhere near her.'

'Don't worry!' said Mrs. Pepperpot. 'I want you to put me down on the *opposite* side of the road—I have a little plan.'

So the wagtail did as she asked and flew out of harm's way as fast as it could go.

Mrs. Pepperpot crouched down in the long grass; she could see the cat's tail waving to and fro in the ditch

on the other side of the road. Soon she heard the clump, clump, clump of Mrs. Calamity's boots as she walked down the road.

Just as she came past where Mrs. Pepperpot was

hiding, Mrs. Pepperpot made the noise of a wagtail calling. The black cat heard it and, like a streak of lightning, shot across the road, right in front of Mrs. Calamity.

Mrs. Calamity stood stock-still with fright. 'A black cat!' she screamed. 'That means *three* years' bad luck!

Oh Calamity, what shall I do?' She was so alarmed she didn't dare go on; instead, she took the path through the wood to her house.

Meanwhile the cat was going in the same direction, for by now Mrs. Pepperpot was riding on her back. 'Have you seen any magpies about?' she asked the cat.

'I should think I have!' said the cat. 'There's a pair of them in that birch-tree over there; they tease me and

pull my tail whenever they get the chance. Look!
They're waiting for me now!'

'Then you can drop me here,' said Mrs. Pepperpot.
'Come and see me tomorrow and I'll give you a bowl
of cream.'

The cat did as she asked, and a moment later Mrs.
Pepperpot was talking to the magpies in the birch-tree.

'Good afternoon,' she said. 'I wonder if you would
have such a thing as a key-ring in your nest?'

'Oh no,' said the magpies, 'we don't have key-rings,
we only collect broken-mirror bits.'

'The best is good enough,' replied Mrs. Pepperpot.
'I want you to put some nice-looking bits on Mrs.
Calamity's doorstep. If you can do that for me, I'll
keep the curly tail for you when we kill the pig at
Christmas.'

The magpies didn't need to be told twice. A little
heap of broken-mirror bits were on Mrs. Calamity's
doorstep before you could say Jack Robinson.

When she arrived and saw what was waiting for her
Mrs. Calamity sat down and cried.

'Oh, misery me! Oh Calamity! A broken mirror will
give me *seven* years' bad luck!'

But by now Mrs. Pepperpot had grown to her proper
size again; quietly she came round the corner, and her
voice was quite gentle when she spoke.

'Now, now, Mrs. Calamity,' she said, 'you mustn't sit here crying.'

'Oh, Mrs. Pepperpot! It's nothing but bad luck for me from beginning to end.' She sniffed, and she told Mrs. Pepperpot about the wagtail that had faced her, the cat that had jumped across her path and now the broken mirror. When she'd finished she fished for a handkerchief in her apron pocket.

Out fell the geranium cutting!

Mrs. Calamity picked it up and handed it to Mrs. Pepperpot. 'There—take it! I stole it from your house. Now you'd better have it back, for I shall never need geraniums or anything else in this world, I don't suppose!'

'Don't be silly,' said Mrs. Pepperpot. 'Let's forget about all this nonsense, shall we? I'm going to *give* you the cutting as a present. You plant it, and I'm sure you'll find that it'll grow into the finest flower you ever had.'

She was right. The tiny cutting grew into a huge geranium with bright red blooms, and that in spite of the fact that Mrs. Calamity not only thanked Mrs. Pepperpot, but shook hands as well, which is the worst thing you can do if you believe in bad omens.

But from then on she changed her ideas, and people no longer called her Mrs. Calamity, but plain Mrs. Brown instead.

Mrs. Pepperpot and the moose

IT WAS winter-time, and Mrs. Pepperpot was having trouble getting water. The tap in her kitchen ran slower and slower, until one day it just dripped and then stopped altogether. The well was empty.

'Ah, well,' thought Mrs. Pepperpot, 'it won't be the first time I've had this kind of trouble, and it won't be the last. But with two strong arms and a good sound bucket, not to mention the lucky chance that there's another well down by the forest fence, we'll soon fix that.'

So she put on her husband's old winter coat and a pair of thick gloves and fetched a pick-axe from the wood-shed. Then she trudged through the snow down the hill, to where there was a dip by the forest fence. She swept the snow away and started breaking a hole in the ice with the pick-axe. Chips of ice flew everywhere as Mrs. Pepperpot hacked away, not looking to left or right. She made such a noise that she never heard the sound of breaking twigs, nor the snorting that was coming from the other side of the fence.

But there he was; a huge moose with great big antlers, not moving at all, but staring angrily at Mrs. Pepperpot. Suddenly he gave a very loud snort and leaped over the fence, butting Mrs. Pepperpot from behind, so that she went head-first into a pile of snow!

'What the dickens!' cried Mrs. Pepperpot as she scrambled to her feet. But by that time the moose was back on the other side of the fence. When she saw what

it was that had pushed her over, Mrs. Pepperpot lost no time in scrambling up the hill and into her house, locking the door behind her. Then she peeped out of the kitchen window to see if the moose was still there. He was.

'You wait, you great big brute!' said Mrs. Pepperpot. 'I'll give you a fright you won't forget!'

She put on a black rain-cape and a battered old hat, and in her hand she carried a big stick. Then she crept out of the door and hid round the corner of the house.

The moose was quietly nibbling the bark off the trees and seemed to be taking no notice of her.

Suddenly she stormed down the hill, shouting, 'Woollah, Woollah, Woollah!' like a Red Indian, the black rain-cape flapping round her and the stick waving in the air. The moose *should* have been frightened, but he just took one look at the whirling thing coming towards him, leaped the fence and headed straight for it!

Poor Mrs. Pepperpot! All she could do was to rush back indoors again as fast as she knew how.

'Now what shall I do?' she wondered. 'I must have water to cook my potatoes and do my washing-up, and a little cup of coffee wouldn't come amiss after all this excitement. Perhaps if I were to put on my old man's trousers and take his gun out . . . I could pretend to aim it; that might scare him off.'

41

So she put on the trousers and took out the gun; but this was the silliest idea she had had yet, because, before she was half-way down the hill, that moose came pounding towards her on his great long legs. She never had time to point the gun. Worse still, she dropped it in her efforts to keep the trousers up and run back to the house at the same time. When the moose saw her disappear indoors, he turned and stalked down the hill again, but this time he didn't jump back over the fence, but stayed by the well, as if he were guarding it.

'Ah well,' said Mrs. Pepperpot, 'I suppose I shall have to fill the bucket with snow and melt it to get the water I need. That moose is clearly not afraid of anything.'

So she took her bucket and went outside. But just as she was bending down to scoop up the snow, she turned small! But this time the magic worked quicker than usual, and somehow she managed to tumble into the bucket which was lying on its side. The bucket started to roll down the hill; faster and faster it went, and poor Mrs. Pepperpot was seeing stars as she bumped round and round inside.

Just above the dip near the well a little mound jutted out, and here the bucket made a leap into space. 'This is the end of me!' thought Mrs. Pepperpot. She waited for the bump, but it didn't come! Instead the bucket seemed to be floating through the air, over the

fence and right into the forest. If she had had time to think, Mrs. Pepperpot would have known that the moose had somehow caught the bucket on one of his antlers, but it is not so easy to think when you're swinging between heaven and earth.

At last the bucket got stuck on a branch and the moose thundered on through the undergrowth. Mrs. Pepperpot lay there panting, trying to get her breath back. She had no idea where she was. But then she heard: 'Chuck, chuck! Chuck, chuck!'—the chattering of a squirrel as he ran down the tree-trunk over her head.

'Hullo!' said the squirrel, 'if it isn't Mrs. Pepperpot! Out for a walk, or something?'

'Not exactly a *walk*,' said Mrs. Pepperpot, 'but I've had a free ride, though I don't know who gave it to me.'

'That was the King of the Moose,' said the squirrel. 'I saw him gallop past with a wild look in his eyes. It's the first time I have ever seen him afraid, I can tell you that. He is so stupid and so stuck-up you wouldn't believe it. All he thinks of is fighting; he goes for anything and anybody—the bigger the better. But you seem to have given him the fright of his life.'

'I'm glad I managed it in the end,' said Mrs. Pepperpot, 'and now I'd be gladder still if I knew how to get myself home.'

But she needn't have worried, because at that moment she felt herself grow large again, and the next thing she knew she had broken the branch and was lying on the ground. She picked herself and her bucket up and started walking home. But when she got to the fence she took a turn down to the well to fill the bucket.

When she stood up she looked back towards the forest, and there, sure enough, stood the moose, blinking at her. But Mrs. Pepperpot was no longer afraid of him. All she had to do was to rattle that bucket a little, and the big creature shook his head and disappeared silently into the forest.

From that day on Mrs. Pepperpot had no trouble fetching water from the well by the forest fence.

Mrs. Pepperpot finds a hidden treasure

IT WAS a fine sunny day in January, and Mrs. Pepperpot was peeling potatoes at the kitchen sink.

'Miaow!' said the cat; she was lying in front of the stove.

'Miaow yourself!' answered Mrs. Pepperpot.

'Miaow!' said the cat again.

Mrs. Pepperpot suddenly remembered an old, old rhyme she learned when she was a child. It went like this:

> The cat sat by the fire,
> Her aches and pains were dire,
> Such throbbing in my head,
> She cried; I'll soon be dead!

'Poor Pussy! Are your aches and pains so bad? Does your head throb?' she said, and smiled down at the cat.

But the cat only looked at her.

Mrs. Pepperpot stopped peeling potatoes, wiped her hands and knelt down beside the cat. 'There's something you want to tell me, isn't there, Pussy? It's too bad I can't understand you except when I'm little, but it's

46

not my fault.' She stroked the cat, but Pussy didn't purr, just went on looking at her.

'Well, I can't spend all day being sorry for you, my girl, I've got a husband to feed,' said Mrs. Pepperpot, and went back to the potatoes in the sink. When they were ready she put them in a saucepan of cold water on the stove, not forgetting a good pinch of salt. After that she laid the table, for her husband had to have his dinner sharp at one o'clock and it was now half past twelve.

Pussy was at the door now. 'Miaow!' she said, scratching at it.

'You want to get out, do you?' said Mrs. Pepperpot, and opened the door. She followed the cat out, because she had noticed that her broom had fallen over in the snow. The door closed behind her.

And at that moment she shrank to her pepperpot size!

'About time too!' said the cat. 'I've been waiting for days for this to happen. Now don't let's waste any more time; jump on my back! We're setting off at once.'

Mrs. Pepperpot didn't stop to ask where they were going; she climbed on Pussy's back. 'Hold on tight!' said Pussy, and bounded off down the little bank at the back of the house past Mrs. Pepperpot's rubbish-heap.

'We're coming to the first hindrance,' said Pussy; 'just sit tight and don't say a word!' All Mrs. Pepperpot could see was a single birch-tree with a couple of magpies on it. True, the birds seemed as big as eagles to her now and the tree was like a mountain. But when the magpies started screeching she knew what the cat meant.

'There's the cat! There's the cat!' they screamed. 'Let's nip her tail! Let's pull her whiskers!' And they swooped down, skimming so close over Mrs. Pepperpot's head she was nearly blown off the cat's back. But the cat took no notice at all, just kept steadily on down the hill, and the magpies soon tired of the game.

'That's that!' said the cat. 'The next thing we have to watch out for is being hit by snowballs. We have to cross the boys' playground now, so if any of them start aiming at you, duck behind my ears and hang on!'

Mrs. Pepperpot looked at the boys; she knew them all, she had often given them sweets and biscuits. '*They* can't be dangerous,' she said to herself.

But then she heard one of them say: 'There comes that stupid cat; let's see who can hit it first! Come on,

boys!' And they all started pelting snowballs as hard as they could.

Suddenly remembering how small she was, Mrs. Pepperpot did as the cat had told her and crouched down behind Pussy's ears until they were safely out of range.

The cat ran on till they got to a wire fence with a hole just big enough for her to wriggle through.

'So far, so good,' she said, 'but now comes the worst bit, because this is dog land, and we don't want to get caught. So keep your eyes skinned!'

The fence divided Mrs. Pepperpot's land from her neighbour's, but she knew the neighbour's dog quite well; he had had many a bone and scraps from her and he was always very friendly. 'We'll be all right here,' she thought.

But she was wrong. Without any warning, that dog suddenly came bearing down on them in great leaps and bounds! Mrs. Pepperpot shook like a jelly when she saw his wide-open jaws all red, with sharp, white teeth glistening in a terrifying way. She flattened herself on the cat's back and clung on for dear life, for Pussy shot like a Sputnik across the yard and straight under the neighbour's barn.

'Phew!' said the cat, 'that was a narrow squeak! Thanks very much for coming all this way with me; I'm afraid it wasn't a very comfortable journey.'

'That's all right,' said Mrs. Pepperpot, 'but perhaps you'll tell me now what we've come for?'

'It's a surprise,' said Pussy, 'but don't worry, you'll get your reward. All we have to do now is to find the hidden treasure, but that means crawling through the hay. So hang on!'

And off they went again, slowly this time, for it was difficult to make their way through the prickly stalks that seemed as big as bean-poles to Mrs. Pepperpot. The dust was terrible; it went in her eyes, her mouth, her hair, down her neck—everywhere.

'Can you see anything?' asked the cat.

'Only blackness,' answered Mrs. Pepperpot, 'and it seems to be getting blacker.'

'In that case we're probably going the right way,' said Pussy, crawling further into the hay. 'D'you see anything now?' she asked.

'Nothing at all,' said Mrs. Pepperpot, for by now her eyes were completely bunged up with hay-seed and dust.

'Try rubbing your eyes,' said the cat, 'for this is where your hidden treasure is.'

So Mrs. Pepperpot rubbed her eyes, blinked and rubbed again until at last she could open them properly. When she did, she was astonished; all round her shone the most wonderful jewels! Diamonds, sapphires, emeralds—they glittered in every hue!

'There you are! Didn't I tell you I had a hidden treasure for you?' said the cat, but she didn't give Mrs. Pepperpot time to have a closer look. 'We'll have to hurry back now, it's nearly time for your husband's dinner.'

So they crawled back through the hay and, just as they got out in the daylight, Mrs. Pepperpot grew to her ordinary size. She picked the cat up in her arms and walked across the yard with her. The dog was there, but what a different dog! He nuzzled Mrs. Pepperpot's skirt and wagged his tail in the friendliest way.

Through the gate they came to the place where the boys were playing. Everyone of them nodded to her and politely said 'Good morning'. Then they went on up the hill, and there were the magpies in the birch-tree. But not a sound came from them; they didn't even seem to notice them walking by.

When they got to the house Mrs. Pepperpot put the cat down and hurried indoors. It was almost one o'clock. She snatched the saucepan from the stove—a few potatoes had stuck to the bottom, so she threw those

out and emptied the rest into a blue serving-bowl. The saucepan she put outside the back door with cold water in it.

She had only just got everything ready when Mr. Pepperpot came in. He sniffed suspiciously. 'I can smell burnt potatoes,' he said.

'Nonsense,' said Mrs. Pepperpot, 'I dropped a bit of potato-skin on the stove, that's all. But I've aired the room since, so just you sit down and eat your dinner.'

'Aren't you having any?' asked her husband.

'Not just now,' answered Mrs. Pepperpot, 'I have to go and fetch something first. I won't be long.' And Mrs. Pepperpot went back down the hill, through the gate to her neighbour's yard, and into the barn. But this time she climbed *over* the hay till she found the spot where her hidden treasure lay.

And what d'you think it was?

Four coal-black kittens with shining eyes!

Mr. Pepperpot

Now you have heard a lot about *Mrs.* Pepperpot, but hardly anything about *Mr.* Pepperpot.

He usually comes in at the end of the stories, when Mrs. Pepperpot is back to her normal size and busy with his dinner. If the food isn't ready he always says 'Can't a man ever get his dinner at the proper time in this house?' And if it is ready, he just sits down to eat and says nothing at all. If it's cold out, he says 'Brrrrrrr!' and if it's very hot, he says 'Pheeew!' If Mrs. Pepperpot has done something he doesn't like, he says 'Hmmmmm!' in a disapproving tone of voice. But if he himself is thinking of doing something he doesn't want Mrs. Pepperpot to know about, he goes round the house whistling to himself and humming a little tune.

One evening when he came home, he went up to the attic. Now, Mrs. Pepperpot had hidden four black kittens up there, because Mr. Pepperpot didn't like kittens when they were small (some people don't, you know). So, when Mr. Pepperpot came down from the attic, he stood in the middle of the floor and said 'Hmmmm!' And a little while later he started whistling and humming his tune.

Mrs. Pepperpot said nothing, though she knew what it meant. She just took his old winter coat from its peg and started mending a tear in it.

'What are you mending that for?' asked Mr. Pepperpot.

'The weather's getting so bad, you'll need it,' said Mrs. Pepperpot.

'Who said I was going out?' asked Mr. Pepperpot.

'You can do as you like,' said his wife, 'I'm staying right where I am.'

'Well, maybe I *will* take a turn outside, all the same,' said Mr. Pepperpot.

'I thought you would,' she said.

Mr. Pepperpot went back to the attic, found a big sack and popped the four kittens inside. But when he got to the bottom of the stairs, he thought he would put on the old winter coat. So he put the sack down and went into the kitchen. There he found the coat hanging over a chair.

'I'm going out now!' he called, thinking his wife must be in the sitting-room. He got no answer, but he didn't bother to call again, as he was afraid the kittens might get out of the sack which wasn't properly tied. Quickly he slung it over his shoulder and went out.

It was a nasty night; the wind blew sleet in his face and the road was full of icy puddles.

'Ugh!' said Mr. Pepperpot, 'this weather's fit to drown in!'

'Isn't that just what you're going to do to us poor kittens?' said a tiny voice close by.

Mr. Pepperpot was startled. 'Who said that, I wonder?' he said. He put the sack down to look inside, but as soon as he opened it out jumped one of the kittens and ran off in the darkness.

'Oh dear, what shall I do?' he said, tying up the sack again as quickly as he could. 'I can't leave a kitten running about on a night like this.'

'He won't get any wetter than the rest of us by the time you've finished with us,' said the little voice again.

Mr. Pepperpot untied the sack once more to find out who was speaking. Out jumped the second kitten and disappeared in the sleet and snow. While he hurriedly tied a knot to stop the rest from getting out, he said to himself:

'What if the fox got those two little mites? That would be terrible!'

'No worse than being in *your* hands,' said the tiny voice.

This time, Mr. Pepperpot was very careful to hold his hand over the opening as he untied it. But his foot slipped on the ice and jogged the sack out of his hand, and another kitten got away.

'Three gone! That's bad!' he said.

'Not as bad as it'll be for me!' came the voice from the sack.

'I know who it is now,' said Mr. Pepperpot; 'it's my

old woman who's shrunk again. You're in that sack, aren't you? But I'll catch you! You just wait!' And with that he opened the sack again.

Out jumped the fourth kitten and ran off, lickety-split!

'You can run, I don't care!' said the old man. 'I'm going to catch that wife of mine—it's all her fault!' He got down on his knees and rummaged round in every corner of the sack. But he found nothing—it was quite empty.

Now he really was worried; he was so worried he started sobbing and crying, and in between he called 'Puss, Puss!' and searched all over the place.

A little girl came along the road. 'What have you lost?' she asked.

'Some kittens,' sniffed Mr. Pepperpot.

'I'll help you find them,' said the little girl.

Soon they were joined by a little boy, and he had a torch which made it easier to search. First the little girl found one kitten behind a tree-stump, then the boy found two kittens stuck in a snow-drift, and Mr. Pepperpot himself found the fourth one and put them all back in the sack, tying it very securely this time.

'Thank you for your help,' he said to the children and asked them to take the kittens back to his house and put them in the kitchen.

When they had gone, he started looking for his little old woman. He searched for an hour—for two hours; he called, he begged, he sobbed, he was quite beside himself. But in the end he had to give up. 'I'll go home now,' he said to himself, 'and try again tomorrow.'

But when he got home, there was Mrs. Pepperpot, as large as life, bustling round the kitchen, frying a huge pile of pancakes! And by the kitchen stove was a wicker basket with the mother cat and all four kittens in it.

'When did you come home?' asked the astonished Mr. Pepperpot.

'When did I come home? Why, I've been here all the time, of course,' she said.

'But who was it talking to me from the sack, then?'

'I've no idea,' said Mrs. Pepperpot, 'unless it was your conscience.' And she came over and gave him a great big hug and kiss.

Then Mr. Pepperpot sat down to eat the biggest pile of pancakes he had ever had and all with bilberry jam, and when he was full the kittens finished off the last four.

And after that Mr. and Mrs. Pepperpot lived happily together, and Mrs. Pepperpot gave up shrinking for a very long time indeed—that's why the next story is a made-up story about an OGRE and not about Mrs. Pepperpot at all, at all.

The ogres

IT IS time we made up a story about *ogres*. You see we have to make it up, because there aren't any ogres, really.

First we must have an ogre and he must have a name. Let's call him GAPY GOB, because he's very fond of eating and is always opening his mouth for more.

Good. Gapy Gob has two servants, a little girl and a little boy. The little girl spends all *her* time cooking porridge for her master, so we can call her KATIE COOK. The little boy spends all *his* time chopping wood to burn in the stove on which Katie cooks the porridge. So we can call him CHARLIE CHOP.

Katie Cook and Charlie Chop aren't really ogres at all; they're just ordinary children, but they have no home of their own, so Gapy Gob lets them stay with him. They are very happy there, except for one thing; on the other side of the hill lives an ogress by the name of WILY WINNIE and her servant, a very cunning cat called RIBBY RATSOUP.

Now I think we have enough ogres and people to start the story, don't you?

Wily Winnie was very set on marrying Gapy Gob, because she knew he had a large ham hanging in his larder. Not only that, but Gapy Gob had a much better house than her own and she wanted to live in it. But first she had to get rid of the ogre's two servants, Katie Cook and Charlie Chop.

Several times she had tried to persuade him to send them away, but each time the children had told Gapy Gob that Wily Winnie was just after his ham and that her cat was waiting to eat up all the herrings they had salted down.

One morning early, when Gapy Gob was sitting at the table waiting for Katie to finish stirring his porridge, and

Charlie was sharpening his axe ready for the day's work,
there was a knock at the door.

'Come in,' said Katie.

The door opened, and there stood Ribby Ratsoup,
Wily Winnie's cat.

'Good morning,' she said, trying to curtsey politely,
but it was difficult because she was wearing riding-boots
and carried a large bucket over one paw.

'Good morning,' said Katie. 'If you've brought that

bucket for salt herrings, you can spare yourself the trouble; you're not having any.'

'No, no, nothing of the kind!' said the cat. 'I just called to see if anyone here would like to go bilberry-picking with me.'

'Bilberry-picking?' said Gapy Gob. 'You going bilberry-picking? What a clever cat you are! But I don't think Katie and Charlie have time to go with you today.' The ogre was a bit put out because he had had to wait for his porridge.

'I was just asking,' said Ribby in a sugary voice. 'You see, at *our* house we get up early. I get all the work done before breakfast. So my mistress told me to go berrying today, and of course I do as I am told. Well, bye-bye for now!'

When the cat had gone, the ogre said, 'I don't really see why you shouldn't go bilberrying too; they're very nice to eat. . . .' And he licked his chops.

'Just as you like,' said Charlie. 'We don't mind going. But then you'll have to look after yourself while we're out.'

'Don't touch the matches, whatever you do!' warned Katie.

'And if anybody knocks, be sure *not* to open the door,' said Charlie.

'I won't,' said Gapy Gob.

But as soon as the children had gone, Wily Winnie came panting over the hill, her skirts flying.

'Hullo, hullo! How are you, Gapy Gob?' she shouted, and marched straight into the kitchen.

Gapy Gob backed away from her into a corner. 'I'm not supposed to open the door if anyone knocks,' he said.

'Ah, but I *didn't* knock. I came straight in!' said the ogress. 'How nice to see you again, dear Gapy Gob. My cat has gone bilberry-picking, so I was all alone!'

'The children have gone as well,' said Gapy Gob.

'How lovely!' cried Wily Winnie. 'Then you can come home with me for a while. We can sit and talk while we wait for them to bring back the berries. I wonder who will bring the most? Come along now, Gapy, let me help you on with your coat. First this arm; that's right, and now this one. There now, we're ready to go!'

So Gapy Gob went home with Wily Winnie and sat in her house all day, while Katie Cook and Charlie Chop searched the wood for all the bilberries they could find. They each had a punnet to pick in, and when they were full they tipped them into their bucket which stood under a fir-tree.

But what d'you think Ribby Ratsoup had been doing all this time? Well, she hadn't been picking bilberries, I

can tell you that much! She spent the day scampering through the forest, chasing squirrels and field mice and birds. Late in the afternoon she came across the children's bucket, filled almost to the brim with bilberries. Katie and Charlie were out of sight, picking their last punnet each.

Ribby, as I told you before, was a very cunning cat. She emptied all the berries into her own bucket and one of her boots. Then she ran home to her mistress as fast as she could go.

Back in Wily Winnie's house the ogre and ogress were getting on fine together. They had come to an agreement that if the *cat* came home with most bilberries, Gapy

Gob would send Katie and Charlie away, but if the *children* had most, Ribby Ratsoup would have to go.

Suddenly they saw something come streaking across the hill-top. It was the cat with her bucket and her boot full of bilberries.

Wily Winnie clapped her hands. 'My cat's won! My cat's won! Look what a lot she's brought!'

'Ah, you wait and see what the children bring!' said Gapy Gob. He was so fond of the children, he didn't want to lose them.

A little while later they saw Katie and Charlie come over the hill-top. But they were walking very, very slowly. And their bucket was—empty.

'What did I tell you, Gapy Gob?' shouted the ogress. 'Those children are no good. Send them away, Gapy, send them away!'

So Gapy Gob went out in the yard and said to the

children: 'Charlie and Katie, you can go. I don't want you any more; you can't even pick bilberries.' And he turned away, for he had tears in his eyes.

'I see,' said Charlie.

'Very well,' said Katie.

'Ribby is much better at picking than you are,' said Gapy Gob.

'Is that so?' said Charlie. 'Then perhaps Madam Ratsoup wouldn't mind showing us her paws?'

'My paws?' said the cat. 'Certainly you can see my paws.' And she held them up.

'Hmm!' said Charlie. 'Very strange. The cat has picked a whole bucket and a boot full, yet her paws are as clean as if she'd been licking them all day. *We*, who have no bilberries to show for it, have our arms stained blue right up to the elbows. Ribby Ratsoup is a thief; she has stolen our berries and now she can give them back to us, every single one, or it will be the worse for her!'

The cat saw the game was up and quickly handed back the berries. Then the children took Gapy Gob by the hands and they all three went home together.

But Wily Winnie was so angry, she shut the cat up in the barn without any supper.

That's the end of this story. Now it's your turn to make one up about the ogres, and we'll see which is the best.

The good luck story

ONCE upon a time there was a little old woman—no, what am I saying? She was a little girl. But this little girl worked every bit as hard as any grown-up woman. Her name was Betsy; she wore a scarf round her head like the women did, and she could weed a field of turnips with the best of them. If any of the big boys started throwing stones or lumps of earth at her, she tossed her head and gave them a piece of her mind.

She was weeding in the field one day when a lady-bird settled on her hand.

'Poor little ladybird! What do you want on my thumb?' said Betsy, at the same time trying to think of a really good wish. For ever since she was tiny she had been told to make a wish when a ladybird flew from her finger.

'I wish . . . I wish I had a new skipping-rope to take to school,' she said quickly. But then she remembered that she had borrowed a skipping-rope from her friend, Anna, and lost it. If she got a new one now she would *have* to give it to Anna.

The ladybird crawled slowly out on Betsy's thumbnail, and she was terrified it would fly away before she had had time to wish for all the things she wanted. Luckily, the ladybird changed its mind when it reached the top; it crawled down again and started up the first finger.

'Now I shall wish—I wish I could have some money,' said Betsy, but was sorry as soon as she had said it. After all, she would *get* some money when she had finished her weeding. And, anyway, the money would have to go to Britta from Hill Farm to pay for the old bicycle Betsy had bought from her in the spring.

The ladybird crawled right out on the top of Betsy's first finger. Then it stopped to consider, and slowly

turned round and climbed down again to start on the second finger.

'Now I must hurry up and wish before it flies off the top of this finger,' said Betsy, while the ladybird climbed steadily upwards.

'I wish I were a real princess,' she said, but then she thought: 'How stupid of me—how can I be a real princess if I haven't been one before? Unless, of course, a prince came along and asked me to marry him. That would look funny, wouldn't it? A prince in a turnip field!' And she laughed at herself.

The ladybird was stretching one wing now and hovering.

'Don't fly yet, little ladybird! I don't want to be a princess at all. I want something quite different. I want my mother to be rid of her rheumatics when I get home tonight.'

This was a good wish, and Betsy was pleased with it. You see, it was a great trouble to her when her mother had the rheumatics; then Betsy had to dress all her little brothers and sisters and give them their dinner. It would be nice not to have to work so hard.

But the ladybird didn't take off even from this finger. Slowly it turned round and made its way to the bottom of the finger and then on to Betsy's hand. Then it stopped; it didn't seem to want to go on at all. But Betsy gave it a gentle little push and got it on to her third finger.

Now she knew what to wish; that her father could get the job he was after that day. Because if he did, he had said he would buy her a whole sheet of pictures to stick in her scrap-book.

But the ladybird had its own ideas; it crawled more and more slowly up Betsy's third finger, and every now and then Betsy had to poke it to get it out on the nail. Then all of a sudden the ladybird rolled off and fell on to the ground.

Betsy lay down flat among the turnips and managed to coax the creature on to her little finger. It didn't move. So Betsy lifted it gingerly out on the nail. Still it didn't move, and she thought she must have hurt it. 'You poor thing! Did I squeeze you too hard? Oh, please, little ladybird, do fly now! Because I want to wish that Daddy could get the job he's after!'

And suddenly the ladybird opened its wings and flew off—straight up towards the sun.

And do you know? When Betsy got home that night her mother was feeling better than she had been for a long while. Her father had got the job and had remembered the pictures for her scrap-book, and her friend Anna had been to see her. She had found the lost skipping-rope and brought it for Betsy, because she had a new one herself. Not only that, but Britta from Hill Farm had been to say that if Betsy would mind her baby for her twice that week, she needn't pay any more for the old bicycle!

What more could you want from a lucky ladybird?

Mr. Big Toe's journey

MR. BIG TOE lived with his four brothers in a little sock, and the sock lived in a shoe which belonged to a little boy who was walking down the lane eating a very big sandwich.

Mr. Big Toe said: 'Now I've been stuck in this place so long, I think it's time I did some travelling.'

When his brothers asked him where he was going, he answered: 'Oh, I expect I shall sail across the ocean.'

'But how will you get through the wall?' they asked him—they meant the sock, of course.

'That's easy for someone as big as I am. I shall just scratch a hole.'

'Will we never see you again?' asked the one who was closest to Mr. Big Toe.

'Maybe not. But I'll ring you up and tell you how I'm getting on. Well, I'm off now, so goodbye!'

Then Mr. Big Toe started scratching a hole, and it didn't take long before he had wriggled through. The rest of the toes sat waiting for the telephone message.

Soon the little boy started running and Mr. Big Toe sent his first message:

'Hullo, hullo! I've started on my travels. It feels rather strange at first, of course, and I miss you a bit. But I expect you miss me much more. Be good. I'll ring you up again when I get on the boat.'

After a time the little boy found a puddle and began dipping his shoe in it. Mr. Big Toe got on the telephone again.

'Hullo boys, I've just got to the edge of the ocean; in a few moments I'll be sailing to the far shore. It's a dangerous journey, but don't worry, I'll manage! The waves are enormous! Still, the boat seems strong and seaworthy. It won't be long now before I meet the African Chief's Big Toe and all his little black brothers. I'll tell them I've left *my* four brothers at home. They'll be glad to hear about you, I expect. . . . Bye, bye, I must ring off now till we get to the far shore.'

The boy waded out into the middle of the puddle, but it was deeper than he thought, and while the other toes were lying inside the sock, thinking of their big brother alone on the stormy sea, they had another call from him.

'Hullo there! This is getting more and more danger-ous; the boat is out in the middle of the ocean, and it's leaking badly. If you don't hear anything more for a

bit, it's because I have to use my nail to bail the water out. It's difficult, but I'm not a bit afraid!'

'Poor Big Toe!' the brothers said to each other and huddled closer together inside the sock.

The little boy had splashed through the puddle by now. Next he found a tricycle and got on it. He rode it as fast as he could and stuck both his legs straight out in the air.

Mr. Big Toe's telephone rang again. 'Hullo boys, hullo! It's your brother Big Toe calling. I'm floating in mid-air. I'm in an aeroplane, but you needn't worry, it's quite safe. The boat sank, though I did my best to bail all the water out. I was alone, you see, that made it very difficult. However, you'll be pleased to know I'm on my way home now. See you all soon!'

The boy went indoors to change his wet socks. The five toes got a new home to live in and the boy set out again with another big sandwich in his hand.

'Fancy you coming home to us!' said all the brothers to Mr. Big Toe, and they curled themselves round him to make him feel warm and cosy.

'Yes, yes, home is all right when the sock is dry and clean,' said Mr. Big Toe. 'But I don't suppose it will be long before I take another journey.'

A concertina concert

Do YOU remember the story we made up? The one about the ogres, Gapy Gob and Wily Winnie? Gapy Gob had two servants, Katie Cook and Charlie Chop, who were not ogres at all, but just ordinary children. Wily Winnie had a cat to look after her, called Ribby Ratsoup, a very cunning cat. These two would sit at home in the evenings and talk about how they could get Gapy Gob to marry Wily Winnie. Then one day, just after New Year, the cat had an idea.

'I know how to get Gapy Gob to marry you,' she said. 'Tell him you have learned to play the concertina. Gapy likes concertina music better than anything.'

'You have some bright ideas, I must say!' said Wily Winnie scornfully. 'You know I can't play the concertina.'

'Don't worry about that,' said Ribby. 'I met a musician in the forest this morning; that's what made me think of it. Wait here till I fetch him.'

So the cat went into the forest and there, under a fir-tree, sat a very small, thin musician. He had been

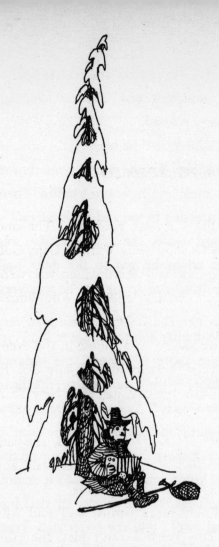

playing his concertina at village gatherings all through
Christmas and now he was anxious to get home as
quickly as possible. But when Ribby had met him that
morning, the little musician had lost his way in the
forest. So Ribby had promised to come back and guide
him if he would wait there.

'You can play me a tune in return,' the cat had said.

Now, when the musician saw the cat trotting towards him he was very pleased.

'Shall I play you a tune now?' he asked.

'Not just yet,' said Ribby. 'I want you to come home with me first to eat a meal and have some coffee. Then you can play your concertina to me and my mistress.'

This sounded a good idea to the musician, who was hungry by now. But when he got to the door and saw that the cat's mistress was an ogress, he was very frightened.

At first Wily Winnie did her best to be nice to him, but as this only made him more frightened, she ordered Ribby to lock the door. 'Now,' she said to the little musician, 'you'll do as we say!' And she brought out a large orange-box and put it in the middle of the floor.

'Get in that box, quick sharp!' said the ogress. And the musician had to crawl inside, whether he liked it or not.

Then Wily Winnie said: 'You're to stay in that box and not make a sound until I give the box a kick. Then you must play "A Life on the Ocean Wave" on your concertina.'

'Do I have to sing as well?' asked the musician, whose knees were knocking together with fear.

'Certainly,' said Wily Winnie. 'What's more, you've to make up a song about Gapy Gob and me this instant

—something about how I love him and would like him
to marry me.'

The musician thought as quickly as he could, and
then he sang this song:

> 'Gapy Gob is bright and fair,
> Combing down his yellow hair,
> He's my ain for ever mair,
> Bonny Gapy Gob—o!'

'Not my own idea, I'm afraid,' said the musician,
'but it's rather difficult to make up songs sitting in an
orange-box.'

'It'll do,' said Wily Winnie. Then she sent the cat to
fetch Gapy Gob, and smartened herself up as well as she
could. Suddenly she remembered she would have to
have a concertina herself, or Gapy Gob would never
believe she was playing it.

'I must have a concertina,' she said.

'You'll find an old broken one in my sack,' said the musician. 'It hasn't a note in it.'

'Good,' said Wily Winnie. So she sat down and waited for Ribby to come back with Gapy Gob. But they were a very long time.

'I think I shall have to go and see what has happened to my cat,' said the ogress. 'You wait there.' And she left the musician sitting in the box. He hadn't been there long, however, before the door opened. Can you guess who came in? Katie Cook and Charlie Chop.

When the cat had arrived to invite Gapy Gob to come and listen to Wily Winnie playing the concertina, the children were quite sure something was up. So they had slipped out the back way and taken a short cut through the forest to the ogress's house. They had just seen Wily Winnie leave so they knew it was safe to go in.

'I wonder what's in that orange-box?' said Charlie Chop.

'It's me!' said the musician, and he told the children the whole story of what had happened to him after he had got lost.

'I'll show you the way home,' said Katie, 'but we'll have to be quick; the others will be here any moment now. Follow me!'

The musician crawled out of the box and ran out of the house with Katie as fast as his thin legs could carry him.

Charlie had borrowed the good concertina; now he crept into the box in the musician's place.

After a time the cat came back with Wily Winnie and Gapy Gob. The ogress was in high spirits. 'Now you just listen, Gapy Gob,' she said. 'I'm going to sit on this orange-box and play "A Life on the Ocean Wave" and you'll be *amazed*.' She picked up the old broken concertina, gave the box a kick, and started pretending to play.

But what came out was *not* 'A Life on the Ocean Wave' because, of course, it was Charlie Chop who was inside the box, and he made the most horrible noise he could on the concertina.

'Oh no, please stop!' said Gapy Gob, holding his ears. 'That was the most frightful noise I ever heard!'

'Perhaps you would like me to sing for you instead,' said Wily Winnie, and gave the box another kick. This was the signal for the musician to sing his song about Gapy Gob—you know, the one that went like 'Bobby Shaftoe':

> 'Gapy Gob is bright and fair,
> Combing down his yellow hair,
> He's my ain for ever mair,
> Bonny Gapy Gob—o!'

But this is what Charlie sang instead:

> 'Gapy is the ugliest fellow,
> Ever since I first could bellow,
> I have wished he was a toad
> So I could chase him down the road.'

'Well!' said Gapy Gob. 'I must say! If you've brought me all this way to make a fool of me, I'll go home this minute, and that's flat! Toad, indeed!' And with that he stumped out of the house, slamming the door behind him.

'Wait, Gapy! Dear Gapy! I can explain!' wailed the ogress as she hurried after him. Charlie Chop took this chance to get out of the box and run home by the short cut.

All this time Ribby Ratsoup had been in the kitchen cooking a celebration feast for his mistress and Gapy Gob. She couldn't understand why everything was so quiet suddenly, so she came in to have a look. There was nobody there. Not even in the orange-box, though she got inside it to make sure.

Just at that moment Wily Winnie came back; she was *not* in high spirits *now*. 'So it's you who's been sitting in there mocking me!' she shouted. 'You wait till I get my broom! I'll give you the hiding of your life!'

Late that night, when the little musician had long since reached home, and Gapy Gob had had his supper, and Katie Cook and Charlie Chop had finished all their work for the day, two dark figures could be seen leaping from hill-top to hill-top; it was Wily Winnie chasing Ribby Ratsoup with her broom.

A birthday party in Topsy Turvy Town

IN TOPSY TURVY TOWN, where the sun rises in the West and goes down in the North, and three times fourteen is four, the Mayor was going to have his fiftieth birthday. His little girl, Trixie, was busy baking cakes, but she couldn't get on, because the Mayor *would* keep bothering her to know how much longer it would be before his birthday.

'Do stop bothering me, Daddy dear,' she said. 'When you've slept one more night it will be your birthday. So run along to your office now, please, and write out invitations to the people you want to come to your party.'

'I won't ask the Postmaster, anyway,' said the Mayor.
'Why ever not?'

'He always teases me about my big ears,' answered the Mayor.

'That's only when he's with the Smith,' said Trixie. 'You always play perfectly well when the Smith isn't there.'

'But I want to ask the Smith,' said the Mayor. 'I'm sure he'll behave if he knows we're having birthday cake.'

'Well, you'd better ask them both, then.'

'I want to ask the Doctor and the Dentist as well,' said the Mayor.

'I only hope the Doctor will be well enough to go out,' said Trixie. 'I spoke to his little girl yesterday, and she

told me he had had a very bad night, tossing and turning. She was afraid he might be sickening for something. But I expect you'd better ask him all the same.'

'Oh yes, otherwise he'd sulk,' said the Mayor. 'So would the Dentist.'

'You do as you like,' said Trixie, 'but you know he isn't allowed any sweet things like chocolate cake with icing on.'

'I know. But we could give him apples and rusks instead,' said the Mayor.

'That's a good idea. Are you asking any more?'

'What a question! I can't leave the Baker out, can I?'

'Now, now, that's not the way for a Mayor to talk to his little girl!' said Trixie. 'Anyway, if you ask him you can't have any more; there isn't room.' Then she told him to put the invitations through the letter-boxes and come straight home to bed to have a good sleep before the great day.

The next day the Mayor was very excited. He sat in his office and looked at the clock till it was time to go home. Then he raced back to put on his Grand Chain of Office and went and stood by the door to welcome his guests.

The first to arrive was the Smith. He had his hands in his pockets.

'Many Happy Returns of the Day,' he said.

'Thank you,' said the Mayor, holding out his hand for the present.

'Haven't brought a present,' said the Smith.

'Never mind,' said Trixie soothingly. 'Wouldn't you like to take off those big heavy boots before you come in?'

'No,' said the Smith.

'Why not?' asked the little girl.

'Hole in my sock,' said the Smith.

'You can borrow my daddy's slippers. And then what about taking your hands out of your pockets?'

'No,' said the Smith.

'Why not?'

'Dirty,' said the Smith.

'Oh, we'll soon deal with that!' said Trixie. 'You come along to the bathroom with me; I'll help you

wash them. You'll have to let the others in by yourself, Daddy dear.'

Next came the Doctor and the Dentist. They walked hand-in-hand and each had a little parcel under his arm.

'Many Happy Returns,' they said, both together.

'Thank you very much,' said the Mayor, and started

unwrapping. The Doctor's present was a stethoscope, but it was only a toy, because it was broken. The Dentist gave him a nice thing to squirt his mouth with.

Then came the Postmaster, and he brought a packet

of stamps which were very unusual, because all the edges had been cut off.

Last of all came the Baker. He brought a large slab of chocolate, and when he had wished the Mayor many happy returns he broke the chocolate in two, gave one half to the Mayor and stuffed the other half in his pocket.

'Come in, all of you,' Trixie said, as she came out of the bathroom with the Smith. His hands were now so clean, he was ashamed to show them.

In the dining-room there was a fine spread, with a huge birthday cake in the middle of the table decorated with fifty candles.

'Now do sit down and help yourselves,' invited Trixie. 'I'm just going to telephone.' And she shut the door. She picked up the receiver. 'Hullo, can you please give me the little girl in Flat 2?'

'There you are,' said the operator.

'Hullo, is that you, Kitty? This is Trixie.'

'Oh, hullo Trixie! What do you want?'

'Could you come and help me this afternoon? My daddy is having a birthday party and there *is* so much to do!'

'Yes, all right. But I'll have to bring my doll's ironing; there's a whole heap of it,' said Kitty on the telephone.

'We can iron together, then. *I* have a whole heap to do as well,' said Trixie.

As she put the 'phone down, Trixie heard a terrible crash from the dining-room, and when she opened the door what a sight met her eyes! There was birthday cake plastered all over the walls, and cups and saucers were strewn about the floor!

'What is the meaning of this?' she demanded sternly.

It was the Postmaster who answered. 'Well, you see, the Mayor tried to blow out the candles and he couldn't do it, so we all had a go and none of us could do it. Except the Smith.'

Trixie frowned. 'How did *you* manage it when the others couldn't do it?' she asked.

'Had my bellows,' said the Smith, staring up at the ceiling.

'Oh dear,' sighed Trixie. 'I suppose I shall have to clean up the mess. But then you really must behave. I have someone coming to see me, and we shall be in the nursery. So you're not to come in there. You can play in the sitting-room when you have finished your tea.' Then she left them to get on with it.

Trixie and her friend Kitty were ironing their dolls' clothes and having a very interesting talk together when suddenly there was another awful crash from the room where the party was going on. The Mayor came and knocked on the nursery door.

'What is it?' asked Trixie.

'It's the Postmaster,' said the Mayor; 'he's started teasing me again; I want him to go home.'

Trixie had to go and make peace. 'I really don't know why you can't play nicely instead of quarrelling,' she said.

The Postmaster was standing next to the Smith, staring at the floor. The Smith was looking at the ceiling, as usual.

'What did the Postmaster say?' asked Trixie.

'He said my ears were so big he would put a stamp on my forehead and send me by air-mail,' said the Mayor.

'*We* never put stamps on people and send them by air-mail,' said the Doctor and the Dentist, both together.

'Oh, how silly!' said Trixie. 'Now please be good boys and play a game, or something. What about Blind Man's Buff? Then I'll go and cook some lovely hot sausages for you.'

Trixie called to Kitty. 'I'll have to stop ironing dolls' clothes now, I must cook the sausages.'

'I'll come and help you,' said Kitty. 'I've finished my ironing.'

'Good,' said Trixie. But no sooner had they got to work in the kitchen than the door of the sitting-room flew open, and the Baker rushed out, grabbing his coat from the peg. Then he shot through the front door and down the main stairs, taking two at a time.

'*Now* what's happened?' asked Trixie.

The Mayor, who was nearly crying, came out in the kitchen. 'The Baker snatched his present back and ran off, just because he couldn't catch any of us in Blind Man's Buff,' he said.

'Oh dear! Oh dear!' said Trixie.

'*We* don't snatch our presents back and run off home,' said the Doctor and the Dentist.

'Of course not. You're *good* boys,' said Trixie, 'and I have some nice hot sausages for you.' Suddenly she noticed the Dentist's face. 'Goodness Gracious!' she exclaimed. 'What's that swelling you have on your cheek?' She beckoned to Kitty to have a look. 'I do believe he's got an ab—ab—what's it called?'

'You mean an abscess,' said Kitty, who was very clever. She climbed on the Dentist's knee. The Dentist opened his mouth wide, and, sure enough, he had an abscess!

'You'll have to go home to your little girl at once,' said Trixie, 'and get her to pull out the tooth for you.'

'He's not the only one who'll have to go home,' said Kitty. 'Look at the Doctor, he's coming out in spots all over his face. I expect he's getting measles.'

'Goodness Gracious!' cried Trixie. 'You'll all have to go at once before you catch the measles. Hurry and get your things on!'

So they all put on their coats and shook hands and said 'thank you' before they went home.

All except the Smith. He sat in the hall and took a very long time to put on his boots.

'You must go home to *your* little girl now,' said Trixie.

'Haven't got one,' said the Smith, with his eyes on the ceiling.

Trixie and Kitty both said 'Oh, you poor thing!' and they gave him all that was left of the birthday cake and a bucket, full of sausages, to take home.

The Mayor walked round the dining-room table, scraping all the plates and drinking all the cold tea. He thought it had been a wonderful party.

Father Christmas and the carpenter

THERE was once a carpenter called Anderson. He was a good father and he had a lot of children.

One Christmas Eve, while his wife and children were decorating the Christmas tree, Anderson crept out to his wood-shed. He had a surprise for them all: he was going to dress up as Father Christmas, load a sack of presents on to his sledge and go and knock on the front door. But as he pulled the loaded sledge out of the wood-shed, he slipped and fell right across the sack of presents. This set the sledge moving, because the ground sloped from the shed down to the road, and Anderson had no time even to shout 'Way there!' before he crashed into another sledge which was coming down the road.

'I'm very sorry,' said Anderson.

'Don't mention it; I couldn't stop myself,' said the other man. Like Anderson, he was dressed in Father Christmas clothes and had a sack on his sledge.

'We seem to have had the same idea,' said Anderson. 'I see you're all dressed up like me.' He laughed and shook the other man's hand. 'My name's Anderson.'

'Glad to meet you,' said the other. 'I'm Father Christmas.'

'Ha, ha!' laughed Anderson. 'You will have your little joke, and quite right too on a Christmas Eve.'

'That's what I thought,' said the other man, 'and if you agree we can change places tonight, and that will be a better joke still; I'll take the presents along to *your* children, if you'll go and visit *mine*. But you must take off that costume.'

Anderson looked a bit puzzled. 'What am I to dress up in then?'

'You don't need to dress up at all,' said the other. 'My children see Father Christmas all the year round, but they've never seen a real carpenter. I told them last Christmas that if they were good this year I'd try and get the carpenter to come and see them while I went round with presents for the human children.'

'So he really *is* Father Christmas,' thought Anderson to himself. Out loud he said: 'All right, if you really want me to, I will. The only thing is, I haven't any presents for your children.'

'Presents?' said Father Christmas. 'Aren't you a carpenter?'

'Yes, of course.'

'Well, then, all you have to do is to take along a few pieces of wood and some nails. You have a knife, I suppose?' Anderson said he had and went to look for the things in his workshop.

'Just follow my footsteps in the snow; they'll lead you to my house in the forest,' said Father Christmas. 'Then I'll take your sack and sledge and go and knock on your door.

'Righto!' said the carpenter.

Then Father Christmas went off to knock at Anderson's door, and the carpenter trudged through the snow in Father Christmas's footsteps. They led him into the forest, past two pine-trees, a large boulder and a tree-stump. There, peeping out from behind the stump, were three little faces with red caps on.

'He's here! He's here!' shouted the Christmas children as they scampered in front of him to a fallen tree, lying with its roots in the air. When Anderson followed them round to the other side of the roots he found Mother Christmas standing there waiting for him.

'Here he is, Mum! Here's the carpenter Dad promised us! Look at him! Isn't he tall!' The children were all shouting at once.

'Now, now, children,' said Mother Christmas, 'anybody would think you'd never seen a human being before.'

'We've never seen a proper *carpenter* before!' shouted the children. 'Come on in, Mr. Carpenter!'

Pulling a branch aside, Mother Christmas led the way into the house. Anderson had to bend his long back double and crawl on his hands and knees. But once in, he found he could straighten up. The room had a mud floor, but it was very cosy, with tree-stumps for chairs, and beds made of moss with covers of plaited grass. In the smallest bed lay the Christmas baby and in the far corner sat a very old Grandfather Christmas, his red cap nodding up and down.

'Have you got a knife? Did you bring some wood and some nails?' The children wanted to know everything at once and pulled at Anderson's sleeve.

'Now, children,' said Mother Christmas, 'let the carpenter sit down before you start pestering him.'

'Has anyone come to see me?' croaked old Grandfather Christmas.

Mother Christmas shouted in his ear. 'It's Anderson, the carpenter!' She explained that Grandfather was so old he never went out any more. 'He'd be pleased if you came over and shook hands with him.'

So Anderson took the old man's hand which was as hard as a piece of bark.

'Come and sit here, Mr. Carpenter!' called the children.

The eldest one spoke first. 'D'you know what I want you to make for me? A toboggan. Can you do that—a little one, I mean?'

'I'll try,' said Anderson, and it didn't take long before he had a smart toboggan just ready to fly over the snow.

'Now it's my turn,' said the little girl who had pigtails sticking straight out from her head. 'I want a doll's bed.'

'Have you any dolls?' asked Anderson.

'No, but I borrow the field-mice sometimes, and I can play with the baby squirrels as much as I like. They *love* being dolls. Please make me a doll's bed.'

So the carpenter made her a doll's bed. Then he asked the smaller boy what he would like. But he was very shy and could only whisper, 'Don't know.'

' 'Course he knows!' said his sister. 'He said it just before you came. Go on, tell the carpenter.'

'A top,' whispered the little boy.

'That's easy,' said the carpenter, and in no time at all he had made a top.

'And now you must make something for Mum!'
said the children. Mother Christmas had been watching,
but all the time she held something behind her back.

'Shush, children, don't keep bothering the carpenter,'
she said.

'That's all right,' said Anderson. 'What would you
like me to make?'

Mother Christmas brought out the thing she was
holding; it was a wooden ladle, very worn, with a crack
in it.

'Could you mend this for me, d'you think?' she asked.

'Hm, hm!' said Anderson, scratching his ear with his
carpenter's pencil. 'I think I'd better make you a new
one.' And he quickly cut a new ladle for Mother Christmas. Then he found a long twisted root with a crook at

one end and started stripping it with his knife. But, although the children asked him and asked him, he wouldn't tell them what it was going to be. When it was finished he held it up; it was a very distinguished-looking walking-stick.

'Here you are, Grandpa!' he shouted to the old man, and handed him the stick. Then he gathered up all the chips and made a wonderful little bird with wings outspread to hang over the baby's cot.

'How pretty!' exclaimed Mother Christmas and all the children. 'Thank the carpenter nicely now. We'll certainly never forget this Christmas Eve, will we?'

'Thank you, Mr. Carpenter, thank you very much!' shouted the children.

Grandfather Christmas himself came stumping across the room, leaning on his new stick. 'It's grand!' he said. 'It's just grand!'

There was a sound of feet stamping the snow off outside the door, and Anderson knew it was time for him to go. He said goodbye all round and wished them a Happy Christmas. Then he crawled through the narrow opening under the fallen tree. Father Christmas was waiting for him. He had the sledge and the empty sack with him.

'Thank you for your help, Anderson,' he said. 'What did the youngsters say when they saw you?'

'Oh, they seemed very pleased. Now they're just waiting for you to come home and see their new toys. How did you get on at my house? Was little Peter frightened of you?'

'Not a bit,' said Father Christmas. 'He thought I was you. "Sit on Dadda's knee," he kept saying.'

'Well, I must get back to them,' said Anderson, and said goodbye to Father Christmas.

When he got home, the first thing he said to the children was, 'Can I see the presents you got from Father Christmas?'

But the children laughed. 'Silly! You've seen them already—when you were Father Christmas; you un-packed them all for us!'

'What would you say if I told you I had been with Father Christmas's family all this time?'

But the children laughed again. 'You wouldn't say anything so silly!' they said, and they didn't believe him. So the carpenter came to me and asked me to write the story down, which I did.

Mrs Pepperpot to the Rescue

WHEN IT IS breaking-up day at the village school, and the summer holidays are about to begin, all the children bring flowers to decorate the school. They pick them in their own gardens or they get them from their uncles and aunts, and then they carry their big bunches along the road, while they sing and shout because it is the end of term. Their mothers and fathers wave to them from the windows and wish them a happy breaking-up day.

But in one window stands a little old woman who just watches the children go by. That is Mrs Pepperpot.

She has no one now to wish a happy breaking-up day, for all her own children are long since grown up and gone away, and none of the young ones think of asking her for flowers.

At least, that's not quite true; I do know of one little girl who picked flowers in Mrs Pepperpot's garden. But that was several years ago, not long after the little old woman first started shrinking to the size of a pepperpot at the most inconvenient moments.

9

That particular summer Mrs Pepperpot's garden was fairly bursting with flowers: there were white lilac with boughs almost laden to the ground, blue and red anemones on strong, straight stalks, poppies with graceful nodding yellow heads and many other lovely flowers. But no one had asked Mrs Pepperpot for any of them, so she just stood in her window and watched as the children went by, singing and shouting, on their way to the breaking-up day at school.

The very last to cross the yard in front of her house was a little girl, and she was walking, oh, so slowly, and

carried nothing in her hands. Mrs Pepperpot's cat was lying on the doorstep and greeted her with a 'Miaow!' But the little girl only made a face and said, 'Stupid animal!' And when Mrs Pepperpot's dog, which was chained to the wall, started barking and wagging his tail the little girl snapped, 'Hold your tongue!'

Then Mrs Pepperpot opened the window to throw a bone out to the dog and the little girl whirled round and shouted angrily, 'Don't you throw that dirty bone on my dress!'

That was enough. Mrs Pepperpot put her hands on her hips and told the little girl that no one had any right to cross the yard in front of her house and throw insulting words at her or her cat and dog, which were doing no harm to anybody.

The little girl began to cry. 'I want to go home,' she sobbed. 'I've an awful pain in my tummy and I don't want to go to the breaking-up party! Why should I go when I have a pain in my tummy?'

'Where's your mother, child?' asked Mrs Pepperpot.

'None of your business!' snapped the girl.

'Well, where's your father, then?' asked Mrs Pepperpot.

'Never you mind!' said the girl, still more rudely. 'But if you want to know why I don't want to go to school today it's because I haven't any flowers. We haven't a garden, anyway, as we've only been here since Christmas. But Dad's going to build us a house now that he's working at the ironworks, and then we'll have a garden. My mum makes paper flowers and does the paper round, see? Anything more you'd like to know? Oh well, I might as well go to school, I suppose. Teacher can say what she likes—I don't care! If *she'd* been going from school to school for three years she wouldn't know much either! So blow her and her flowers!' And the little girl stared defiantly at Mrs Pepperpot.

Mrs Pepperpot stared back at the little girl and then

she said: 'That's the spirit! But I think I can help you with the flowers. Just you go out in the garden and pick some lilac and anemones and poppies and anything else you like. I'll go and find some paper for you to wrap them in.'

So the girl went into the garden and started picking flowers while Mrs Pepperpot went indoors for some paper. But just as she was coming back to the door she shrank!

Roly Poly! And there she was, tucked up in the paper like jam in a pudding, when the little girl came running back with her arms full of flowers.

'Here we are!' shouted the little girl.

'And here *we* are!' said Mrs Pepperpot as she disentangled herself from the paper. 'Don't be scared; this is something that happens to me from time to time, and I never know when I'm going to shrink. But now I've got an idea; I want you to pop me in your satchel and take me along with you to school. We're going to have a game with them all! What's your name, by the way?'

'It's Rita,' said the little girl who was staring at Mrs Pepperpot with open mouth.

'Well, Rita, don't just stand there. Hurry up and put the paper round those flowers. There's no time to lose!'

When they got to the school the breaking-up party was well under way, and the teacher didn't look particularly pleased even when Rita handed her the lovely bunch of flowers. She just nodded and said, 'Thanks.'

'Take no notice,' said Mrs Pepperpot from Rita's satchel.

'Go to your desk,' said the teacher. Rita sat down with her satchel on her knee.

'We'll start with a little arithmetic,' said the teacher. 'What are seven times seven?'

'Forty-nine!' whispered Mrs Pepperpot from the satchel.

'Forty-nine!' said Rita.

This made the whole class turn round and stare at Rita, for up to now she had hardly been able to count to thirty! But Rita stared back at them and smiled. Then she stole a quick look at her satchel.

'What's that on your lap?' asked the teacher. 'Nobody is allowed to use a crib. Give me your satchel at once!'

So Rita had to carry it up to the teacher's desk where it was hung on a peg.

The teacher went on to the next question: 'If we take fifteen from eighteen what do we get?'

All the children started counting on their fingers, but Rita saw that Mrs Pepperpot was sticking both her arms and one leg out of the satchel.

'Three!' said Rita before the others had had time to answer.

This time nobody suspected her of cheating and Rita beamed all over while Mrs Pepperpot waved to her from between the pages of her exercise book.

'Very strange, I must say,' said the teacher. 'Now we'll have a little history and geography. Which country is it that has a long wall running round it and has the oldest culture in the world?'

Rita was watching the satchel the whole time, and now she saw Mrs Pepperpot's head pop up again. The little old woman had smeared her face with yellow chalk and now she put her fingers in the corners of her eyes and pulled them into narrow slits.

'China!' shouted Rita.

The teacher was quite amazed at this answer, but she had to admit that Rita was right. Then she made an announcement.

'Children,' she said, 'I have decided to award a treat to the one of you who gave the most right answers. Rita gave me all the right answers, so she is the winner, and she will be allowed to serve coffee to the teachers in the staff-room afterwards.'

Rita felt very pleased and proud; she was so used to getting meals ready when she was alone at home that she was sure she could manage this all right. So, when the other children went home, she took her satchel from the teacher's desk and went out into the kitchen. But, oh dear, it wasn't a bit like home! The coffee-pot was far too big and the huge cake with icing on it was very different from the plate of bread-and-dripping she usually got ready for her parents at home. Luckily the cups and saucers and plates and spoons had all been laid out on the table beforehand. All the same, it seemed too much to Rita, and she just sat down and cried. In a moment she heard the sound of scratching from the satchel, and out stepped Mrs Pepperpot.

'If you're the girl I take you for,' said the little old woman, putting her hands on her hips, 'you won't give up half-way like this! Come on, just you lift me up on the table, we'll soon have this job done! As far as I could see from my hiding place, there are nine visiting teachers and your own Miss Snooty. That makes two cups of water and two dessertspoons of coffee per person—which makes twenty cups of water and twenty dessertspoons of coffee in all—right?'

'I think so. Oh, you're wonderful!' said Rita, drying her tears. 'I'll measure out the water and coffee at once, but I don't know how I'm going to cut up that cake!'

'That'll be all right,' said Mrs. Pepperpot. 'As far as I can see the cake is about ninety paces—my paces—round. So if we divide it by ten that'll make each piece nine paces. But that will be too big for each slice, so we'll divide nine by three and make each piece three paces thick. Right?'

'I expect so,' said Rita, who was getting a bit lost.

'But first we must mark a circle in the middle of the cake,' went on Mrs Pepperpot. 'Lift me up on your hand, please.'

Rita lifted her carefully on to her hand.

'Now take me by the legs and turn me upside down. Then, while you swing me round, I can mark a circle with one finger in the icing. Right; let's go!'

So Rita swung Mrs Pepperpot round upside down and the result was a perfect little circle drawn right in the middle of the cake.

'Crumbs are better than no bread!' said Mrs Pepperpot as she stood there, swaying giddily and licking her finger. 'Now I'll walk right round the cake, and at every third step I want you to make a little notch in the icing with the knife. Here we go!

> 'One, two, three, notch!
> One, two, three, notch!
> One, two, three, notch!'

And in this way Mrs Pepperpot marched all round the cake, and Rita notched it so that it made exactly thirty slices when it was cut.

When they had finished someone called from the staff-room: 'Where's that clever girl with the coffee? Hurry up and bring it in, dear, then you can fetch the cake afterwards.'

Rita snatched up the big coffee-pot, which was boiling now, and hurried in with it, and Mrs Pepperpot stood listening to the way the teachers praised Rita as she poured the coffee into the cups with a steady hand.

After a while she came out for the cake. Mrs Pepperpot clapped her hands: 'Well done, Rita! There's nothing to worry about now.'

But she shouldn't have said that, for while she was listening to the teachers telling Rita again how clever she was, she suddenly heard that Miss Snooty raising her voice:

'I'm afraid you've forgotten two things, dear,' she said.

'Oh dear!' thought Mrs Pepperpot, 'the cream-jug and the sugar-bowl! I shall have to look and see if they are both filled.'

The cream-jug was full, but when Mrs Pepperpot leaned over the edge of the sugar-bowl she toppled in! And at the same moment Rita rushed in, put the lid on the sugar-bowl and put it and the cream-jug on a little tray. Then she turned round and went back to the staff-room.

First Mrs Pepperpot wondered if she should tell Rita where she was, but she was afraid the child might drop the tray altogether, so instead she buried herself well down in the sugar-bowl and hoped for the best.

Rita started carrying the tray round. But her teacher hadn't finished with her yet. 'I hope you remembered the sugar-tongs,' she said.

Rita didn't know what to say, but Mrs Pepperpot heard the remark, and when the visiting head teacher took the lid off, Mrs Pepperpot popped up like a jack-in-the-box holding a lump of sugar in her outstretched hand. She stared straight in front of her and never moved

an eyelid, so the head teacher didn't notice anything
odd. He simply took the sugar lump and waved Rita on
with the tray. But his neighbour at the table looked hard
at Mrs Pepperpot and said: 'What very curious sugar-
tongs—I suppose they're made of plastic. Whatever will
they think of next?' Then he asked Rita if she had
brought them with her from home, and she said yes,
which was strictly true, of course.

After that everyone wanted to have a look at the
curious sugar-tongs, till in the end Rita's teacher called
her over.

'Let me have a look at those tongs,' she said. She
reached out her hand to pick them up, but this was too
much for Mrs Pepperpot. In a moment she had the
whole tray over and everything fell on the floor. The

cream-jug was smashed and the contents of the sugar-bowl rolled under the cupboard, which was just as well for Mrs Pepperpot!

But the teacher thought it was she who had upset the tray, and suddenly she was sorry she had been so hard on the little girl. She put her arms round Rita and gave her a hug. 'It was all my fault,' she said. 'You've been a very good little parlourmaid.'

Later, when all the guests had gone, and Rita was clearing the table, the teacher pointed to the dark corner by the cupboard and said, 'Who is that standing there?'

And out stepped Mrs Pepperpot as large as life and quite unruffled. 'I've been sent to lend a hand with the washing-up,' she said. 'Give me that tray, Rita. You and I will go out into the kitchen.'

When at last the two of them were walking home, Rita said, 'Why did you help me all day when I was so horrid to you this morning?'

'Well,' said Mrs Pepperpot, 'perhaps it was because you *were* so horrid. Next time maybe I'll help that Miss Snooty of yours. She looks pretty horrid too, but she might be nice underneath.'

Mrs Pepperpot on the Warpath

IT WAS the day after Mrs Pepperpot had helped Rita at the school party, and the little old woman was in a terrible rage. You see, if there's anything Mrs Pepperpot hates, it's people being unkind to children. All night she had been thinking about it, and now she had made up her mind to go and tell Rita's teacher just what she thought of her. So she put on her best hat and her best frock, straightened her back and marched off to the school.

'I hope I don't shrink this time,' she thought, 'but it's not likely to happen two days running. Anyway, today I must have my say or I shall burst. Somebody's going to say she's sorry or my name's not Pepperpot!'

She had reached the school gate and swung it open. Then she walked up to the teacher's front door and knocked twice smartly. Then she waited.

No one said, 'Come in!'

Mrs Pepperpot knocked again, but there was still no answer. So she decided to try the latch. 'If the door isn't locked I shall go straight in,' she said to herself. She pressed the latch and the door opened. But no sooner had she put a foot over the threshold than she shrank and fell head over heels into a travelling-rug which was rolled up on the floor just inside the door! Next to it stood a suitcase and a hatbox.

'Oh, calamity!' cried Mrs Pepperpot, 'let's hope she's not in after all now!' But she was unlucky, for now she could hear footsteps in the corridor and the teacher came towards the front door dressed in her going-out clothes.

'What an old dolt I am!' thought Mrs Pepperpot. 'Fancy me not remembering the summer holidays have started today and she'll be going away, of course. Oh well, she's not gone yet. If I can manage to stay near her

for a little while longer I may still get my chance to give her a piece of my mind.' So she hid in the rug.

The teacher picked up the suitcase in one hand, then she threw the travelling-rug over her shoulder and picked up the hatbox in the other hand and walked out of the house, closing the door behind her. And Mrs Pepperpot? She was clinging for dear life to the fringe of the rug and she was still as angry as ever.

'Very nice, I must say!' she muttered. 'Going away on a holiday like this without a thought for Rita and all the harm you did her. But you wait, my fine lady, very soon it'll be my turn to teach you a thing or two!'

26

The teacher walked briskly on, with Mrs Pepperpot dangling behind her, till they got to the station. Then she walked over to the fruit-stall and put the rug down on the counter, and Mrs Pepperpot was able to slip out of it and hide behind a bunch of flowers.

The teacher asked for two pounds of apples.

'That's right!' fumed Mrs Pepperpot to herself. 'Buy two pounds of apples to gorge yourself with on the train!'

'And eight oranges, please,' continued the teacher.

'Worse and worse!' muttered Mrs Pepperpot.

'And three pounds of bananas, please,' said the teacher.

Mrs Pepperpot could hardly contain herself: 'If I was my proper size now, I'd give you apples and oranges and bananas, and no mistake!'

Then the teacher said to the lady in the fruit-stall:

'Do you think you could do me a favour? I want all this fruit to go to one of my pupils, but I have to catch the train, so I've no time to take it to her myself. Could you deliver it to Rita Johansen in the little house by the church and tell her it's from me?'

On hearing this, Mrs Pepperpot's ears nearly fell off with astonishment. It was just as if someone had taken a sweet out of her mouth and left her nothing to suck; what was she going to say now?

'I'll do that for you with pleasure, miss,' said the fruit-lady. 'That'll be twelve shillings exactly.'

'Oh dear!' exclaimed the teacher, rummaging in her purse, 'I see I shan't have enough money left after buying my ticket. Would you mind if I owed you the twelve shillings till I come back from my holidays?'

'The very idea! Asking me to deliver goods you can't

even pay for! I shall have to have the fruit back, please,' the fruit-lady said, and held out her hand.

The teacher said she was sorry, put the bag of fruit back on the counter and went off to board her train, but Mrs Pepperpot had taken the chance to jump into the bag.

Silently she wished the teacher a good holiday: 'You're not so bad after all, and you needn't worry; I'll see that Rita gets her bag of fruit somehow. But *somebody*'s going to get the edge of my tongue before the day's out!'

Of course the fruit-lady could no more hear what Mrs Pepperpot was saying than the teacher could. She was busy getting ready to shut up shop and go home. But when she had put her hat on and opened the door she suddenly turned round and picked up the bag of fruit on the counter.

Mrs Pepperpot had just been wondering if she was going to be locked in the fruit-stall all night, and now here she was, being taken on another journey!

'I suppose you're going to eat all this yourself, you selfish old thing, you!' thought Mrs Pepperpot, getting worked up again. 'The teacher may be snooty, but at least she has a kind heart underneath. You're just plain mean! But just you wait till I grow again!'

The fruit-lady walked on and on, until at last Mrs

Pepperpot could hear her opening a door and going into a room. There she set the bag down with a thump on the table, and Mrs Pepperpot was able to climb over an orange and peep out of the top.

She saw a man banging on the table, and he was as cross as a sore bear. 'What sort of time is this to come home?' he roared. 'I've been waiting and waiting for my supper. Hurry up now! What's in that bag, anyway?'

'Oh, it's only some fruit for a little girl,' said his wife. 'The school-teacher wanted to send it to Rita Johansen, but she found she hadn't enough money, so I took it back. Then when she'd gone I felt sorry, so I thought I'd take it along to the child myself.'

This time Mrs Pepperpot was really amazed: 'Well, I never!' she gasped, 'here's another one who turns out to be nice. Still, I'm sure her husband won't; he looks as if he could do with a good ticking off!'

The fruit-lady's husband certainly was a cross-patch and no mistake. He banged his fist on the table and shouted that no wife of his was going to waste money and time running errands for silly school-teachers and brats.

'Give me that bag!' he roared. 'I'll take it right back to the shop this minute!' And he snatched up the bag from the table. Poor Mrs Pepperpot was given an awful shaking and landed up jammed between two bananas.

Taking long strides, the man walked off down the road.

'Bye-bye, fruit-lady!' whispered Mrs Pepperpot. 'You have a nasty husband, but I'll deal with him shortly, don't you worry!'

Squeezed and bruised, the little old woman lay there in the bag while the man strode on. But after a while he walked more slowly and at last he stopped at a house and knocked on the door.

'Surely this isn't the station?' wondered Mrs Pepperpot.

She heard the door open and the man spoke: 'Are you Rita Johansen?'

Then she heard a little girl's voice, 'Yes, that's me.'

'Your teacher sent you this,' said the man and handed over the bag; 'it's fruit.'

'Oh, thank you!' said Rita. 'I'll just go and get a bowl to put it in.' And she set the bag on a chair.

'That's all right,' said the man, and he turned on his heel and walked away.

32

When Rita came back with the bowl she thought she heard the door close, but she didn't take much notice in her eagerness to see what the teacher had sent her.

But it was actually Mrs Pepperpot who had slipped out, for she was now her usual size and she wanted time to think; it had all been so surprising and not at all what she expected. As she walked she began to hurry. For now she knew who was going to get a piece of her mind, and rightly so! Someone who made her more angry than anyone else just now!

When she got home she marched straight to the mirror. Putting her hands on her hips she glared at the little old woman she saw there. 'Well!' she said, 'and who do you think you are, running round the country-side, poking your nose in where you're not wanted? Is it any of your business, may I ask, who the school-teacher buys fruit for? What d'you mean by hiding in people's travelling-rugs and spying on them? You ought to be ashamed of yourself, an old woman like you, behaving like a senseless child. As for the fruit-lady, why shouldn't she be cross? How was she to know if she could trust the teacher? And her husband; I suppose he can bang his fist on his own table if he likes without you interfering? Are you listening? Wouldn't you be pretty mad if you'd come home hungry and the wife wasn't there to cook your meal, eh? I'm disgusted with you! *They* were sorry for what they did and made amends, all three of them, but *you*, you just stand there glaring at me as if nothing had happened. Wouldn't it be an idea to say you were sorry?'

Mrs Pepperpot turned her back on the mirror and took a deep breath. 'That's better!' she said. 'I've got it all off my chest at last. Now I can give my tongue a rest and get on with the housework.'

But first she took one more look in the mirror, smiled shyly and bobbed a little curtsy.

'I'm sorry!' she said.

And the little old woman in the mirror smiled back at her and bobbed a little curtsy too.

The Nature Lesson

EVERY MORNING, when Mrs Pepperpot sits at her window with her after-breakfast cup of coffee, she watches a little boy who always walks across her yard on his way to school. The boy's name is Olly and he and Mrs Pepperpot are very good friends, though not in the way grown-ups usually are friends with children. Quite often Olly rushes past Mrs Pepperpot's window without even saying 'Good morning', because he is in such a hurry. But then Mrs Pepperpot has never even asked him his name or how old he is or what he wants for Christmas. She just watches him every morning and says to herself, 'There goes the little boy on his way to school.' As for Olly, he just glances up at her window and thinks, 'There's the old woman, drinking her coffee.'

Now with animals it is different: if Olly sees the cat sitting on Mrs Pepperpot's door-step he can't resist stopping to stroke her. He'll even sit down on the door-step and talk to her.

'Hullo, pussy,' he'll say. 'There's a lovely pussy!' And then, of course, he has to go and see the dog outside his kennel as well, in case he should get jealous.

'Hullo, boy! Good dog, good dog! You didn't think I'd forgotten you, did you? Oh, I wouldn't do that! There's a good dog!' And by the time he's made a fuss of them both he's late for school.

This is Olly's trouble: he's *very* fond of animals. He loves to play hide-and-seek with the squirrel he sees on his way to school, or to have a whistling-match with a blackbird. And as for *rainy* days, well, he spends so much time trying not to step on the worms wriggling by the puddles in the road that he's *always* late for school.

This won't do, of course, and when he's late his teacher gets cross, and she'll say, 'It's all very well being fond of animals; it's quite right that you should be, but it's no excuse for being late for school.'

But that wasn't what I was going to tell you. What I was going to tell you was how Mrs Pepperpot had a nature lesson one day. So here we go!

It was a lovely spring day, and Mrs Pepperpot was sitting by the window as usual, enjoying her cup of coffee and watching Olly come across the yard. He was walking rather briskly this time—watching some bird or animal had probably made him late again—so he had

36

only time to say 'Hullo, puss!' to the cat on the door-step and 'Hi, boy!' to the dog by the kennel.

But suddenly he stopped dead, turned round on his heel and started running back across the yard. Mrs Pepperpot had just come to the door to give the dog his breakfast and Olly rushed past her as fast as he could go.

Mrs Pepperpot called to him: 'Whatever's the matter with you, boy? The police after you?'

'Forgot my nature textbook!' answered Olly over his shoulder, and started off again.

'Wait a minute!' called Mrs Pepperpot. Olly stopped. 'You can't go all the way home again now; you'll be much too late for school. No, you go on and *I'll* go back for your book and bring it to you at school.'

Olly shuffled his feet a bit and looked unhappy; he didn't much like the idea of an old woman turning up in school with his nature textbook.

'Don't stand there shuffling, boy!' said Mrs Pepperpot. 'Where did you leave the book?'

'On the window-sill,' he answered; 'the window is open.'

'All right. Where do you want me to put the book when I get to the school? Come on, hurry up; we haven't got all day!' said Mrs Pepperpot, trying to look severe.

'There's a hole in the wall, just by the big birch tree; there's an old bird-nest there you can put it in.'

'In the old nest in a hole in the wall by the birch tree; right!' said Mrs Pepperpot. 'Now, off you go and see if you can be on time for a change! I'll see to the rest.'

'Righto!' said Olly and was off before you could say Jack Robinson.

Mrs Pepperpot took off her apron, smoothed her hair and stepped out into the yard. And then, of course, the inevitable thing happened; she shrank!

'This is bad,' thought Mrs Pepperpot, as she peeped over the wet grass by the door-step, 'but I've known worse.' She called to the cat: 'Come here, puss! You'll have to be my horse once again and help me fetch Olly's nature book from his house.'

'Miaow! All right,' said the cat, as she allowed Mrs Pepperpot to climb on her back. 'What sort of a thing is a nature book?'

'It's a book the children use in school to learn about animals,' answered Mrs Pepperpot, 'and one thing it says about cats is that you are "carnivores".'

'What does that mean?' asked the cat.

'That you eat meat, but never mind that now; all you have to do is to take me straight down the road till we get to the stream. Then we take a short cut across. . . .'

But, as they came near the stream, the cat said, 'Doesn't the book say anything about cats not liking to get their feet wet?' And then she stopped so abruptly that poor Mrs Pepperpot toppled right over her head and fell plump into the water!

'Good job I can swim,' spluttered Mrs Pepperpot as she came to the surface, 'humans aren't meant to live under water on account of the way they breathe with their lungs. Phew! It's hard work all the same; I'll take a rest on this stone and see if something turns up.'

While she was getting her breath a tiny animal stuck its nose out of the water, and started snarling at her. Now Mrs Pepperpot knew what that was, but you probably wouldn't, because it only lives in the faraway places, and it is called a lemming. Its fur is dappled brown and fawn, so that it looks a bit like a guinea-pig in summer, but in winter it turns white as the snow around it.

As I say, Mrs Pepperpot knew all about lemmings, so she snarled back at the little creature, making as horrible a noise as she could. 'I'm not afraid of you!' she said, 'though the book says you're the worst-tempered of all the little rodents and don't give way to a fierce dog or even a grown man. But now you can just stop showing off and help me out of this stream like a good lemming.'

41

'Well, blow me down!' said the lemming. 'I never saw a woman as small as you and with such a loud voice. Get on my back and I'll take you across. Where are you going, by the way?'

'To fetch a nature book from the house over there for a little boy at school,' said Mrs Pepperpot. 'And in that book there is quite a bit about you.'

'Oh? And what does it say?' asked the lemming, crawling out on to the grass with Mrs Pepperpot.

'It says that once every so many years lemmings come down from the mountains in great swarms and eat up all the green stuff they can find till they get to the sea.' Then she stopped, because she remembered that when the lemmings reach the sea in their search for food, thousands of them get drowned.

'We do get rather hungry,' said the lemming; 'as a matter of fact, I'm on my way now to join my mates in a little food-hunt. . . .'

'Couldn't you just take me down to the house?' pleaded Mrs Pepperpot; she didn't like the idea that he might drown in the sea. But the lemming's empty tummy was telling him to go, so he told Mrs Pepperpot she would have to manage by herself, and he ran off muttering to himself about juicy green leaves.

Before Mrs Pepperpot had had time to wonder what

would happen to him, another head appeared above a little wall. This time it was a stoat.

'Hullo, Mr Nosey Parker,' she greeted him, 'what are you looking for?'

'I thought you were a mouse, but I see you're a little old woman, and I don't eat women,' said the stoat. 'Have you by any chance got a silver spoon?' he added.

'I have something you like even better than silver spoons,' answered Mrs Pepperpot, 'a whole packet of tin-tacks, and you can have them if you'll take me to that house over there. I have to fetch a book from the window-sill for a little boy in the school.'

'All right,' said the stoat, 'hop up!'

So Mrs Pepperpot got on his back. But it was a most

uncomfortable journey, because stoats, like weasels, move by rippling their long bodies, and though they have short legs, they can run very fast. Mrs Pepperpot had a job keeping on and was glad when they reached the wall under the window.

The stoat scrambled up to the window-sill, and presently he came back with the book—under his chin.

'Why do you carry the book that way?' asked Mrs Pepperpot.

'How else?' answered the stout. 'I always carry eggs under my chin.'

'Eggs?' Mrs Pepperpot pretended to be surprised. 'I didn't know stoats laid eggs.'

'Ha, ha, very funny!' said the stoat. 'I suppose you don't eat eggs?'

'Oh yes,' said Mrs Pepperpot, 'but I don't steal them out of wild birds' nests.'

'That's my business,' said the stoat. 'Now you'd better think how you're going to get this book to school; I can't carry both you and the book.'

'That's true!' said Mrs Pepperpot. 'I'll have to think of something.'

But it wasn't necessary, for the next moment Mrs Pepperpot was back to her proper size. As she bent down to pick up the book she whispered to the little stoat, 'The tin-tacks will be waiting for you in that nest you robbed in the stone wall by the school.' And she thought she heard him chuckle as he rippled away in the grass.

When she reached the school the bell was ringing for break, and she just had time to pop the book into the empty nest before Olly came running out with the other children. Mrs Pepperpot gave the tiniest nod in the direction of the wall and then she walked briskly away.

But the next morning Olly brought a lovely bone for her dog and from his milk bottle he poured a good saucer-full of milk for her pussy.

Mrs Pepperpot opened the window. 'Would you do something for me this morning?' she asked.

'As long as it won't make me late for school,' answered Olly.

'Good,' said Mrs Pepperpot. Then she fetched a packet of tin-tacks from the toolshed and gave them to Olly. 'Put those in the empty nest in the wall, will you? They're for a friend of mine.'

The Shoemaker's Doll

THERE WAS once a shoemaker who won a doll in a raffle at a bazaar. But a doll was no good to him, living alone as he did in a little cottage where the floor was strewn with old soles and bits of leather and where everything he touched was covered in glue.

For, with all the village shoemaking to be done before he could do his own housework, you can imagine what the shoemaker's home looked like. And now there was this doll. When he had brought it home he stood looking round the little room and wondering where on earth he could put it. At last he decided to set the doll on top of the chest of drawers next to a half-loaf of bread and a rubber boot. Then he went to bed.

In the night he dreamed that the doll came over to his bed and said:

> 'I can scrub, I can sweep,
> Make a bed and house-keep;
> If *you* won't, *I* will!'

47

When the shoemaker opened his eyes next morning and saw the doll on the chest of drawers he remembered the dream and laughed to himself.

'So you can scrub and sweep and make beds, can you, my little flibberty gibbett? Still, I suppose I had better do it myself to save you spoiling your pretty frock,' he said. So he made his bed, which hadn't been done properly for fifteen years, and underneath he found the old gold watch his grandfather had left him. Until that moment he thought it was lost for ever. After that he washed the floor and found a half-crown lying in a corner behind the cupboard. Then he swept out all the rubbish from the drawer in his work-bench, and what do you think?

Right at the bottom he found a little ring with a red stone in it!

At first the shoemaker was astonished, but then he remembered:

'Yes, yes, of course! It was that little girl from Crag House; she did tell me she had lost her ring here once. She came to ask me about it several times. I'll put it on the shelf here and give it to her when I see her. And now I suppose I'd better tidy up the chest of drawers for you, my little slave-driver!'

He started by removing the rubber boot. But he decided to leave the half-loaf, because he liked to take a bite from time to time while he was mending the shoes.

Later in the day a village woman came in. When she

saw how tidy the room was she clapped her hands and exclaimed: 'Well I never! What a change! You must have had a lot of time to spare getting the place so ship-shape. I suppose you have my shoes ready as well, then?'

The shoemaker pushed his spectacles up on his fore-head and stared at the woman. Then he said, 'Come again Tuesday!'

'But it's Tuesday today,' objected the woman.

The shoemaker let his spectacles fall back on his nose.

'Come again Wednesday!' he snapped and went on with his work.

'Oh, you're just the same old lazy sour-puss that you always were!' said the woman, and left him to it.

In the afternoon a little boy started playing in the

street outside the house. He came to the door and asked the shoemaker to button his jacket because his fingers were too cold to manage the buttonhole.

'Come again Thursday!' said the shoemaker in his snappy voice.

'But I'm cold today, mister!' said the little boy.

'Come again Friday!' said the shoemaker.

'You're just a grumpy old toad, so you are!' said the little boy, and went away.

'Good riddance!' said the shoemaker, and he didn't even turn round, but went on with his work, mending and patching till it was too dark to work any more. Then he ate up the rest of the loaf and climbed into bed. But in his sleep he dreamed that the doll came over to him and this is what she said:

> 'I can button, mend a hose,
> I can wipe a runny nose,
> If *you* won't, *I* will!'

'You're a proper fusspot, aren't you?' said the shoemaker when he woke in the morning and remembered his dream. 'I'd better get those shoes finished for Mrs Butt. Then when I take them along to her I can take the ring for the little girl as well.'

So he sat down at his bench and finished mending Mrs Butt's shoes.

Meanwhile the little boy had started playing outside the window again; the shoemaker called him in.

'Come here, boy, let me button your coat for you,' he said. 'Would you like me to wipe that nose of yours too? You can tell me if it hurts.'

' 'Course it doesn't hurt,' said the little boy, blowing into the hankie like a trumpet and waving his fingers in the air; they were quite stiff and blue with cold. 'Not so cross today, are you?' he said, and then he added: 'I'd like to help *you* now. Got any messages for me to take?'

'Well yes, I have, as a matter of fact,' said the shoemaker. 'You can take these shoes to Mrs Butt at the corner, and while you're at it you can take this ring and give it to the little girl at Crag House; she lost it here a long time ago.'

'All right!' said the little boy and ran off with the things.

It wasn't long before he was back with a message from Mrs Butt. 'Mrs Butt told me to tell you that if you want your Sunday suit cleaned and pressed she'd be glad to do it for you. And that girl at Crag House told me to thank you and ask if you'd like to go to her birthday party tomorrow—she's asked me too, wasn't that nice of her?'

The shoemaker was staring in front of him, thinking hard. 'Very nice of her, I'm sure. But, as for me, I've been on my own for so long now I wouldn't know how to behave with other folks at a party. No, I'd better not go.'

But when the little boy had gone away and the shoemaker had got into bed he dreamed again that the doll came over to speak to him:

'I always smile when folks are kind,
Not turn my back and act so blind,
If *you* won't, *I* will!'

53

Next morning the shoemaker remembered and said to himself, 'I shall have to go, then.' And he has never regretted it. For one thing, he wore his Sunday suit, all neatly cleaned and pressed by Mrs Butt, and, for another, he had three different kinds of cake to eat, and, most important of all, he found out that it is good for people to get together now and then and not always to be moping on their own.

Ever since that day the shoemaker's cottage has been as clean as a new pin, and the shoemaker himself whistles and sings as he goes about his housework. He makes his bed and scrubs the floor, he buttons boys' coats and wipes their noses and he mends the shoes in double-quick time.

Every now and again, when there's something he *doesn't* want to do, he takes a quick look at his doll on the chest of drawers, and he always ends up by doing whatever it is he has to do. For if *he* won't, *she* will.

Mrs Pepperpot is taken for a Witch

MRS PEPPERPOT lives in a valley in Norway, and in summertime in that part of the world the nights hardly get dark at all. On Midsummer's Eve, in fact, the sun never quite goes down, so everybody, young and old, stays up all night to dance and sing and let off fireworks round a big bonfire. And because there's magic abroad on Midsummer's Eve they sometimes see witches riding on broomsticks through the sky—or they think they do, anyway.

Now the only two people in that valley who never used to go to the bonfire party were Mr and Mrs Pepperpot. Not that Mrs Pepperpot didn't want to go, but Midsummer's Eve happened to be Mr Pepperpot's birthday as well, and on that day it was he who decided what they did. He never liked mixing with a crowd on account of that shrinking habit of Mrs Pepperpot; he was always afraid that she would suddenly turn the size of a pepperpot and disappear, leaving him standing there looking a proper fool.

But this year Mrs Pepperpot *did* go to the party, and this is how it happened.

It started the night before Midsummer's Eve. Mrs Pepperpot had been to the store and was walking slowly home with her basket on her arm. She was wondering how she could persuade her husband to go to the bonfire when suddenly she had an idea.

'I could ask him if there was something he really wanted for his birthday, and then I could say I would give it to him if he promised to take me to the bonfire party.'

As soon as she got inside the door she jumped on her husband's knee and gave him a smacking kiss on the tip of his nose.

'Dear, good hubby,' she said, 'have you got a very special wish for your birthday tomorrow?'

Her husband was quite surprised. 'Have you had sunstroke or something? How could you buy anything? Why, money runs through your fingers like water.'

'Sometimes it does, and sometimes it doesn't,' said Mrs Pepperpot, looking sly; 'there are such things as hens, and hens lay eggs and eggs can be sold. Just now I have quite a tidy sum put by, so just you tell me what you would like and the present will be laid out here on the table as sure as my name's Pepperpot.'

'Well,' he said, 'if you think you have enough money to buy that handsome pipe with the silver band that's lying in the store window, I'll promise you something in return.'

'Done!' cried Mrs Pepperpot at once, 'and the thing I want you to promise me is to take me to the bonfire party on Windy Ridge tomorrow night!'

So Mr Pepperpot had to agree and the next day Mrs Pepperpot filled her pockets with all the sixpennies, pennies and threepenny bits she had earned from the eggs and set off to the store.

'I want to buy the pipe with the silver band,' said Mrs Pepperpot, when it came to her turn to be served.

But the grocer shook his head. 'Sorry, Mrs Pepperpot,'

he said, 'but I'm afraid I sold that pipe to Peter Poulsen yesterday.'

'Oh dear,' said Mrs Pepperpot, 'I'll have to go and see if he'll let me buy it off him,' and she hurried out of the door, letting the door-bell jingle loudly as she went.

She took the shortest way to Peter Poulsen's house, but when she got there only his wife was at home.

'I was wondering if your husband would sell me that pipe he bought in the store yesterday?' said Mrs Pepperpot. 'I'd pay him well for it,' she added, and patted her pocketful of coins.

'That pipe is no longer in the house,' said Mrs Poulsen, who had a sour look on her face. 'I wasn't going to have tobacco smoke in my curtains, no *thank* you! I gave it to some boys who were having a sale; they said they were collecting money for fireworks for tonight's bonfire, or some such nonsense.'

Mrs Pepperpot's heart sank; did Mrs Poulsen know where the sale was being held?

'Up on Windy Ridge, near the bonfire, the boys said,' answered Mrs Poulsen, and Mrs Pepperpot lost no time in making her way up to Windy Ridge.

But it was a tidy walk uphill and when she got to the top she found the boys had sold everything. They were busy tidying up the bits of paper and string and cardboard boxes and carrying them over to the bonfire.

Mrs Pepperpot was so out of breath her tongue was hanging out, but she managed to stammer, 'Who got the pipe?'

'What pipe?' asked one of the boys.

'The one with the silver band that Mrs Poulsen gave you.'

'Oh that,' said the boy; 'my brother bought it. But then he tried to smoke it and it made him sick. So he got fed up with it and tied it to a long pole and stuck it at the top of the bonfire. There it is—look!'

Mrs Pepperpot looked, and there it was, right enough, tied to a pole at the very top of the huge bonfire!

'Couldn't you take it down again?' she asked the boy.

'Are you crazy?' said the boy. 'Expect us to upset the bonfire when we've got everything piled up just nicely? Not likely! Besides, we're going to have some fun with that pipe; you wait and see! But I can't stand talking now, I must go and get a can of petrol to start it off.' And he ran off with the other boys.

'Oh dear, oh dear, oh dear!' wailed Mrs Pepperpot

to herself. 'I see there's nothing for it but to climb that bonfire and get it down myself.' But she looked with dismay at the mountain of old mattresses, broken chairs, table-legs, barrows, drawers, old clothes and hats, car-tyres and empty cartons.

'First I shall have to find a stick to poke the pipe off the pole when I do get up aloft,' she thought.

Just at that moment she turned small, but for once Mrs Pepperpot was really pleased. 'Hooray!' she shouted in her shrill little voice. 'It won't take long for a little thing like me to get that pipe down now, and I don't even need to upset the bonfire!'

Quick as a mouse, she darted into the big pile and started climbing up from the inside. But it was not as easy as she had thought; climbing over a mattress she got her heel stuck in a spring and it took her quite a while to free herself. Then she had difficulty in climbing a slippery chair-leg; she kept sliding back. But at last she managed it, only to find herself entangled in the lining of a coat. She groped about in this for some time before she found her way out of the sleeve.

By now people had started gathering round the bonfire.

'All right, let them have a good look,' she thought. 'Luckily I'm too small for them to see me up here. And nothing's going to stop me from getting to the top now!'

Just then she lost her grip and fell into a deep drawer. There she lay, puffing and blowing, till she managed to catch hold of a bonnet string which was hanging over the edge of the drawer.

'Not much further to go, thank goodness!' she told herself, but when she looked down she almost fainted; it was fearfully far to the ground, and now there were crowds of people standing round, waiting for the bonfire to be lit.

'No time to lose!' thought Mrs Pepperpot, and heaved herself on to the last obstacle. This was easy, because it was an old concertina, so she could walk up it like a staircase.

Now she was at the foot of the pole and at the top was the pipe, securely tied!

'However am I going to get up there?' she wondered, but then she noticed the rim of an empty tar-barrel right next to her. So she smeared a little tar on her hands to give them a better grip, and then she started to climb the pole. But the pole and the whole bonfire seemed to be heeling a little over to one side, and when she looked down she nearly fell off with fright: *the boys had lit the bonfire!*

Little flames were licking up round the mattresses and the broken furniture.

Then people started cheering and the children chanted: 'Wait till it gets to the pipe at the top! Wait till it gets to the pipe at the top!'

'Catch me waiting!' muttered Mrs Pepperpot. 'I've got to get there *first!*' and she climbed on up till her hands gripped the stem of the pipe. Down below she could hear the children shouting:

'Watch the flames when they reach the pole! There's a rocket tied to the pipe!'

'Oh, good gracious!' cried Mrs Pepperpot, clinging on for dear life. BANG! Up into the cold night sky shot the rocket, the pole, the pipe *and* Mrs Pepperpot!

Round the bonfire everyone suddenly stopped shouting. A thin woman in a shawl whispered to her neighbour:

'I thought I saw someone sitting on that stick!'

Her neighbour, who was even thinner and wore two shawls, whispered back, 'It could have been a witch!' and they both shuddered. But from behind them came a man's voice:

'Oh, it couldn't be her, could it?' It was Mr Pepperpot who had just left off working and had taken a ride up to the mountain to have a look at the bonfire. Now he swung himself on his bicycle again and raced home as fast as he could go, muttering all the way, 'Let her be at home; oh, please let her be at home!' When he reached the house and opened the door his hand was shaking.

There stood Mrs Pepperpot, quite her normal size and with no sign of a broomstick. She was decorating his birthday cake and on the table, neatly laid on a little cloth, was the precious pipe with its silver band.

'Many Happy Returns of the Day!' said Mrs Pepperpot. 'Come and have your meal now. Then you can put

on a clean shirt and take your wife to dance all night at the bonfire party!'

'Anything you say!' said Mr Pepperpot; he was so relieved she hadn't gone off with the witches of Midsummer's Eve.

The Little Mouse who was Very Clever

THERE WAS once a little mouse called Squeak, who sat behind the door in his mousehole, waiting for his mother to come home from the larder with some food.

Suddenly there was a knock at the door.

'Who is that?' asked little Squeak.

'Peep, peep, let me in, it's your mother,' said a voice outside, but it didn't sound a mousy sort of voice.

'Why are you knocking at our door?'

'I forgot to take the key,' said the voice.

'We don't use a key for this door,' said the little mouse.

'It's bolted on the inside and I'm not opening it for *you*!'

Whoever it was went away and Squeak waited for some time before there came another knock.

'Who is that?' asked Squeak.

'It's Peter,' said a voice, but it didn't sound like Peter, the little boy who lived in the house.

'Why are you knocking at our door?'

'Because you've been using my shawl for your bed,' said the voice.

'If you're a little boy, you won't want a shawl,' said Squeak. 'I'm not opening the door for you!'

After he had waited some time there was another knock.

'Who is that?' he asked.

'Peter's mother,' came the reply; 'let me in.'

'Why are you knocking at our door?'

'Because I think you must have hidden my braces down your hole,' said the voice, which sounded rather purry for a lady.

'If you are Peter's mother,' said little Squeak, 'I'm sure you don't need braces. I'm not opening the door for *you*!'

Again he had to wait a long time before the next knock.

'Who is that?' said Squeak.

'This is Peter's father,' said a voice that was very croaky. 'Let me in at once!'

'Why are you knocking at our door?' asked the little mouse.

'My tail went in the honey-pot and I want you to clean it.'

'If you are Peter's father,' said Squeak, 'why have you got a tail? I'm not opening the door for *you*!'

After that there was a long, long silence, and then at last there was a tiny little knock.

'Who is that?' asked Squeak.

'It's your mother, darling.'

But the little mouse wanted to make quite sure:

'Why are you knocking at our door?'

'Because I want my clever Squeak to unbolt it as he always does,' said the voice. Then he knew it was his mother, and the little mouse, who was too clever to be tricked by a cat with many voices, unbolted the door and let his mother in.

And because he'd been so clever his mother gave him an extra large lump of cheese for his supper.

Mrs Pepperpot's Birthday

IT WAS Mrs Pepperpot's birthday, so she had asked her neighbours in to coffee at three o'clock. All day she had been scrubbing and polishing, and now it was ten minutes to three and she was putting the final touches to the strawberry layer cake on the kitchen table. As she stood balancing the last strawberry on a spoon, she suddenly felt herself shrinking, not slowly as she sometimes did, but so fast that she didn't even have time to put the strawberry on a plate. It rolled on to the floor and Mrs Pepperpot tumbled after it. But she quickly picked herself up and jumped into the cat's basket. Puss was a bit surprised, but allowed her to snuggle down with the kittens. In her black-and-white-striped skirt and white blouse, she hoped the guests would take her for one of the cat-family, until the magic wore off and she could be her real size again. For you may remember that Mrs Pepperpot never liked anyone to see her when she was tiny.

There was a knock at the door, and, when it wasn't

answered, Sarah from South Farm walked into the little front hall, carrying a huge bunch of lilac.

'Many Happy Returns of the Day!' said Sarah. There was no reply, so she peered into the kitchen, thinking Mrs Pepperpot might be in there, though, naturally, she didn't look in the cat-basket. Somehow she managed to knock over the flower-vase on the hall table, and the water spilled on the tablecloth and on to the floor.

'Oh dear, oh dear!' thought Sarah. 'I shall have to mop that up before anybody notices.'

But at that moment there was another knock at the

door. So Sarah ran into the kitchen and hid in a cupboard.

In came Norah from North Farm, and she was carrying a very nice tablecloth.

'Many Happy Returns!' she said, but, as she got no answer, she looked round for Mrs Pepperpot, and her parcel swept the vase off the table on to the floor.

'That's bad!' thought Norah. 'I must put it back before anybody comes.'

But before she could do it there was another knock on the door and Norah hurried into the bedroom and crept under the bed.

Esther from East Farm came in, carrying a handsome glass bowl for Mrs Pepperpot. When she had said 'Many Happy Returns!' and no one answered, she walked

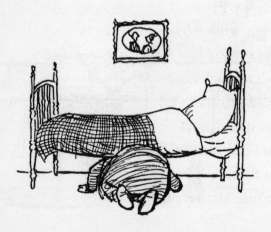

straight into the living-room. Carrying the bowl in front of her, she didn't notice the vase on the floor and put her foot straight on it. There was a nasty crunch and there it lay, in smithereens!

'Goodness gracious, what have I done?' thought Esther. 'Perhaps if I hide behind this curtain no one will know who did it!' So she quickly wrapped herself in one of the curtains.

At that moment the clock struck three, and the magic wore off; there was Mrs Pepperpot as large as life, walking through the kitchen. 'Coo-ee!' she called. 'You can all come out now!'

So Sarah stepped out of the cupboard, Norah crawled from under the bed, while Esther unwrapped herself from the curtain in the living-room.

At first they looked a bit sheepish, but then they said 'Many Happy Returns!' all over again and they had a good laugh, while Mrs Pepperpot swept up the broken vase, threw away the dead flowers and put the wet tablecloth in the wash-tub.

Then she thanked them for their fine presents; the table was spread with Norah's tablecloth, Esther's glass bowl was filled with fresh water, and the huge bunch of lilac that Sarah had brought was put into it.

After that Mrs Pepperpot brought in the coffee and

cakes and they all sat down to enjoy themselves. But on
the strawberry layer cake there was one strawberry
missing.

'You see,' said Mrs Pepperpot, when they asked her
what had happened to it, 'my *first* visitor this afternoon
was the little old woman who shrinks, and she was so
tiny today that one strawberry was all she could manage
to eat. So I gave her that and a thimble of milk to wash
it down.'

'Didn't you ask her to stay, so that we could see her?'
asked Sarah, for they were all very curious about the
little old woman who shrank, and nobody thereabouts
had ever seen her.

'She was sorry, she said, but she was in a tearing hurry; she had some business with a mouse, her night watchman or something. But she told me to tell you she did enjoy our little game of hide-and-seek!'

The Dancing Bees

_____

YOU HAVE probably been told that bees are very busy, hardworking creatures, collecting honey from the flowers from morning till night all through the summer to store it up for food in winter.

But now you shall hear about a she-bee who spent her time in quite a different way; she did nothing but dance. And what gave her this curious idea? Well, wait till I tell you.

One evening in June this she-bee was on her way home to the hive from the meadows, but she hadn't found any honey that day. So when she saw a beautiful flower right below her she swooped down and settled on it. But the flower was swinging round because it was fixed to a hat, and the hat was on the head of a girl, and the girl was dancing with her young man to the band in People's Park.

At first the little she-bee was disappointed to find no honey in the flower, but soon she forgot all about it; it

was such a delicious feeling to sway up and down in time to the music.

'It's like hearing a thousand bumble-bees humming over a field of clover,' she murmured happily as she swayed round and round.

'Yes, isn't it?' said a voice quite close to her. And there, on the boy's hat, sat another bee!

'I shouldn't talk to strangers, I know,' said the little she-bee, 'but this music is making me so giddy I don't really know what I'm doing.'

'Nothing wrong in talking, surely?' said the other bee, who was, of course, a he-bee. 'Allow me to say that you dance superbly, and it's not so easy to hang on to a flower that is swinging round and round. I know what I'm talking about; there were two young lady bees here earlier this summer and I tried to dance with them, but they both fell off after just a few turns. I always hold on to the young man's hat-brim; in any case, this is my second season here, so I've had plenty of practice. Ah, the music is stopping; that means it's time for refreshments. Just stay where you are.'

The girl and the young man moved over to the refreshment tent and the bees went with them on their hats.

'Do you live far from here?' asked the he-bee.

'It's quite a long flight,' said the she-bee, 'but I simply daren't let anyone see me home, as we have such a very strict doorkeeper.'

'I quite understand,' he replied, 'but perhaps you will permit me to fetch you a little drink of fruit-juice?'

He flew down on to the table and a moment later brought back a drop of fruit-juice on one of his wings. 'Excuse my wing, but it is the only way I can manage it.'

'Very nice of you to bother; thank you very much,' said the little she-bee. 'Aren't you having any yourself?'

'Not for me, thanks, I'm driving—at least, it's not exactly *me* driving, but I daren't take any risks, all the same. I shall have to get back to my own hat now, I see they're starting the show.'

The little she-bee would have liked to ask what a 'show' was, but she felt shy, so she just rubbed her wings with her feet.

'Tonight there's a fellow with a guitar—forgotten his name, but he's very famous,' the he-bee told her. 'One young lady bee told me she once sat on his guitar while he played "Rocking round the Clock", and she'll never forget it as long as she lives, she said.'

The little she-bee listened while the man on the platform sang and played his guitar, and very funny he looked. First he sang quite quietly, but suddenly he went into shrieks and sobs and then he fell right down on his knees and shuffled off the platform backwards.

'What happened? Did a bee sting him?' asked the she-bee.

'No, no, that was the high spot,' answered her new friend.

'The high spot? Oh yes, I've heard that high spots can sting very badly—the poor man!' And the little she-bee felt quite sorry for the man. But then the music began once more. 'Isn't it wonderful!' she cried, and clapped her front pair of feet.

They sailed out on the dance-floor again, she on her flower and he on his hat-brim.

'I'm afraid that's the last dance tonight,' he said. 'I can see they're beginning to put out the lights.'

'How sad! I shall have to hurry home now,' said the little she-bee, 'but thank you so much for a lovely evening.'

'You're welcome! Perhaps we could meet another time?'

'That would be very nice,' she answered.

When she got back to the hive the doorkeeper would not let her in at first because she had no honey with her. But in the end he relented.

Next evening she went dancing again. But this time

she was careful to hide a little honey in a tree-stump close to the hive, so that she could pick it up on her way home after the dance.

The he-bee on his hat-brim was very pleased to see her. 'I have been thinking about you all day,' he said.

'Very kind of you, I'm sure,' she said, looking very demure.

Like the evening before, there was music, there was dancing, the he-bee brought her fruit-juice, and then there was the show. Afterwards he persuaded her to take a little ride in the young man's car, but when the he-bee asked if he might sit on *her* hat the little she-bee said firmly, 'No.'

Later, when she got back to the hive, she had no difficulty in getting past the doorkeeper, as she had remembered her store of honey in the tree-stump.

And so it went on every evening all through the summer, and no one in the hive knew anything about it. But one day, while the she-bee was flying round looking for honey, she forgot herself; instead of her ordinary buzzing song she started to sing 'Waltzing Matilda'.

'Whatever are you buzzing?' asked the bee who was flying nearest to her.

The little she-bee got quite confused. 'It's—it's only a little waltz tune I heard,' she stammered. Then, of course, she had to explain *where* she had heard it. But this was just as well, for she could not have kept the secret to herself much longer.

As the day went on other bees kept flying up to her wanting her to tell them about the dancing, the music and the show, and about her dancing partner on the hat-brim.

'Can't you take us along with you tonight?' they all pleaded.

'Not tonight,' she said, 'but perhaps tomorrow, if my partner gives his permission.'

That evening was as delightful as all the rest, but the young man didn't have his car with him, so he and the girl and the bees all went for a walk in the wood instead.

'It is really just as pleasant, don't you think, to go for a walk on such a lovely evening?' said the he-bee. 'And if I'm not mistaken we're heading for that little bank with the bluebells on it.' He was right; the young man and the girl sat down on the flowery bank, and so did the two bees.

The young man spoke softly to the girl, and she bent her head so far forward that the bee had to hold on tight not to fall off the flower.

'Why does she bend her head like that?' she asked.

'He is proposing to her,' said the he-bee. 'You had

better let me come over and hold you so you don't fall off.' And he took off from the hat-brim and made an elegant landing on the flower. Then he put his wing protectingly round the little she-bee. This time she did not protest.

'What does "propose" mean?' she asked, though deep inside she had a feeling she knew what it meant already.

'He is asking if she will be his wife and stay with him for ever.'

'Oh, how wonderful!' cried the little she-bee before she could stop herself.

'Do you really think so? Then I shall propose to you this very minute,' said the he-bee, 'even though this isn't the usual way for bees to behave, I'm sure. But it's difficult, you will agree, not to be carried away in these beautiful surroundings and hearing so much love-talk!'

'Oh yes!' sighed the little she-bee, and hung her head bashfully just like the young girl.

The next day there was a terrific hullabaloo in the hive. The bees who knew about the dancing had told a lot more bees, and now it had got all round the hive. There they were, a great black swarm of them, thronging round the entrance, all demanding to go to People's Park like the little she-bee.

'Show us the way!' they kept crying. 'Show **us** the way and we'll follow you!'

The little she-bee hesitated at first, but then she said: 'All right, I will. You can all come with me.' Secretly she was longing for the music and for her partner in the park.

So the whole swarm rose in the air and flew off after the she-bee. But this was in the middle of the day and there was not a soul to be seen in People's Park when they got there. No sign of the flower on the hat, or, for that matter, of the girl and the young man and the he-bee. The she-bee was lost and she knew it, but she couldn't stop now.

On, on she flew, and the swarm after her, over fields and meadows, over roads and hedges, until quite suddenly the little she-bee caught sight of something hanging on the branch of an apple tree.

It was the hat with the flower on it! She was saved!

'Come on, all of you!' she buzzed as loudly as she could. She flew to the flower and clung there. And all the other bees clung to her, till they looked like a huge black cluster of grapes shining in the sunshine.

Someone came into the orchard; it was the girl. When she saw what was happening to her hat she gave a shriek of alarm. She shouted out to someone inside the house, and out came the young man with a great big net. He put it carefully over the swarm of bees and carried it over to an empty hive. There he shook the net so that they all tumbled in, and then he put the lid on firmly.

As luck would have it, the he-bee was still perched on the young man's hat-brim, so he was able to slip into the hive with the rest of them.

After they had time to settle down in their new home the bees made the little she-bee their queen. But, from what I've heard, she was not a bit kind to the he-bee when he became her husband. And if he or any of the other bees ever dared to dream about going dancing in People's Park they soon discovered that it was the queen who called the tune from now on; their dancing days were over for good.

How the King Learned to Eat Porridge

THERE WAS once a king who was wise and good and mighty and rich, but he had one fault. Not a very big fault, mind you, but annoying enough. And do you know what it was?

He would not eat porridge.

Now this wouldn't have mattered so much if he had kept it to himself. After all, a king has so many other things to eat. But he was an honest king, so he could not lie, and he told both the government and the people that he did not like porridge.

'I detest porridge!' he declared. 'It tastes of glue and tufts of wool. Ugh!'

And when the people of his realm heard that they wouldn't eat porridge either. They wanted to be like the king—especially the children, who thought it was wonderful not to eat porridge, and whooped with delight. On the national flag-day they walked in the procession carrying big banners saying 'Long Live the King! Down with Porridge!'

But far up in the mountains there lived a peasant with his daughter, and they had only one tiny field of their own. On this field they grew oats, and their whole livelihood depended on it. So when everyone stopped buying oats they made less and less money.

'This can't go on!' said the peasant's daughter one day. 'People not eating porridge like this. I shall have to go to the palace and give that stupid king a piece of my mind!'

'Take care, my child, you might make the king angry,' said her father.

'He'd better take care himself,' she answered, 'or *I* might get angry.' And she slung a bag of oatmeal over her shoulder and set off for the palace.

In the palace garden she met a man, but the country girl did not know he was really the king.

'Where are you off to?' asked the man.

'I'm going to the palace to teach the king to eat porridge,' she answered.

This made the man laugh. 'If you can do that,' he said, 'you're a very clever girl!' Then he went into the royal kitchen and told the royal cook that he could take a day off, as a country girl had come to town to teach him, the king, to eat porridge.

Next day, when the king was at breakfast, the

peasant's daughter brought in a big steaming bowl of porridge. She was a little taken aback when she saw who the man was she had spoken to in the garden. But the king smiled at her and said:

'Come along now, you must teach me to eat this porridge of yours.'

'Oh no,' she said, 'not after making such a fool of

myself, I couldn't. Anyway, I don't suppose you even know which hand to hold the spoon in?'

'I think I do,' said the king, and picked up the spoon in his right hand.

'Just as I thought!' said the girl. 'Never in all my life have I seen anyone eat porridge with the right hand!'

'All right,' said the king, 'I'll try with my left hand.'

'That's better,' said the girl, 'but I've never seen anyone with a bowl of porridge on the table while they sat on a chair to eat it. Get up on the table and put the bowl on the chair in the proper manner!'

The king was beginning to enjoy himself. First he got

up on the table and then he tried to set the bowl on the chair. But this was not so easy; he nearly lost his balance several times before he managed it.

'There, now you can start eating,' said the girl.

The king held the spoon in his left hand and bent down to the bowl. It was awkward, but he succeeded at last in getting a spoonful up to his mouth and swallowing it.

'Just a minute,' said the girl, 'you have to hold your left ear with your right hand while you're eating.'

'I expect I can manage that too,' said the king, and balanced another spoonful up to his mouth.

'That's only two spoonfuls,' she said. 'Wait till you get to the bottom of the bowl; that's when it gets really difficult.'

'Don't worry, I'll do it!' said the king, and, do you know, he didn't give in till he had scraped the bowl clean!

'There you are!' he shouted proudly.

'There you are yourself!' said the girl. 'Now I have taught the king to eat porridge!'

At first the king was a little put out that she had tricked him in this way. But then he had to laugh.

'You're a very cunning little girl,' he said. 'I almost think I'll marry you—that is, if you're willing?'

'I might as well,' said the girl.

*   *   *   *   *

So they were married, and at the wedding a huge pot of hot, steaming porridge was set up in the middle of the market place, and the king commanded his people, including the whole court and all his ministers, to come and learn how to eat porridge.

The queen stood on a high tribune to teach them, and they all laughed and enjoyed themselves like anything. But when they had had their lesson the queen said:

'Now I know you can all eat porridge; so from this day on you may sit on your chairs and put your porridge bowls on the table and eat it the way you do any other food.'

But many people, especially the children, preferred the way the queen had taught them and went on doing it—secretly.

Mrs Pepperpot Turns Fortune-Teller

EVERY MORNING when Mr Pepperpot goes off to work
Mrs Pepperpot stands at the window and watches him
till he disappears round the bend to the main road. Then

she settles down in the chair by the kitchen table, picks up her empty coffee cup and starts reading her fortune in it.

Now you probably didn't know that Mrs Pepperpot could read fortunes in a cup. Well, she can; she can tell from the way the coffee grounds lie what road she will take that day and whether she will meet joy or sorrow before nightfall. Sometimes she sees the shape of a heart in the cup and that means she will have a new sweetheart. But that makes Mrs Pepperpot laugh, for to her it means she will probably get a new pet to look after—perhaps a poor little bird with a broken wing or a stray kitten on her doorstep, getting tamer and tamer as it laps up the food and milk she gives it.

But if the grounds form a cross she knows she must watch her step, for that means she will break something; it could be when she is washing up or when she is scrubbing the floor. If she sees a clear drop of coffee running down the side of the cup that means she will hurt herself in some way and will need not only a bandage but maybe a doctor as well. And so it goes on; there are many more signs that she can read, but she only does it for herself, never for other people, even if they ask her. It's just an amusement, she says, something to while away the time when she is at home alone all day.

Well, this day—it was a Friday too—Mrs Pepperpot had planned to give the house a good clean out and then she was going to bake a cake for Mr Pepperpot. Apart from that she was just going to take it easy for a change. So, when she had watched her husband turn the corner, she picked up their two coffee cups and was just about to put them in the sink. But then she stopped herself.

'There, what am I doing? I nearly forgot to have a look at my fortune for today!' So she took one of the cups back to the table and sat down. 'Let's see, now,' she said and turned the cup round and round in her hand. 'Oh dear, oh dear!' she exclaimed, 'what's this I see? A big cross? I shall have to mind how I go today and no mistake!'

At that very moment she shrank, and in no time at all she was no bigger than the coffee cup and both she and the cup fell off the chair on to the floor.

'That was a bit of a come-down!' she said, and felt both her arms and her legs to see if there were any bones broken. But when she found she was still all in one piece she lay still for a moment, not daring to look at the cup. For it was one of her best ones, and she was sure it must have been broken by the fall.

At last she said to herself, 'I suppose I shall have to have a look.' And when she did she found to her

great surprise that the cup was not even cracked or
chipped.

But she was still worried. 'If that isn't it there'll be
something else for me to break today,' she said miserably
as she squatted down to look into the cup, for it was
lying on its side.

'Oh me, oh my!' she cried. 'If this isn't my unlucky
day!' She had caught sight of a large clear drop on the
side of the cup. 'This means tears, but I wonder what
will make me cry?'

Suddenly there was a loud BANG! inside the kitchen
cupboard. Mrs Pepperpot nearly jumped out of her skin
with fright.

'There! Now isn't that just like Mr P., setting a mouse-trap in the cupboard, although he knows it's not necessary now that I have a mouse for a night watchman. It's only now and again that a baby mouse gets into the cupboard by mistake—before he's learned the mouse rules. It's not as if they *mean* to do any damage, so it's silly to take any notice. I wonder if I dare open the door a little to see what's happened? I suppose I'd better; the little thing might just have caught its tail and I could free it. But, of course, it might be worse than that; the cup said tears, and tears it will be, no doubt!'

So Mrs Pepperpot went over to the cupboard and pulled gently at the door. But she closed her eyes to keep back the tears which were ready to come at any moment. When she had the door opened enough to look in she opened first one eye, then the other, and then she flopped down on the floor, clapping her hands on her knees, and burst out laughing.

Right enough, the trap had snapped, but there was nothing in it. Instead two baby mice were happily playing just beside it with two empty cotton-reels. Mrs Pepperpot thought it was the funniest sight she'd ever seen.

'Hullo, Mrs Pepperpot!' squealed one of the baby mice. 'Have you shrunk again?'

'We hoped you would!' said the other one, ' 'cos my brother and I had never seen you small before, and

Granny said we could come in here and have a peep—
just in case you shrunk. We weren't being naughty—just
playing cars—and then we bumped into that nasty thing
which went snap over there.'

'Will you play with us?' asked the first little mouse.
'You sit in the car and we'll pull you along.'

And when Mrs Pepperpot looked closer she saw that
the baby mice had fixed a matchbox over the cotton-reels
and the whole contraption really moved.

'Let's go!' shouted Mrs Pepperpot, and jumped into
the box.

So they played at cars, taking turns to sit in the
matchbox, and Mrs Pepperpot laughed while the baby
mice squealed with delight, till, all of a sudden, they
heard a scratching sound above them.

'That's enough, children!' called granny mouse,

whose head had appeared in a hole in the back wall. 'The cat's on top of the cupboard and the door is open!'

Before you could say 'knife' the two baby mice had disappeared through the hole, squeaking 'Thanks for the game!' as they went.

'Thank you!' said Mrs Pepperpot, and stepped out of the cupboard to see what that cat was up to.

There she was, standing on top of the cupboard waving her tail expectantly when Mrs Pepperpot came out. But Mrs Pepperpot was not standing any nonsense; she shouted at the cat: 'What are you doing up there? You get down at once or I'll teach you a lesson as soon as I grow again! Maybe it's you who are going to break something for me today? Yes, I can feel it in my bones. I know if I have another look in that cup there'll be more calamity there for me.'

By now she was just as worked up as she had been before her little game with the mice. But she couldn't resist having another look in the cup. 'Goodness gracious!' she cried. 'It's just as I thought, doctor and bandages, ambulances and everything! As if I hadn't trouble enough already! Down you get, cat, and make it quick!'

'All right! Keep your hair on,' said the cat. 'I was only doing my duty when I heard a suspicious noise in the cupboard. I'm coming down now.'

'Mind how you go! Be careful! I don't want anything broken. I'll stand here below and direct you,' said Mrs Pepperpot.

'Anybody would think I'd never jumped off a cupboard before, and I'm not in the habit of breaking things,' answered the cat, as he made his way gingerly past a big china bowl. But just on the edge of the cupboard lay a large pair of scissors, and neither the cat nor Mrs Pepperpot had seen them.

Mrs Pepperpot was busy with her warnings: 'Mind that bowl!' she shouted, standing right beneath those scissors.

The cat was being as careful as she could, but her tail brushed against the scissors, sending them flying, point downwards, to the floor. There they stood quivering!

Mrs Pepperpot had just managed to jump out of the way, but now she was too frightened to move. 'So that was it!' she stammered at last. She felt herself all over again, for this time she was *sure* she must be hurt. But she couldn't find as much as a scratch!

A moment later she was her normal size. So she pulled the scissors out of the floor and lifted the cat down out of harm's way. Then she set to work cleaning the house and just had time to bake her cake before she heard her husband at the door.

But what a state he was in! The tears were pouring out of his eyes because of the bitter wind outside, and anyway he had a bad cold. One hand he was holding behind his back: he had fallen off his bicycle, had broken his cycle lamp and cut his hand on the glass!

As she hurriedly searched for something to tie round his hand, Mrs Pepperpot thought how odd it was that it was Mr Pepperpot who had tears in his eyes; it was Mr Pepperpot that had broken something, and had hurt himself so that he had to have a bandage on. Very odd indeed!

But if you think this cured Mrs Pepperpot of reading her fortune in a coffee cup you are very much mistaken. The only thing is, she *does* take more care not to pick up the wrong cup and read her husband's fortune instead of her own.

Mrs Pepperpot in the Magic Wood

MRS PEPPERPOT, as you may remember, lives on a hillside in Norway. Behind her house there is an old fence with a gate in it. If you walk through that gate, says Mrs Pepperpot, you walk straight into the Magic Wood.

It's really just a little copse with larch and spruce and birch trees, but in spring the ground is covered with snowdrops—the whitest carpet you ever saw, and round a big mossy stone a patch of violets make a bright splash of colour. The birch trees seem more silvery in here and the pale green branches of the larch trees more feathery as they sway over the stream that trickles down the hillside. And in and out of the long grass the weasel has made a pattern of little winding paths. It is very beautiful.

But Mrs Pepperpot likes it even better in winter when the Magic Wood has a thick carpet of snow and the icicles sparkle from the branches. Then all is silent except for the scrunch, scrunch of Mrs Pepperpot's boots as she walks through the snow.

7

It was a day before Christmas, and Mrs Pepperpot had asked her husband to cut her a small Christmas tree in the Magic Wood. But he was so busy at his work that he hadn't had time to do it, so Mrs Pepperpot decided to take the axe and cut it down herself. As the snow was slippery, she took a stick with her. She soon reached the little fir-tree and, after marking a circle round it with her stick, she lifted the axe to start chopping.

Then the awful thing happened! You know, the thing that keeps happening to Mrs Pepperpot at the most inconvenient moments: she shrank to the size of a pepperpot.

'I'll have to find a small stick,' she said, 'it'll help me to plough a path through the snow. Ah well, I could be in a worse fix, I suppose, and I ought to be used to it by now.'

'Hi!' shouted a small voice quite close above her.

'What was that?' said Mrs Pepperpot, who had nearly jumped out of her skin, she was so surprised.

'It's me!' said the little voice. And now Mrs Pepperpot could see a tiny boy no bigger than herself, standing by her side.

'Well, come on; don't just stand there! They're all sitting inside, crying their hearts out because they think the ogre has eaten you. We must hurry home and surprise them.'

Without waiting for an answer, the little fellow bent down to a hole in the snow and started to crawl into it.

'Well,' thought Mrs Pepperpot, 'I may as well go and see what this is all about; he seems to know me, even if I don't know him.'

She left the axe and tucking the stick she had found under her arm she bravely crawled after the boy into the hole. It was quite a long tunnel which led to a little door. The boy knocked, but from behind the door there was such a noise of wailing and weeping that at first no one answered his knock. But when he had knocked again the bolt slid back and the door was opened by a young girl with a ladle in her hand. The room was brightly lit by a fire over which hung a steaming pot. Mrs Pepperpot,

who was hidden behind the boy in the dark tunnel, could see three people inside and they were all looking most dejected as they went on with their crying.

The little boy stamped his foot. 'Stop that noise!' he shouted. 'Can't you see I've brought Betty Bodkin back?' and with that he took hold of Mrs Pepperpot's arm and dragged her into the middle of the room.

For a moment everyone stared at Mrs Pepperpot and then the wailing began afresh!

'Little Dick, what have you done? This isn't Betty Bodkin!' said the girl with the ladle.

Little Dick turned and had a good look at Mrs. Pepperpot. Then he shook his fists at her and threw himself on the floor in what can only be described as a temper tantrum.

But Mrs Pepperpot had had enough of this nonsense: 'When you've all finished your catawauling,' she said, 'perhaps someone will tell me who you are and who I'm *supposed* to be. Then maybe I'll tell you who I *really* am.'

'It is a bit confusing,' said a fat little man who sat nearest the fire, 'we thought you were one of us, you see.'

'So I hear, but who are *you*?' Mrs Pepperpot was losing patience.

'Let me explain,' said the girl with the ladle, and as no one tried to stop her, she continued: 'You may not recognise us, but when you were little you knew us well enough. D'you remember your mother taking you on her lap sometimes to cut your nails? You probably didn't like it, and she would hold your hand and count your fingers one by one.'

'That's right,' said Mrs Pepperpot, 'and then she would sing me a little ditty that went like this:

> Here is Thumbkin, fat and tubby,
> Here is Lickpot, always grubby,
> Longman next: he has his fiddle,
> Now Betty Bodkin with her needle,
> And little Dick who's just a tiddle.

They all clapped their hands. 'There you are!' cried the girl, 'you haven't forgotten. And that's who we are— the finger people who live in the Magic Wood. This is Thumbkin,' she said, pointing to the fat little man by the fire.

'Pleased to meet you,' said Thumbkin, as Mrs Pepperpot shook hands with him.

'I used to find you a very comforting person,' said Mrs Pepperpot smiling.

'This is Longman, as you can see,' went on the girl, but the tall, thin fellow was so shy he held his fiddle behind his back and looked as if he'd like to vanish right away. 'I'm Lickpot. I do the cooking, you see,' said the girl.

Little Dick had now got over his disappointment. Taking another look at Mrs Pepperpot he said: 'You're so very like Betty Bodkin!'

'Just what happened to Betty Bodkin?' asked Mrs Pepperpot.

Immediately they all started talking at once: 'It was like this—we were out in the wood—we always wish the moon a Happy Christmas—it was such a glorious night!'

'One at a time, please!' said Mrs Pepperpot, holding her ears.

Lickpot raised her ladle to get order: 'Quiet now! I'll explain. As they said, we went for a walk to greet the moon. Suddenly a huge ogre came along the path and we all had to rush into the tunnel to get out of his way. But Betty Bodkin tripped over her needle, and didn't manage it. The ogre picked her up in his great hand and put her in his pocket. Now we're all so worried about what has happened to her, and Christmas won't be Christmas without Betty Bodkin!'

'Perhaps the ogre has eaten her up!' said Little Dick, and he started to cry again.

'Oh, ogres aren't as bad as they once were!' said Mrs Pepperpot to comfort him. 'Besides, if she's as used to being small as I am, she'll know how to get out of tight corners.'

'If only we could find where the ogre lives, then perhaps we could rescue her,' said Lickpot.

'I'm sure we could, if we all pull together,' said Mrs Pepperpot. 'I think I have an idea where that ogre lives.'

'Will you show us the way?' asked Little Dick excitedly, and they all crowded round Mrs Pepperpot, tugging at her skirt.

'There's no time to lose,' she said immediately and started crawling back through the tunnel. The others followed, but when they got outside they found the road blocked by an enormous snowdrift.

'We'll never get through that!' said Thumbkin and looked quite ready to creep back to his warm fire inside.

It was quite a problem, and Mrs Pepperpot shut her eyes so as to think better. Suddenly she remembered something very important; they were in the Magic Wood, where wishes come true if you wish hard enough. 'Quiet everybody! I'm going to make a wish!' she said.

While they all stood very still she touched the snowdrift with her stick and said loudly: 'I wish this snowdrift to turn into a polar bear—a *friendly* polar bear—who can carry us all on his back and take us to the ogre's house.'

As soon as she finished speaking the snowdrift began to rise under them and they found themselves sitting on a soft, warm, white rug. Then the rug began to move forward, and Mrs Pepperpot could see two ears in front

14

of her. She had ridden on a bear before, so she knew what bears like most—to be tickled between the ears. Gingerly she crawled towards the ears and perched herself between them.

'Do be careful!' warned Lickpot, who was clinging with all her might to the bear's fur. Longman was so frightened he was lying full length with his face buried, but Thumbkin and Little Dick were beginning to enjoy themselves, looking all around from their high seat.

When the bear felt his ears being tickled he purred—or rather, he rumbled—with contentment, and in no time at all he had carried Mrs Pepperpot and the finger-people to the edge of the wood where there was a fence and a gate in it.

'Open the gate with your muzzle!' commanded Mrs Pepperpot, and the big polar bear did just as she said and opened the gate.

Then they came to a house with a lighted window.

'Now I want you to lie down outside the door,' said Mrs Pepperpot, 'and you must wait there till I come out again—is that clear?'

The great creature just nodded his head slowly and settled down on the doorstep.

Mrs Pepperpot turned to the finger people: 'I'm pretty certain that I'll find the ogre inside this house,' she said.

'Don't you want us to help you rescue Betty Bodkin?' asked Little Dick, who was feeling quite chirpy now.

'No thanks, I think I can manage this by myself,' said Mrs Pepperpot. 'I just want you to wait here with Mr Polar Bear. If Betty Bodkin is there I'll bring her out to you, and then you can all go home.'

They all shook her hand warmly and wished her luck.

'Trust in me!' said Mrs Pepperpot, and swung her leg over the door-sill.

Just as she disappeared into the dark hall she grew to her normal size and walked into the dining-room.

There sat Mr Pepperpot; the tears were rolling down

16

his cheeks and his sharp nose was quite red with crying. On the table by his side stood a small doll's bed Mrs Pepperpot had bought to give a little girl for Christmas, and in the bed lay Betty Bodkin, trying very hard to look like a doll! There were medicine bottles on the table as well, and a box of liquorice pills.

Mrs Pepperpot put her hands on her hips and said: 'Just what are you carrying on like this for?'

At the sound of her voice Mr Pepperpot looked up. He couldn't believe his eyes!

'Is that you? Is that really you, my own wife?' he cried, and caught hold of her skirt to see if she wasn't a ghost.

'I thought I'd lost you this time! I was going through the wood, searching for you, when I saw . . .' He stopped and stared at the little old woman in the doll's bed. 'But then, who's this? I picked her up in the snow and brought her home, thinking it was you who had shrunk again.'

'You silly man! Mixing me up with a doll that someone has dropped on the path!' said Mrs Pepperpot. Then, standing between him and the doll's bed, she carefully

lifted Betty Bodkin up and wiped away the sticky medicine and liquorice pills her husband had tried to dose her with. Betty was just about to thank her, but Mrs Pepperpot made a sign for her to keep quiet and carried her towards the front door.

But Mr Pepperpot was so afraid his wife might vanish once more that he followed, holding on to her coat. As she leaned out of the door he asked: 'What are you putting the doll in that snowdrift for?'

'To get her back where she belongs,' said Mrs Pepperpot. 'Come and have your supper now.'

'Just a minute. I want to shovel that snowdrift away from the door-step first,' Mr Pepperpot said.

'Why? Are you afraid it'll walk in? Come on now, supper's ready.'

So Mr Pepperpot went into the kitchen to wash his hands and didn't hear his wife whisper to the snowdrift: 'Turn about, quick march and get them home as fast as you can!'

Later that night, when she was washing up, Mrs Pepperpot amused herself by singing the old ditty:

> Here is Thumbkin, fat and tubby,
> Here is Lickpot, always grubby,
> Longman next: he has a fiddle,
> Now Betty Bodkin with her needle,
> And Little Dick who's just a tiddle.

Mrs Pepperpot and the puppet show

IT WAS a lovely summer's day, just the day for an outing. The village sewing club had been invited to a television show in the nearest town and they were going by special coach.

Mrs Pepperpot was going too, and very excited she was, as she had never watched a TV show in a theatre before. Nor had any of the others, for that matter, and they had all put on their best summer frocks and straw hats with flowers.

On the way they prattled, as women do, and wondered what it would be like. They were going to see a puppet show, and Sarah South was sure that everyone else in the village would be envying them.

When they got to the town the bus stopped in the market square and they all got off. As they walked into the hall Norah North said: 'One thing we shouldn't do—smile at the camera—it looks so silly when you're watching TV.'

'Especially if you have gaps in your teeth,' said Mrs East, who could be a bit sharp when she liked.

They felt rather shy when they were given the front row of seats, but soon they were all comfortably seated with little bags of peppermints to munch. All except Mrs Pepperpot. Where was she?

Well, you know how she likes to poke her nose into things, and as they were walking along the passage to their seats, Mrs Pepperpot heard someone sniffing and crying in a little room next to the stage.

'That's funny!' she thought and peeped through the door. There she saw a full-grown man with a top hat and long moustachios, sitting on a chair, crying like a baby.

'Well, I never!' said Mrs Pepperpot, but before she had time to follow the rest of her party, she SHRANK!

As she stood there, a tiny figure by the door in her bright summer dress and little straw hat, the puppet-man saw her at once. Quick as a knife he stretched out his hand and picked her up.

'*There* you are!' he said, holding her tightly between finger and thumb. 'I thought I'd lost you!'

Mrs Pepperpot was so terrified she didn't move, but when the man had had a closer look he said: 'But you're *not* my Sleeping Beauty puppet at all!'

'Of course I'm not!' said Mrs Pepperpot. The very idea!

'All the same,' said the puppet-man, 'as I can't find my most important puppet, you'll have to play her part. You'll look fine with a blonde wig and a crown and a veil, and I'll make your face up so that you'll be really beautiful.'

'You let me go this minute!' shouted Mrs Pepperpot, struggling to get out of the man's grip. 'Whoever heard of an old woman like me playing Sleeping Beauty?'

'Now, now! You have talent—you can act, I'm sure of it. And that's more than can be said of my other puppets who have to be handled with sticks and threads. You can walk and talk by yourself; you're just what I've always dreamed of and you'll bring me success and lots of money, you'll see.'

'Over my dead body!' said Mrs Pepperpot, who was still furious. 'I don't even remember the story of Sleeping Beauty.'

'I shall be telling the story,' explained the puppet-man, 'and you just have to do the things I say. But you don't come into the first act at all, so you can stand at the side and watch the other puppets through that crack in the curtain. Now it's time for the show to start, so be a sport and stay there, won't you?'

'I may and I mayn't,' said Mrs Pepperpot, so he lifted her gingerly down on the side of the puppet-stage which was set up in the middle of the real theatre stage.

Then the lights in the hall went out and those on the little stage went on. Mrs Pepperpot peeped through the hole in the curtain. The scene was a magnificent marble hall and she could see a puppet king and queen sitting on their thrones with their courtiers standing round. They were looking at a baby doll in a cradle.

The man began to speak behind the stage.

'There was once a king and a queen who had been blessed with a baby princess.'

'Lucky he didn't want me to lie in the cradle!' thought Mrs Pepperpot.

The man read on, telling how the good fairies were asked to the christening party and how they each gave the little princess a gift. Waving their wands over her cradle the fairies came in one by one.

'May you have the gift of Beauty!' said one.

'May you have the gift of Patience!' said another.

'I could certainly do with that gift,' said Mrs Pepperpot to herself. 'If there's anything I lack it's patience!'

When all the good fairies except one had waved their wands over the cradle, there was a terrible clap of thunder and the stage went completely dark for a moment.

'Goodness Gracious!' cried Mrs Pepperpot, 'I hope they haven't had a break-down!' She was beginning to get excited about the play now.

The lights came on again, and there was the bad fairy leaning over the baby with her wand.

'Ha, ha!' said the puppet-man in an old witch sort of voice. 'Today you are all happy, but this is *my* gift to the princess; in your fifteenth year may you prick your finger on a spindle and die!' And with that the bad fairy vanished in another clap of thunder and black-out.

'Well, if I'm the Sleeping Beauty, I'm a good deal more than fifteen years old and I'm still hale and hearty!' thought Mrs Pepperpot.

The puppet-man had now brought on another fairy to tell the king and queen that their daughter would not really die, but only go into a long, long sleep.

'One day a prince will come and wake her up,' said the fairy and that was the end of the first act.

The puppet-man was glad to see Mrs Pepperpot still standing there, but he didn't take any chances and caught her up roughly before she could protest. No matter how much she wriggled, she was dressed in the princess's blonde wig with a crown on top and a veil down her back. The worst part was when the puppet-man made up her face: Ough! It tasted like candle grease!

But when at last he put her down in front of a little mirror, she had to admit she looked rather wonderful.

'Now listen,' said the puppet-man. 'I don't mind if you make up your own speeches, but you must follow the story as I tell it, and one thing you must remember; no advertising! It's strictly forbidden on this TV station.'

'Is it indeed!' said Mrs Pepperpot, who had not forgiven him for the rough treatment she had had—why, he'd even pulled her hair! 'We'll see about that!' she muttered.

But there was no time to argue, as the puppet-man was preparing to raise the curtain again. The scene was the same as before, but at first it was empty of puppets while the puppet-man read the introduction to the next part of the story.

'The king was so anxious to keep his only child safe from all harm, that he ordered every spindle in the country to be burned and forbade any more to be made. Meanwhile the princess grew up with all the gifts she had received from the fairies; she was good and beautiful, modest and patient, and everyone loved her. Then one day when she was fifteen years old the king and queen had gone out and she was all alone in the palace. She thought she would explore a bit.'

The puppet-man stopped reading and whispered to Mrs Pepperpot: 'This is where you come in! Walk across the marble hall and up the winding staircase in the corner. You'll find the witch at the top, spinning.'

He gave her a little push, and Mrs Pepperpot, in all her princess finery, walked on to the stage as grandly as she could. In the middle of the marble hall she stood still and looked for the staircase. When she saw it she turned to the audience and, pointing to the stairs, she said: 'I have to go up there; I hope it's safe! Always buy planks at Banks, the lumber man!' And up she went, holding her long skirt like a lady.

At the top of the stairs she found the witch puppet sitting, turning her spindle in her hand.

'Why, whatever are you doing with that old-fashioned thing?' asked Mrs Pepperpot.

'I am spinning,' said the puppet-man in his old witch voice.

'I call that silly,' said Mrs Pepperpot, 'when you can buy the best knitting wool in town at Lamb's Wool Shop!'

The audience laughed at this, but the puppet-man was

27

not amused. However, he couldn't stop now, so he went on with the play, saying in his old witch voice: 'Would you like to spin, my child?'

'I don't mind if I do,' said Mrs Pepperpot. As she took the spindle from the witch's hand, the puppet-man whispered to her to pretend to prick herself.

'Ouch!' cried Mrs Pepperpot, sucking her finger and shaking it, 'I need a plaster from Mr Sands, the chemist!'

Again the audience laughed. The puppet-man now whispered to her to lie down on the bed to sleep. She asked if he wanted her to snore to make it more life-like.

'Of course not!' he said angrily, 'and I don't want any advertising for sleeping pills either!'

'Not necessary!' said Mrs Pepperpot, making herself comfortable on the bed. Then she raised her head for a moment and in a sing-song voice she spoke to the people in the audience.

> The moment you recline
> On a mattress from Irvine
> You will fall into a sleep
> That is really quite divine!

The puppet-man had difficulty in getting himself heard through the shouts of laughter that greeted this outrageous poem. But at last he was able to go on with the story how the princess slept for a hundred years and everyone in the palace slept too. When he got to the bit about the rose-hedge growing thicker and thicker round the walls of the palace, Mrs Pepperpot popped her head up again and said:

> Quick-growing roses
> From Ratlin and Moses.

and then pretended to sleep again. She was really getting her revenge on the puppet-man, and she was enjoying every minute of it.

The puppet-man struggled on, but now the audience laughed at everything that was said, and he began to wonder if he should stop the show. He tried reading again: 'At length the king's son came to the narrow stairs in the tower. When he reached the top he opened the door of the little chamber, and there he saw the most beautiful sight he had even seen—the Sleeping Beauty.'

While the gramophone played soft music to suit the scene, the puppet prince walked up the stairs and came through the door. Mrs Pepperpot winked one eye at the audience and said:

> I owe my beautiful skin
> To Complexion-Milk by Flyn.

The puppet prince walked stiffly over to her bed and stiffly bent down and planted a wooden kiss on her cheek. But this was too much for Mrs Pepperpot: 'No, no!' she shrieked, jumping out of bed and knocking the prince flying, so that all his threads broke and he landed in an untidy heap at the bottom of the stairs.

Down the stairs came Mrs Pepperpot herself, and, jumping over the fallen prince, she rushed across the stage and out through the curtain, while the audience rolled in their seats and clapped and shouted for the princess to come back.

But once safely in the dressing-room, Mrs Pepperpot only just had time to snatch off her wig and veil and crown before she grew to her normal size. The little things she put in her handbag and she walked through the door as calmly as you please, only to be met by the poor puppet-man, who was wringing his hands and crying even worse than before the show.

'Whatever's the matter?' asked Mrs Pepperpot.

'My show's ruined!' he wailed. 'They'll never put it on TV again after all that advertising!'

'Advertising?' Mrs Pepperpot pretended to be surprised. 'Wasn't it all part of the play?'

But the puppet-man wasn't listening to her: 'Oh dear, oh dear! What will become of me? And now I have no Sleeping Beauty at all!'

'You should treat your puppets with more respect,' said Mrs Pepperpot, 'they don't like being pushed about and having their hair pulled!'

With that she left him and walked out to the square to get on the bus. Her friends had all been too busy laughing and discussing the play to notice that she hadn't been with them. She sat down next to Sarah South who asked her if she had enjoyed the show.

'Oh, I had a lovely time! We all did, I mean!' said Mrs Pepperpot.

*   *   *   *   *

A few days later the puppet-man was mending the threads of his puppet-prince. He was feeling happier now, because all the newspapers had written that his way of playing Sleeping Beauty was new and original, and they all praised his performance very highly.

There was a knock on the door and the postman handed him a small parcel. He wondered what it could be, but when he opened it he stared with astonishment: inside was the princess's wig, crown and veil and also a reel of black thread and a little note.

The puppet-man read it aloud:

> As back to you these things I send,
> May I be bold and recommend
> When next your puppet prince you mend,
> Try Jiffy's thread; it will not rend.

Who had sent the parcel? And where did that little puppet go who could walk and talk on its own?

'If only I knew!' sighed the puppet-man.

Midsummer Eve with the ogres

IN NORWAY everybody celebrates Midsummer Eve with bonfires and fireworks and all sorts of fun. It is so far north that the sun hardly goes down at all in June, and on Midsummer Eve even the children stay up all night, dancing and singing with the grown-ups.

Now, although Gapy Gob is a big ogre, he is very much like a little boy as far as parties go; he just loves them, and Katie Cook and Charlie Chop, his two little human servants, take a lot of trouble to make everything nice for him on Midsummer Eve.

This year they hadn't invited any guests: 'Let's just be ourselves,' said Gapy Gob, 'we can have fun together and there'll be more to eat!' The ogre does like his food.

They all worked hard to get ready for the night; even Gapy Gob decided to do his annual clean-out of the cow-shed while their only cow was grazing on the high mountain pasture. Katie was busy cooking in the kitchen; she made Gapy's favourite pudding with cream and best wheat flour and nuts and raisins floating in it. When it was cooked she sprinkled grated lemon rind over the top and put it in the larder. She had baked a special cake with malt beer in it and something else which she and Charlie kept secret from Gapy Gob—it was to be a surprise for him. There was also a big bowl of freshly picked strawberries from their own garden and thick cream to go with it.

Meanwhile Charlie was cutting green branches in the wood and brought them home to decorate the outside

of their little house. He built a most imposing porch over the front door and put green leaves all round the windows. When Katie had finished cooking she went out to pick flowers and made pretty garlands to hang on the

doors; one for the front door, one for the cow-shed door and even one for the larder, which was built on stilts behind the house. The whole place looked really beautiful when they had done, and they looked forward to showing Gapy Gob when he came home from milking the cow.

'We deserve a nice cool drink after all that!' said Katie, and went to the larder to fetch some fruit juice. But a moment later she called out to Charlie: 'Come quick!

Someone's been in the larder and stolen the food!'

Charlie rushed round and, sure enough, not only the cream-pudding and the malt cake had gone, but also a big tall candle that Charlie had made himself for Midsummer Eve.

'But how could anyone get in?' he asked. 'You always carry the key in your belt, Katie.'

'I have the key, all right,' said Katie, 'but I must just have forgotten to lock the door when I went out to pick flowers.'

'Whatever will Gapy say?' Charlie wondered.

'We won't tell him yet. By this evening I'll think up something else we can have and there's still the strawberries and cream.'

So, when the ogre came home with the milk, they said nothing about what had happened.

Gapy admired all their decorations and then he rubbed his hands, saying: 'Oh boy, oh boy, oh boy! Am I looking forward to tonight!' And all the poor children could do was to smile and nod their heads.

Not long after, who should they see come tripping up the path but the ogress, Wily Winnie, and her cat, Ribby Ratsoup.

'What do they want?' said Gapy Gob, and the happy look disappeared from his face. Wily Winnie was very ugly and stupid, but she fancied Gapy Gob as a husband

37

and was always getting her cunning cat to think up ways of getting Gapy to visit her.

'Up to no good, I'll be bound!' said Charlie darkly.

But Wily Winnie was all smiles when she came up to them and wished them a polite 'Good Afternoon.' Ribby stood behind her, smirking and twirling her whiskers.

'It's so long since we saw you, Gapy Gob,' began the ogress, 'I thought it would be nice if you could come to my house tonight to celebrate Midsummer Eve.'

'Well, thanks, Wily Winnie,' said Gapy. 'It's kind of you to ask me, but——'

Katie chipped in and finished his sentence for him: 'We're having our own party here tonight, so he can't come.'

'No, I couldn't leave the children—not tonight!' said Gapy.

'But of course we want them to come too, don't we, Ribby?' cried Wily Winnie, but while she spoke she managed to put her heavy shoe on poor Katie's bare foot. Katie bit her lip; she wasn't going to cry.

'And we love little boys at our parties!' said Ribby, secretly digging her claws into Charlie's leg. He just shut his eyes and said nothing.

'Right oh!' said Wily Winnie. 'Then that's agreed— you'll all come tonight at seven o'clock and we shall have a lovely meal!'

As Gapy Gob couldn't think of any other good reason to say no, he thanked the ogress and she and Ribby Ratsoup danced off down the path again. But as the afternoon wore on, the ogre and the children felt more and more gloomy at the thought of leaving their nice house in the sunshine to go tramping over the other side of the mountain where it was dark and dreary.

'She'll probably give us one of those horrible soups Ribby makes,' said Gapy, 'with rats' tails in it.'

'Better have the soup than no meal at all!' said Charlie, but Katie nudged him with her elbow and said loudly: 'Come along, we might as well go now,' and they set off for the ogress's house.

Wily Winnie and her cat had been decorating too.

Ribby had dragged some fallen fir branches in from the wood because she couldn't use a saw or an axe with her paws. She had scattered them on the path outside the house while her mistress nailed up a crazy arrangement of sticks over the door which she fondly imagined looked very artistic.

Inside Ribby had swept the floor for once, but a heap of fishbones and other rubbish had been left in one corner, and it didn't smell very nice.

Wily Winnie was on the doorstep to greet Gapy. She said: 'I hope your servants won't mind giving Ribby a hand; I see Charlie has brought his axe, so perhaps he could cut us some wood for the cooking stove, and maybe Katie could lay the table, eh?'

'No,' said Katie, 'I couldn't. I'm a guest.'

'Oh, come on, Katie,' said Charlie. 'I don't mind cutting up a few logs, so you can give a hand too.' Then he added in a whisper: 'It'll give us a chance to see what's cooking!'

So the children went out in the kitchen with Ribby, while in the front room Gapy sat down in one rocking chair and Wily Winnie in the other.

'I don't know what you see in those stupid children,' she began.

'They're not stupid,' said Gapy Gob. 'Katie's a wonderful cook, and we always have plenty of wood for the stove with Charlie around.'

'Well, *I* have a proposition to make,' said Wily Winnie.

'A proposition? What's that?' said Gapy, who didn't like long words.

'Let me put it this way!' said the ogress, 'what would you say if you could have just as good food as Katie's and all the wood brought in to keep you warm? Would you need the children then?'

Gapy looked confused: 'But I haven't anyone else to do those things!'

Wily Winnie gave his hand a playful slap: 'You silly!' she said, 'I'm talking about *us*! I mean, if I could give you lovely meals here and keep you warm as well, would you send Katie and Charlie packing—*would* you?' And she put her head on one side and smiled in what she hoped was a winning way.

But Gapy Gob just looked away and didn't answer, because he knew she was trying to catch him again.

'How aggravating you are!' cried the ogress. 'It's very rude not to agree to what a lady proposes, and I would look after you like my own pet lamb, so I would!'

'I'm not a pet lamb!' muttered Gapy, but not too loudly, for he was very scared of Wily Winnie.

'Will you agree,' she went on, 'to send the children away after tonight if you like the food I give you? Say yes or no!'

Miserably Gapy nodded his head, more to stop the argument than anything. All he hoped now was that the food would be bad, so that he wouldn't have to part with Katie and Charlie.

At last the meal seemed to be ready. First Charlie brought in a tall candle and set it in the middle of the table and lit it. Then Ribby carried in the first course, which was a malt cake with a curious hump in the middle.

'D'you always bake your malt cake with a hump?' asked Katie, as they sat down to eat.

'A hump?' said Wily Winnie, noticing it for the first time. 'Oh yes, of course I do. Malt cake *should* have a hump.' She cut them all slices, and Gapy Gob had to admit that it was delicious. But the next moment he spat out a big mouthful; 'I bit on something hard!' he said, and there, right in the middle of the plate, was a tiny horse carved in wood.

'How very odd!' said Charlie Chop. 'That's just like the little horse I carved and put in *our* malt cake when Katie was baking it. I meant it to be a surprise present for Gapy.'

'My Ribby's very good at carving too,' said the ogress hurriedly, 'and she put a horse in our cake, didn't you, Ribby?'

'That's right,' said the cat, 'whittled it with my own

fair paw,' and she held up her right paw that had never done an honest stroke of work in its life. The children gave her such a look that she thought it best to go and fetch the next course in. When she came back with a large bowl of cream pudding, Gapy Gob just stared: 'How did you know that was my favourite pudding?' he asked.

'Ah!' said the ogress. 'A little bird told me that!'

'Flew over here, bowl and all, I suppose!' muttered Charlie, but Gapy was so busy scooping pudding into his mouth he didn't hear.

'It's just like ours at home,' he said between mouthfuls, 'and it has all the right things in it!'

'Oh yes,' said Wily Winnie, 'I always put nuts and raisins in!'

'I don't mean them,' said Gapy Gob, 'I mean the *secret* flavour; it was very clever of you to put that in.'

Wily Winnie couldn't think what that could be, so she turned to Katie and asked if she had put something in the pudding before it was brought in.

'Not in *your* kitchen!' said Katie.

'Well, never mind,' said the ogress, who seemed to be getting nervous: 'I think everyone's had enough. You may clear, Ribby!'

'What's the hurry?' asked Gapy, who was scraping his plate. 'At home Katie lets me have lots and lots of my favourite pudding.'

'You'll get too fat!' said Wily Winnie, as Ribby whisked the bowl away from the table.

'Look who's talking!' whispered Katie to Charlie, for the ogress was just about as wide as she was high.

'What's next?' asked Gapy Gob.

'That's all!' said Wily Winnie. 'Enough's as good as a feast, you know. Now we can all sit and watch the pretty candle burn while we play some guessing games.'

But Gapy was still hungry: 'We always have strawberries and cream at home on Midsummer Eve!' he said.

'We couldn't carry—I mean we don't *grow* strawberries on this side of the mountain,' said Wily Winnie. 'Come on now, what shall we play?'

'Let's guess what's inside the candle,' suggested Charlie.

'That's easy!' said the ogress, 'candles are made of tallow, of course!'

'It has a wick down the middle!' said Ribby.

'Clever Puss!' cried Wily Winnie, clapping her hands.

'Well, *I* guess there's something made of silver halfway down!' said Charlie Chop.

'Nonsense, boy, how could there be anything inside?' said Gapy.

'Wait and see!' said Charlie, so they all watched the candle burn, and when it came to the middle it sputtered and out fell a little silver ring on to the table.

'Well, I never!' said Gapy, 'how did you know?'

'Because I put it there!' said Charlie. 'It was my surprise present for Katie. And now we know who stole my candle!'

'And the malt cake I made and the cream pudding!' chimed in Katie.

'I don't know what you're talking about!' said the ogress.

'Nor do I,' said Gapy. 'Who stole what?'

'We didn't want to spoil your evening, Gapy,' explained Katie 'but our party food was stolen from the larder today when I was out picking flowers and Charlie was building the porch.'

'I *see*,' said Gapy, looking hard at Wily Winnie, who had backed away into a corner. 'So *that's* why the cream pudding tasted so good! It was Katie's all the time!' He was so angry that he pushed the table over and all the plates and dishes fell on the floor.

'Please don't be cross, Gapy!' pleaded the ogress, while her cat hid behind her. 'It was only a joke! Ribby and I wanted to have a little fun on Midsummer Eve, that's all!'

But Gapy Gob didn't even look at her. Taking Katie by one hand and Charlie by the other he led them out of the door; 'We'll go home now, children,' he said.

As they walked back over the mountain, they could

hear the ogress throwing pots and pans at Ribby and shouting at the top of her voice: 'You stupid cat! It's all your fault; you and your crazy ideas! Get out this instant and bring me back enough wood to make a bonfire to roast you on!' and she chased the cat out of the door with a stick. Ribby ran as she had never run before, and she hid in the wood for three whole days and nights till her mistress had had time to cool her temper.

As for Gapy Gob and the children, they had a lovely feast of strawberries and cream when they got home. They sat under Charlie's green porch all night long, singing songs and telling stories. And they didn't even need the candle, because it never got really dark at all.

Mrs Pepperpot and the baby crow

ONE SUMMER'S DAY when Mrs Pepperpot was coming home from picking blue-berries in the forest, she suddenly heard something stir in the heather.

'Oh dear,' she thought, 'I hope it isn't a snake.'

She picked up a strong stick and walked as softly as she could towards the noise.

But it wasn't a snake; it was a baby crow which must have fallen out of its nest. It was flapping its wings and trying so hard to get off the ground.

'Poor wee thing!' said Mrs Pepperpot. 'What shall we do with you?'

Very gently she lifted it up and then she could see it had hurt one of its wings. So she put it into her apron pocket and took it home with her. When she got indoors she found a little doll's bed which she lined with soft flannel, and then she carried the baby crow up to the attic, so that Mr Pepperpot wouldn't know about it. He always got so cross when she brought creatures in.

Whenever her husband was out Mrs Pepperpot would sneak up to the attic with little titbits for the bird and watch it hop around on the floor. When it got stronger it could jump from one beam to the other, and soon the day came when it could really fly.

But by now Mrs Pepperpot had got so fond of the untidy ball of black fluff that she hadn't the heart to let

it go. The days went by till one Monday morning Mrs Pepperpot woke up and said to herself: 'Today's the day. I'll have to let the bird out today.'

But then the weather turned nasty and she thought it would be better to wait till the next day.

On Tuesday morning the sun shone. In fact, it was very hot.

'Oh dear,' said Mrs Pepperpot, 'I'm sure there'll be a thunderstorm. The poor little thing would be frightened to death. We'd better wait till tomorrow.'

On Wednesday Mrs Pepperpot couldn't find the cat, and she was afraid it might be lurking somewhere outside the house, waiting to pounce on the baby crow. So she decided to wait till Thursday.

On Thursday she found the cat and shut it in the shed. The little crow was flying from beam to beam and quite clearly wanted to get out. When Mrs Pepperpot came up to the attic it flew on to her shoulder and pulled her hair with its beak, as much as to say: 'Come on, open that window!'

But Mrs Pepperpot had thought up another excuse. 'You see, my pet,' she said, stroking the little crow's back, 'when people have been ill, they have to rest a bit —they call it convalescing—before they can go out. I think you need a little more convalescing.'

'Caw, caw!' said the crow and flew off into a corner of

the attic where it sulked the rest of the day.

On Friday Mrs Pepperpot spent a lot of time in the attic. She found all sorts of things to do up there, sorting out her boxes of old clothes and quite unnecessarily dusting the shelves. In between she sighed and she sniffed, and by the time her husband came home she was so out of sorts she had forgotten to cook him any supper.

'What's the idea?' said Mr Pepperpot. 'Can't a man even have a meal when he comes back from a hard day's work?'

'Eating! That's all you think of!' snapped Mrs Pepperpot. 'You can come back in half an hour.' And she turned her back on him and made a great noise with the saucepans so that he wouldn't notice she was crying.

'Well!' said Mr Pepperpot, 'I don't know what's the matter with you, but you seem to have lost the *rest* of your wits,' and with that he hurried out of the door, in case his wife should throw a plate after him.

But Mrs Pepperpot was too upset to throw plates; she just stood by the kitchen stove and cried because she couldn't bear to let the little crow fly.

When she went to bed she was feeling more sensible and she told herself she would do it for sure tomorrow. But then she remembered it was Saturday: 'So many people go out shooting on Saturdays, they might shoot my baby by mistake, or think it was lame and "put it

out of its misery", as they say.'

So next day she went to the attic, and when the little crow flew over to her, she took it gently in her hand and talked to it soothingly. 'You must be patient a little longer. Today you might get shot, and tomorrow is Sunday and then there are so many trippers about you might get caught and put in a cage. You wouldn't like that, would you, my pet? No, let's wait till the beginning of the week when all is quiet again.'

The bird seemed to understand what she was saying, because it jumped straight out of her hand and flew up and pecked her nose!

'Temper, temper!' said Mrs Pepperpot and she didn't go near the attic the rest of the day.

On the Sunday she only had time to take some food and water up to the bird in the morning, as she was expecting visitors and, besides, Mr Pepperpot was home all day.

On Monday morning she had some nice bacon-rind which she took up as a special treat.

'Here we are, my little duck, something really nice for you!' she said.

But the little crow just glared at her from the highest beam and wouldn't come down.

There was a bee buzzing round the window, so, as Mrs Pepperpot was afraid it might sting her precious bird, she opened the window and let it out.

At that very moment she SHRANK!

'Caw, caw! At last!' squawked the little crow, and before she had time to get on her feet, Mrs Pepperpot felt herself being lifted into the air by her skirt, and away went the little crow with her out of the window!

As they flew over the roof and the trees they were joined by a whole crowd of big crows, all squawking together.

'Caw, caw! Welcome back!' they squawked.

One big crow flew up beside the young crow. In a deep throaty voice it said: 'Well done, young 'un. Bring her before the council! We'll all be there. Caw, caw!'

'Oh no!' cried Mrs Pepperpot, 'not that again!' Because she remembered the time she had had to sing at the Crows' Festival and they stole all her clothes!

But there was nothing she could do, dangling helplessly, as she was, in the little crow's beak.

All the crows were heading in the same direction and soon they swooped down and landed in a clearing in the forest. The little crow put Mrs Pepperpot down right in the centre, and all the crows stood in a big ring round her. She was very frightened indeed.

The big crow spoke first: 'You may begin, young 'un. Tell us what happened.'

So the little crow told them how Mrs Pepperpot had found it after it had fallen out of the nest, and how she had taken it home.

'Were you frightened?' asked the big crow.

'I suppose I was just as frightened as she is now,' said the little crow, looking at Mrs Pepperpot, who was shaking all over.

'What did the monster do to you?' asked another crow.

'I'm not a monster!' cried Mrs Pepperpot. 'I didn't do anything bad! I just kept him in a nice warm attic till he could fly.'

'That's right,' said the little crow. 'She took pity on me because I had hurt my wing.'

'But after the wing got better,' asked the big crow, 'did she still keep you shut up in the attic against your will?'

'She did,' said the little crow.

'It's a black lie!' shouted Mrs Pepperpot. 'You know I was going to let you out, but I had to be sure you would be safe. The first day you could fly it was raining cats and dogs.'

The big crow looked up at the sky: 'Hm, it looks as if it's going to pour any minute now. We'd better keep the little thing here till tomorrow, or she might get drowned walking home.'

'I'm not a "thing",' said Mrs Pepperpot.

'You called me a "duck",' said the little crow.

'But I *must* get home today,' said Mrs Pepperpot. 'I have to put the peas to soak for our pea-soup tomorrow.'

'And we can't let her go tomorrow, either,' went on the big crow, 'because that's the day we have a visit from Master Fox, and he might take her for a weasel.'

'Stuff and nonsense!' said Mrs Pepperpot.

'That's what I thought,' said the little crow, 'when you told me about the cat.'

'Perhaps we could let her go on Wednesday,' chipped in another crow.

'Wednesday!' cried Mrs Pepperpot. 'I must certainly be there then, because that's the day the fishmonger calls, and I've ordered two pounds of herring from him,' said Mrs Pepperpot.

The big crow shook its head: 'I'm afraid that fish-monger's van is too dangerous. It might run her down. She can go on Thursday.'

'Thursday! I *must* be home then; we get the big saw back from the grinder's that day, and I have to help my husband saw up logs.'

'Tut, tut! A little thing like you can't be allowed to saw logs!' said the big crow. He turned to the others: 'Don't you think it would be safer to keep her till Friday?'

'Yes, yes! Caw, caw!' squawked all the crows.

'Friday is my big cleaning day,' said Mrs Pepperpot, 'and if you don't let me go till then I shall have to do all my washing as well. It's not fair!' and she stamped her foot and shook her fists at the birds.

'Now, now,' said the big crow, 'temper, temper! Friday is an unlucky day, everyone says so. Saturday would be better.'

But this was too much for Mrs Pepperpot. She just sat down and buried her head in her apron and sobbed and sobbed. She thought she'd never get home!

'I only did it to be kind!' she hiccoughed, 'I was so very fond of the little crow!'

Just then she felt herself grow to her usual size, and when she looked round all the crows had scattered and were whirling overhead in the trees, cawing loudly.

Mrs Pepperpot wiped her eyes and straightened her hair. Then she started to walk home. As she walked she thought about the things the crows had said to her.

'I think maybe they're right. It isn't much fun to be in prison like that, day after day.'

But wait till you hear the strangest thing; since that day, whenever Mrs Pepperpot goes up to the attic and opens the window, that little crow comes flying in to sit on her shoulder! It never pecks her nose or pulls her hair, and Mrs Pepperpot always has a titbit for it in her apron pocket.

Mrs Pepperpot learns to swim

As you know, Mrs Pepperpot can do almost anything, but, until last summer, there was one thing she couldn't do; she couldn't swim! Now I'll tell you how she learned.

In the warm weather Mrs Pepperpot always took a short cut through the wood when she went shopping. In the middle of the wood is quite a large pool which the village children use. Here they play and splash about in the water. The older ones, who can swim, dive from a rock and race each other up and down the pool. They teach the younger ones to swim too, as there's no grown-up to show them. Luckily, the pool is only deep round the big rock and those who can't swim stay where it's shallow. But they're all very keen to learn, so they practise swimming-strokes lying on their tummies over a tree-stump and counting one-two-three-four as they stretch and bend their arms and legs.

Mrs Pepperpot always stopped to watch them, and then she would sigh to herself and think: 'If only I could do that!' Because nobody had taught *her* to swim when she was a little girl.

Some of the big boys could do the crawl, and the little ones tried to copy them, churning up the water with their feet and their arms going like windmills while everyone choked and spluttered.

'I bet I could learn that too!' thought Mrs Pepperpot. 'But where could I practise?'

One day when she got home, she decided to try some swimming-strokes in the kitchen, but no sooner had she got herself balanced on her tummy over the kitchen stool, when her neighbour knocked on the door asking to borrow a cup of flour. Another time she tried, she flung out her arms and knocked the saucepan of soup off the stove, and her husband had to have bread and dripping for supper. He was *not* pleased.

Every night she would dream about swimming. One night she had a lovely dream in which she could do the breast-stroke most beautifully. As she dreamed, she stretched forward her arms, bent her knees and then—Wham! One foot almost kicked a hole in the wall, the other knocked Mr Pepperpot out of bed!

Mr Pepperpot sat up. 'What's the matter with you?' he muttered. 'Having a nightmare, or something?'

'Oh no,' answered Mrs Pepperpot, who was still half in a dream. 'I'm swimming, and it's the most wonderful feeling!'

'Well, it's not wonderful for me, I can tell you!' said Mr Pepperpot crossly. 'You stop dreaming and let me have some peace and quiet.' And he climbed into bed and went to sleep again.

But Mrs Pepperpot couldn't stop dreaming about swimming. Another night she dreamed she was doing the crawl—not like the little ones, all splash and noise, but beautiful strong, steady strokes like the big boys, and one arm went up and swept the flower-pots from the window-sill and the other landed smack on Mr Pepperpot's nose.

This was too much for Mr Pepperpot. He sat up in bed and shook Mrs Pepperpot awake.

'You stop that, d'you hear!' he shouted.

'I was only doing the crawl,' said Mrs Pepperpot in a far-away voice.

'I don't care if you were doing a high dive or a somersault!' Mr Pepperpot was very angry now. 'All I know is you need water for swimming and not a bed. If you want to swim go jump in a swimming pool and get yourself a swimming teacher!'

'That's too expensive,' said Mrs Pepperpot, who was now awake. 'I watch the children in the pool in the wood.

One of these days, when they're all gone home, I'll have a try myself.'

'Catch your death of cold, no doubt,' muttered Mr Pepperpot and dozed off again. But a little while later there was a terrible crash, and this time Mr Pepperpot nearly jumped out of his skin.

There was Mrs Pepperpot, on the floor, rubbing a large lump on her forehead. She had been trying to dive off the side of the bed!

'You're the silliest woman I ever knew!' said Mr Pepperpot. 'And I've had enough! I'm going to sleep on the kitchen floor.'

With that he gathered up the eiderdown and a pillow, went into the kitchen and slammed the door.

Mrs Pepperpot was a bit puzzled. 'I can't have done it right!' But then she decided enough was enough and, wrapping herself in the only blanket that was left on the bed, she slept the rest of the night without any more swimming-dreams.

Then came a bright warm day when all the village children were going on a picnic up in the mountains.

'That's good,' thought Mrs Pepperpot, 'there'll be no one in the pool today and I can get my chance to have a try.'

So when she'd cleaned the house and fed the cat and the dog, she walked through the wood to the pool.

It certainly looked inviting, with the sun shining down through the leaves and making pretty patterns on the still water. There was no one else about.

She sat down on the soft grass and took off her shoes and stockings. She had brought a towel with her, but she'd never owned a bathing suit, and it didn't even occur to her to take her skirt and blouse off. Peering over the edge, she could see the water wasn't very deep just there, so she stood up and said to herself: 'All right, Mrs P., here goes!' and she jumped in!

But she might have known it—at this moment she SHRANK!

Down, down she went, and now, of course, the pool seemed like an ocean to the tiny Mrs Pepperpot.

'Help, help!' she cried, 'I'm drowning!'

'Hold on!' said a deep throaty voice from below. 'Rescue on the way!' And a large frog swam smoothly towards her.

'Get on my back,' he said.

Mrs Pepperpot was thrashing about with both arms and legs and getting tangled up in her skirt as well, but she managed to scramble on to the frog's knobbly back.

'Thanks!' she panted, as they came to the top, and she spat out a lot of water.

The frog swam quickly to the rock, which now seemed quite a mountain to Mrs Pepperpot, but she found a foothold all right and sat down to get her breath, while the frog hopped up beside her.

'You're certainly a good swimmer,' said Mrs Pepperpot.

The frog puffed himself up importantly: 'I'm the champion swimming teacher in this pool,' he said.

'D'you think you could teach me to swim?' asked Mrs Pepperpot.

'Of course. We'll begin right away, if you like.'

'The children do the breast-stroke first, I've noticed,' said Mrs Pepperpot.

'That's right, and frogs are very good at that. You

climb on my back and watch what I do,' said the frog, as he jumped in.

It was a bit difficult to get off the rock on to the frog's back, but he trod water skilfully and kept as steady as he could. Soon she was safely perched and watched how the frog moved his arms and legs in rhythm. After a while he found her a little piece of floating wood and told her to hang on to that while she pushed herself along with her legs.

She got on fine with this till she suddenly lost her grip on the piece of wood and found herself swimming along on her own.

'Yippee!' she shouted with excitement, but the frog, who had been swimming close to her all the time, now came up below her and lifted her onto his back.

'That's enough for the moment,' he said, and took her back to the rock for a rest. 'You've got the idea very well, for a beginner.'

Mrs Pepperpot was feeling so pleased with herself, she wanted to go straight on and learn the crawl and swim on her back and everything, but the frog said: 'Not so fast, my dear; you've learned to keep afloat now, but you must go on practising the breast-stroke before you can do the other things.' But when he saw she looked disappointed, he said: 'I'll get my tadpoles to give you a show of water acrobatics, how's that? You get in and swim along with me to the shallow end; that's where they have their water circus.'

So they set off together, the frog making elegant circles round Mrs Pepperpot as she made her way slowly across the pool, trying to remember to keep her arms together and her legs from kicking in all directions. At last they got to the shallow part where there were reeds growing on the sandy bottom, and in and out of these hundreds of tadpoles were darting. There were all sizes from the tiniest things no bigger than a lady-bird to big ones with their front legs showing and some even had their back legs as well and were just about to shed their tails.

The frog found a small flat rock for Mrs Pepperpot to sit on and then he called all the tadpoles round him: 'Come on, children,' he croaked, 'I want you to show this lady all your best tricks. Let's see what you can do and remember what I've taught you.'

All the tadpoles immediately got into line, the biggest at the front, the smallest at the back, so that they looked like a long, winding snake. Talk of follow-my-leader! Whatever the front tadpole did, the others copied so exactly you would think they had all been tied together with string. First they swam to the top of the water, then they dived to the bottom, then they wove in and out of the reeds in a beautiful pattern. Then, like aeroplanes doing aerobatics, they rolled over and over and looped the loop and they even swam backwards, still keeping as smartly in line as any regiment of soldiers.

Mrs Pepperpot was very impressed, and the frog had puffed himself up so much, he was nearly bursting with pride.

When the show was over Mrs Pepperpot looked at the frog very pleadingly and said: 'Don't you think you could just show me how you dive? I *would* like to try that.'

'Well,' he said, 'you won't find it very easy to begin with, but it would do no harm to try at this end, I suppose. I'll give you a demonstration first.' And with that he made a perfect dive off the little rock.

When he came up again he told Mrs Pepperpot to point her arms straight up and to let herself go forwards till they were pointing down into the water.

'Shut your eyes as you go in,' he warned.

Mrs Pepperpot stood on the edge of the rock.

'It looks a bit deep,' she said. She was feeling rather frightened.

'It has to be,' said the frog, 'or you'd knock your head on the bottom. Off you go now; I'll be here to save you!'

So Mrs Pepperpot pointed her arms in the air, held her breath, shut her eyes and let herself fall forward. But instead of the beautiful dive she had hoped to make right under the water and up again, she found herself rolling about in what seemed more like a large puddle than a deep pool; she had GROWN!

As she picked herself up and waded out of the water to the bank she could see no sign of the frog or the tadpoles. Her clothes were clinging to her, and though she tried to dry her arms and legs, it was no use putting on her shoes and stockings, so she hurried home in her bare feet, leaving a great dripping trail behind her.

As soon as she got home she remembered what her husband had said: 'You'll catch your death of cold!' So she changed into dry clothes and hid the wet ones in the attic. Then she quickly set about making her husband's favourite macaroni pie for supper.

*   *   *   *   *

It was several days before Mrs Pepperpot got a chance to go back to the pool. But all the time she was longing to find out if she had really learned to swim. So, when she heard the children going home through the wood one warm evening, she slipped out of the house and made for the pool as fast as she could go. She looked pretty queer, because this time she was wearing an old long bathing suit of her husband's she had found in the attic, and over it she had her winter coat. She just hoped that no one would see her.

When she got to the pool all was quiet. She didn't dare to dive in, but from the big rock she let herself slide into the water, and before she knew it, there she was, swimming along—not quite as stylishly as the frog, rather more like a dog paddling—but still, she was swimming and Mrs Pepperpot felt very proud.

As she turned to swim back to the rock she noticed she was being followed. There was the frog, keeping pace with her, and behind him were all the tadpoles, in close formation, from the largest to the tiniest, no bigger than a lady-bird! For one moment the frog came to the top of the water and gave a loud croak.

'Thanks, Mr Frog,' said Mrs Pepperpot, 'you're the best swimming teacher in the world!'

With an elegant kick of his back legs, the frog did a nose-dive down into the dark depths of the pool, and all the tadpoles followed after and Mrs Pepperpot couldn't see them any more.

So now you know how Mrs Pepperpot learned to swim.

Mrs Pepperpot gives a party

MRS PEPPERPOT likes animals, as you know, but until lately Mr Pepperpot wasn't so keen; in fact, he didn't like *baby* animals at all.

'Messy things,' he used to say, 'always getting in the way and making too much noise!'

'It's all very well for you,' said Mrs Pepperpot, 'out seeing people all day long. But I'm here all alone, and I like to have little creatures round me for company.'

There was no answer to that, so Mr Pepperpot would go off to work muttering: 'Just keep them out of my way, that's all!'

One day when a stray kitten came to the door mewing to come in, Mrs Pepperpot picked it up and brought it indoors. Then she found it had lost a bit of its tail, and though it was mending, it was still very sore.

'Oh, you poor stumpy wee thing!' said Mrs Pepperpot, stroking the kitten, which was trembling with cold and hunger. 'I'll put you in the box under the stove where it's nice and warm, and you shall have some bread and milk.'

Soon the kitten was sleeping contentedly in the box and was so quiet that Mr Pepperpot never noticed it was there when he came home from work.

A few days later, when Mrs Pepperpot was bringing her shopping home from the village, she came past Mr Hog's pig-sty, where the sow had had twelve piglets. She stopped to watch them scampering round, and then she noticed that one of them was limping. It was the smallest of the litter and all the other piglets were pushing it about, so that it couldn't even get to its mother to suckle.

'You're having a pretty thin time, Squiggly,' said Mrs

Pepperpot, as she leaned over the fence and picked up the piglet, which was now squealing loudly. Just then the farmer came out to feed the sow, and Mrs Pepperpot held up the piglet to show him.

'Look, Mr Hog, this piglet has broken its leg!'

'So it has!' said Mr Hog. 'Well, we'll have to have roast suckling pig for dinner this Sunday.'

He reached out to take the animal from her, but Mrs Pepperpot said: 'Oh no, that would be a shame!' and hung on to the piglet which was quietly grunting by now.

'What else can I do? The others will kill it if I leave it in the sty,' said Mr Hog.

'I'll buy it from you and rear it by hand,' said Mrs

Pepperpot, though she wondered how she was going to pay for it.

'I'll give it to you and welcome, Mrs Pepperpot, if you think you can do anything with it,' said Mr Hog.

So Mrs Pepperpot thanked him and went home with the piglet in her arms. When she got there she fixed a little wooden splint on the piglet's broken leg, gave him a good feed of milk and gruel and tucked him up in the box under the stove together with the kitten.

When Mr Pepperpot came home he was a bit startled to hear grunts from under the stove, but Mrs Pepperpot quickly explained that the piglet was a present from Mr Hog.

'It won't cost much to rear,' she said, 'we have plenty of potato peelings and scraps, and then when it's big enough we can sell it.'

This idea appealed to Mr Pepperpot, who liked to make a bit of extra money, so he didn't grumble any more.

Stumpy, the kitten, and Squiggly, the piglet, got on very well together, and Mrs Pepperpot had a lot of fun watching them.

'Good things always come in threes,' she said to herself; 'I wonder what my third pet will be?'

She didn't have long to wait, because the next time she was down at the village store there was a man in there

with a sack on his back. She could see there was something moving in the sack, so when they got outside she
couldn't help asking what it was.

'Oh, it's just a puppy I'm going to drown,' said the man,
who had a nasty leer on his face.

'A puppy?' exclaimed Mrs Pepperpot. 'What's the poor
little thing done that you have to drown it?'

'He was the ugliest of the litter,' said the man, 'and as
he's not pure-bred anyway, nobody wanted him.'

'Not pure-bred, eh?' Mrs Pepperpot was getting angry.
'Ugly, is he? Well, you wouldn't win much of a prize at a

beauty-show yourself, mister! If you don't want the puppy you can give him to me; I'll see he gets a good home.'

'All right, all right, keep your hair on!' said the man, undoing the sack and lifting out a small black and white puppy with a pug-nose and a patch over one eye. 'He's all yours, free and for nothing!'

He handed the puppy to Mrs Pepperpot and walked off quickly before she could change her mind.

Mrs Pepperpot held the whimpering, frightened little puppy and stroked him: 'Well, Ugly, I don't know what Mr Pepperpot's going to say to another baby in the house, but I couldn't let you be drowned, could I?'

When she got home she put him in with the other two, and he wagged his little tail and made friends with the kitten and the piglet with no trouble at all. Mrs Pepperpot decided to tell her husband she was only keeping the puppy till she could find a home for it, but she didn't have to worry, for Mr Pepperpot never noticed the new addition to the family when he got back from work.

He sat down at the table and his eyes had a far-away look as he said: 'D'you know, wife? I've been thinking.'

'What have you been thinking?' asked his wife.

'There's one thing I've never been and I'd really like to be,' said Mr Pepperpot.

'Whatever can that be?' she wondered, thinking of all

sorts of things Mr Pepperpot had never been.

'President of a club or society,' he said.

'Well!' said Mrs Pepperpot, she hadn't expected him to say that. 'Which club or society were you thinking of?'

'I don't know, but Eddie East told me the Sports Club is looking for a new president, and old Hatchet, the president of the Savings Club, died just last week, and then there's the Egg Co-operative Society. . . .'

Mrs Pepperpot thought a bit, then she said: 'The best thing would be to give a party.'

'How d'you mean, give a party?' said Mr Pepperpot, who never liked to ask people to the house in case Mrs Pepperpot did her shrinking act.

'Oh, I don't mean a *big* party, just to ask the Easts and the Wests—he's secretary in the Savings Club, you know —in for coffee and cakes one evening. Then, let me see, who's in the Egg Co-operative? Oh yes, that's Sarah South's husband, so we'll ask them too. What about next Saturday?'

Mrs Pepperpot was getting quite excited at the idea of giving a party, but her husband looked very doubtful. He shook his head: 'Not unless you promise not to shrink,' he said.

'Don't be silly,' said Mrs Pepperpot, 'you know I can't do that. But I *will* promise to get out of the way if I do shrink.'

'That's all very well,' said Mr Pepperpot, 'but how shall *I* know where you are?'

'When you hear a mouse squeak three times, you'll know it's me,' said Mrs Pepperpot, and when her husband still looked worried, she handed him a big plate of his favourite macaroni pie.

'Don't you fret,' she said, 'it'll be all right. Goodness! I've just remembered; if we ask the Easts and the Wests and the Souths, we shall *have* to ask the Norths as well.'

'Why? Ned North isn't in any society that I know of,' grumbled Mr Pepperpot. He wished now that he had never started the idea.

'All the same, we've been to their house, and this is a good way to ask them back. Let me see, that'll be eight guests: I shall have to make two layer cakes and lots of little sandwiches.'

'One thing I do know,' said Mr Pepperpot, 'all those stray animals of yours will have to go out in the shed that night.'

'Certainly not!' cried his wife. 'They'd catch their death of cold! They're very well-behaved and will stay right where they are—under the kitchen stove!'

So the day was fixed and the guests all said they would come.

Mrs Pepperpot spent the whole day cleaning the house and baking layer cakes and making sandwiches. Then she put on her Sunday best and stood at the door to welcome her guests and everyone shook hands.

'Now do sit down and make yourselves at home,' said Mrs Pepperpot, bustling about. To her husband, who was standing in a corner looking helpless she said: 'You'll keep everyone happy, won't you dear, while I go out and heat the coffee?' And then she disappeared out into the kitchen.

Poor Mr Pepperpot! He was so unused to company that he didn't know where to begin, but just stood there shuffling his feet and scratching his head until, luckily, Mr East asked him a question.

'Are you going in for the ski-ing competition this year?' he asked.

'Well, I might,' said Mr Pepperpot, easing himself into a chair next to Mr East. 'I used to be pretty good when I was young, but of course I'm out of training now.'

'Oh, it wouldn't take you long to get back into form!' Mr East assured him and Mr Pepperpot forgot his shyness and was soon talking away about the races he had won and the spills he had had while all the rest of the party listened. It wasn't until he couldn't think of anything more to tell that he noticed his wife hadn't come back from the kitchen.

'Excuse me a moment,' he said, and rushed out, fearing the worst had happened. But there stood Mrs Pepperpot, as large as life, putting the finishing touches to the layer cakes.

'What's the matter?' she asked.

'Thank goodness you're still here!' said Mr Pepperpot.

'Of course I am! Everything's ready now, so hold the door open for me while I carry in the tray.'

They could hear the guests laughing in the living-room, and when they went in they found the piglet had sneaked in and was trying to run round the table.

'Did you ever see a sillier-looking piglet with a wooden splint on?' said Mrs Pepperpot picking him up. 'I call him Squiggly, but my husband is so fond of pigs he wouldn't even let me get rid of the thing.'

Mr Pepperpot was so surprised to hear his wife say this that he took the pig from her and stroked it, muttering, 'Oh yes, I *love* piglets.' Then he handed it to Mrs North who wanted to hold it on her knee.

All went well while they sat at the table; everyone enjoyed the coffee and the delicious sandwiches and layer cake. As they chatted Mrs Pepperpot cleverly brought the conversation round to savings. She told Mr West: 'My husband is such a good manager; he always knows exactly what money we have to spend on what!' Which was true enough, for he usually just said 'no' whenever she asked for money to spend on anything except food.

Mr West said, 'Is that so?' and started asking Mr Pepperpot some questions. Soon they were talking about all sorts of money matters, so Mr Pepperpot didn't notice his wife leaving the room again. When he looked up and found her gone he quickly excused himself to go and look for her.

She was not in the kitchen!

Frantically he called: 'Wife! Where are you?'

'Here I am!' she answered, as calmly as you please. She had been to the bedroom to fetch a pillow for Mrs East's back.

'Oh dear, I don't know where I am when you keep disappearing like this!' said Mr Pepperpot.

'I wish you'd stop fussing and just look after our guests,' Mrs Pepperpot said.

Just then they heard a great noise of laughter and squeaks and yaps, and when they opened the door to the living-room there were Mr North and Mr East on their hands and knees on the floor, while Squiggly the pig and Ugly the pup were chasing each other round and round the two men. Everyone else was laughing and clapping and egging them on.

'You certainly know how to amuse your guests!' said Mr West, who was too fat to join in the fun on the floor.

'My husband just loves to have animals around,' said Mrs Pepperpot. 'I never know what he's going to bring home next.' She gave her husband a great nudge to make

him say something nice, but Mr Pepperpot was so over-come by all the things that were happening he just said, 'Mm, Ah!' and shooed the pup and the piglet back into the kitchen.

Now Mrs Pepperpot thought it was time they talked about hens, as her husband had said that he might like to be president of the Egg Co-operative Society. So she told the guests how well he looked after their hens and what wonderful eggs they produced. She even told them how he always knew what to do if one of the hens became ill.

Her husband listened in astonishment as he knew very well that it was Mrs Pepperpot who looked after the hens and he hardly ever saw them, but he couldn't stop her now, so he just let her talk till the guests got up and said it was time to go home.

'We've had such a nice evening,' said Norah North as they shook hands at the door, and all the others said much the same, while Mr Pepperpot held a torch for them to see their way down the path.

After they were all safely away he came indoors. Taking out his spotted handkerchief, he wiped his face and said: 'Am I glad that's over! All the same I don't really think they'll make me president of any of their societies.'

A squeaky little voice answered: 'You wait and see!'

Startled, Mr Pepperpot looked round: 'Who said that?' he asked.

'Peep, peep, peep!' said the little voice, and then he remembered that this was the signal his wife was to give him if she had turned small.

'Where are you hiding now?' he asked, but she wanted to tease him, so she let him search all through the house before she told him.

'Here I am!' she called at last from a drawer under the kitchen stove. 'I've decided to sleep with *your* pets tonight!'

'*My* pets!' he snorted, 'what's come over you? I never heard you tell so many fibs in all the years we've been married.'

'I was only trying to help,' said Mrs Pepperpot in her tiny voice, 'and, as a matter of fact, I think I managed it rather well! As they were going down the path I heard Ned North say to his wife that he thought you'd be the right person to be President of the Society for the Protection of Helpless Animals.'

'Well, I'll be blowed!' said Mr Pepperpot.

'I hope you're pleased,' said Mrs Pepperpot. 'I did my best. And now I think I'll say good night!' and she snuggled down with Stumpy, the kitten, Squiggly, the piglet and Ugly, the pup.

As for Mr Pepperpot, well, he'd got his wish, they really did ask him to be president of the Society for the Protection of Helpless Animals, and from then on he had to be kind to *all* animals, whether he liked them or not.

Sir Mark the Valiant

THERE WAS ONCE a little boy called Mark who had to stay in bed because he had whooping cough. His friends couldn't visit him in case they too caught the whooping cough, but he didn't really mind, as he had something very special to play with.

That something special was a castle which stood on a little table by Mark's bed. It had a tower and ramparts and a moat with a drawbridge over it, and it was made to look as if it had been built long, long ago. Actually, it was made in a modern factory, and Mark's father had bought it cheaply in a sale. But Mark hated to hear his mother tell people it was cheap; he thought it was so grand and beautiful, it ought to have cost lots and lots of money.

Mark also had a flag which he put on the tower and a handsome knight, dressed in white armour and riding on a white horse with a long mane and tail. The knight he called Sir Guy and he put him on the ramparts to keep a watch for enemies. The horse had its head turned a little, as if it was looking for enemies to come and attack the castle from behind.

There were many windows in the castle; in the tower, which had a winding staircase, there were narrow slits and in the top of the tower there was just one window with bars.

'That is where Sir Guy puts his prisoners,' Mark told his mother.

The little boy played with the castle all day long, and at night when his mother put it back on the table, he would lie gazing at it till he fell asleep. Sometimes the coughing would be so bad that it made his eyes water so that he saw everything through a haze; then the castle seemed to be shimmering with lights from every window —except one; the barred window in the tower was always dark.

'Sir Guy will put the light on when he puts his prisoner there,' said Mark.

One night he had been coughing and whooping so much that both his father and mother had sat with him, one holding his poor head and the other his hand. At last it stopped and he could breathe more comfortably. So his mother gave him some medicine and his father tucked him up, and then they both said good night and put out the light.

Mark was very tired; he lay there rubbing his eyes and

then he looked at the castle. It looked so beautiful with the lights shimmering in every window—*every* window? Mark sat up in bed; even the barred window in the tower was lit up tonight! And what was that? Surely Sir Guy was moving? Yes, his head was moving from side to side, and now he was lifting his hand to shade his eyes, as if he was searching for something in the distance. Now the horse moved its head too and pawed the ground with its right foreleg!

Suddenly Sir Guy dug his spurs in, galloped over the drawbridge and headed his horse straight up the counterpane toward's Mark's chest! It looked as if he were

riding through a flowery meadow and the horse's mane and tail were flying in the wind!

Just before they reached Mark's chin, the knight reined in his horse so that it reared on its hind legs.

'To battle! To battle!' shouted Sir Guy, drawing his sword and waving it over his head. 'Rally to me, my men!' The horse neighed loudly, reared again and waved its hooves so near to Mark's face, he thought he was going to kick him. But he lay quite still, as he didn't want to frighten them away.

'Where are my men?' shouted Sir Guy. 'They have deserted me in my hour of need! Who will follow me now?' he said, and then he pointed his sword at Mark; 'Will you be my squire and fight by my side?'

'I'd like to,' said Mark, 'but who's the enemy?'

'Haven't you heard?' said the knight. 'Didn't you see the light in the prison window? I'm getting ready to capture Sir Hugh. Then I will lock him up in the tower for the rest of his life.'

'How will you find him?' asked Mark.

'A message came to me that he is on his way. But now alas, my men have fled and I have no one to help me except you.'

'I will do my best,' Mark promised, 'but who is Sir Hugh?'

'He is the most fearsome knight in the whole land;

wherever he goes he leaves terror behind, castles burned and people robbed and killed. No one has ever defeated him in battle and it is known that he is afraid of only one thing.'

'What is that?' asked Mark.

'Ah!' cried the knight, 'if we knew that the task would be easy! But he keeps the secret well and no one knows what it is he fears!'

'Oh well,' said Mark, 'he'll have to be pretty big to frighten me!'

At that moment he heard a hollow laugh which seemed to be coming from behind the medicine bottle on the table beside his bed.

'So you're not afraid of me, eh?' It sounded more like a snarl than a voice, and before Mark could answer, a knight in shining red armour from head to foot rushed forward to the edge of the table and took a flying leap right on to the bed! Sir Guy moved a little nearer to Mark's chin.

'I hear you were looking for me, Sir Guy!' shouted Sir Hugh, waving his sword over his head. 'Well, here I am and I challenge you to battle on this plain!' And he pointed to the part of the counterpane that covered Mark's tummy.

Sir Guy had now gathered up his courage; he jumped off his horse, which trotted behind him and he ran full tilt down Mark's chest, shouting: 'Have at you, Sir Hugh, in the King's name!'

The two knights came together in a great clash of swords. They hit each other on their helmets, breastplates and shields. Back and forth they went, and Mark watched spellbound to see which one would go down first.

Suddenly Sir Hugh's sword knocked Sir Guy down and Sir Hugh picked him up and tucked him under one arm and his horse under the other.

'Ah ha!' shouted Sir Hugh, 'I have you at my mercy!'

Then he turned to Mark and shouted at him, 'I challenge you, Moonface, to come to his aid!'

Just then Mark started coughing. He whooped and he whooped and the whole bed shook like an earthquake. Sir Hugh dropped Sir Guy and his horse and they all ran this way and that, trying to find a place where the ground wasn't heaving under them!

*   *   *   *   *

When at last Mark stopped and everything became quiet once more, he saw both the knights pick themselves up and walk towards his face. Sir Hugh was in front and came as close as he dared. Then he said: 'Tell me, Moonface, what caused the earth to tremble? Are you a magician?'

'Oh no, sir,' answered Mark, 'I just have the whooping cough.'

Sir Hugh looked at him with horror in his eyes: 'Did you say whooping cough?'

'That's right,' said Mark, 'I've had it for a week now.'

'Who told you of my one fear in life?' thundered Sir Hugh, shaking his fists at Mark, his face almost as red as his armour.

'No one, sir,' said Mark, 'but it's a very catching illness and I'm afraid the germs will attack you any minute now.'

'Oh no!' shouted Sir Hugh as he ran full tilt to the bottom end of the bed. 'Let me get away from here!'

'If I were you, sir,' said Mark, 'I would lock myself up in a room until the danger of infection is over.'

'I will, I will!' cried Sir Hugh, whose knees were knocking inside his armour by now, he was so frightened. 'But where can I go?'

'Well,' said Mark, 'I suggest you walk across that drawbridge, open the door at the bottom of the tower, climb the winding staircase until you reach the top. There you will find a little room with bars across the window, and if you lock the door you will be quite safe.'

Before you could say knife, that knight was scurrying across the drawbridge and disappearing through the door into the tower! A moment later Mark could see his face peering through the bars of the lighted prison window!

'Hurrah!' shouted Sir Guy, who had been standing near Mark's face, watching. 'That was a master stroke! You have defeated the King's worst enemy, and for this good deed His Majesty will justly reward you!' Facing Mark and raising his sword in his right hand, Sir Guy then said: 'From the bottom of my heart I thank you and salute you, Sir Mark the Valiant!'

'It's very kind of you, sir,' said Mark, 'but I only told him about my whooping cough.'

But Sir Guy paid no attention. He was striding across

the counterpane to where his horse stood. The horse whinnied as the knight swung himself into the saddle, and then it trotted quietly towards the drawbridge. Soon the knight was back in his place on the ramparts, looking into the distance in front of him, while his horse turned its head to see if there were enemies coming up from behind.

*   *   *   *   *

In the morning Mark woke up feeling better. What a strange dream he had had! He looked at the castle to see if he could see Sir Hugh peering through the bars of the lighted prison window. There on one side stood the white horse with Sir Guy on its back, just as he had left it the night before. But there was no light in any of the windows.

Mark's mother came in at that moment with his breakfast.

'Good morning, Mark!' she said, and then she looked at him more closely. 'You look *much* better today,' she said, 'the whooping cough must be nearly over.'

'Yes,' said Mark, 'we had a battle last night and I won! I am now Sir Mark the Valiant and my castle is called "Castle Valiant".'

His mother smiled and said he must have been dreaming, but Mark thought it was all too real to have been a dream.

99

Mrs Pepperpot turns detective

MRS PEPPERPOT has tried her hand at many jobs, but this autumn she has tried something new—she has turned detective.

Of all the seasons Mrs Pepperpot likes autumn best. When anyone complains that it's dark and dreary, she always answers that it's the best time of the year, because then we get the reward for all the hard work we put in in the spring with our digging and sowing and planting.

'But the days get so short and the nights get so long!' they say.

'That makes it all the cosier indoors,' says Mrs Pepperpot, 'and think of all the fun the children have, playing detectives with torches in the dark.'

'All right, but what about the burglars and such-like? They have a much better chance to do their stealing at this time of year.'

So the argument ran, but Mrs Pepperpot said no more, because you see, someone had been stealing from *her*, and she very much wanted to play detective herself.

And what d'you think was being stolen from Mrs Pepperpot? Her potatoes, of all things! Ever since September, when she first started digging them up, she had been finding plants with no potatoes under them; they had been dug up, the potatoes taken off and then the plants stuck back in the soil to make them look as if they were still growing. Wasn't that a cunning trick?

Mrs Pepperpot couldn't think who it could be. If only she were a *real* detective, then she could trace footprints in the mud, perhaps even fingerprints on the leaves of the potato-plants. She could build a secret observation post and carry a gun, and when she had caught the thief red-handed, she would say: 'Hands up!'

At supper one night she was thinking so hard about being a detective that she said 'Hands up!' when she was passing a bowl of hot stew to her husband, and he dropped it all over the clean table-cloth in his fright. For once she couldn't very well scold him.

After supper she remembered she had left her potato bucket out in the field almost full of potatoes. 'I'd better fetch it in, or the thief might take that too,' she thought.

She put a scarf round her head and found the torch, for it was a very dark night. Then she went out to the field and was just bending down to pick up the bucket when she heard someone climbing through the hedge. Quickly she put out the torch and got right down on her knees over the bucket, so that she couldn't be seen.

'I'll catch him this time!' she said to herself and her heart was going pitterpat with excitement! But was she *cross* a moment later, when she found herself sprawling among the potatoes in the bucket; she had SHRUNK, of course.

It wasn't even any good trying to climb out of the bucket; because how could she get through all that mud back to the house while she was tiny? And she did so want to catch the thief! So, there was nothing for it but to lie where she was and try and see what the thief looked like.

First she listened very carefully; there was someone climbing through the hedge, right enough. But what was that? Two more people seemed to be coming

through, and they were not being very quiet about it, either! Now she could hear them whispering to each other: 'Mind how you go!' This was a *boy's* voice.

'I had to pull him through the hedge!' answered a *girl's* voice.

'She hurt me!' wailed another younger voice.

'Ssh!' whispered the big boy, 'or we'll go straight home and not get any potatoes tonight!'

Mrs Pepperpot could hear them coming down one of the rows with a spade. They also had a bucket which rattled. The steps stopped. Now she could hear the spade going into the soil.

'Look, Sis,' said the big boy's voice, 'these are wopping great potatoes. Hold the bucket!'

The smaller child's footsteps started coming in Mrs Pepperpot's direction and in another moment he had found her bucket.

'Tum here, tum here!' he called in a high baby voice, quite forgetting he had promised to keep quiet.

'What is it?' hissed the big boy. 'Don't shout!'

But the little boy went on: 'Lots o' tatoes in a bucket!' he announced.

'I'll give you lots o' 'tatoes in a bucket!' muttered Mrs Pepperpot to herself; 'I'll have you all three arrested when I get back to my proper size.'

Then, as quietly as she could, she worked her way down under the top layer of potatoes, so that the children wouldn't see her. It was only just in time, as the big boy and the girl came over to have a look, and they were so pleased with little brother's find that the big boy lifted up the bucket and made for the hedge.

'You carry the other bucket,' whispered the big boy to the little one, 'it's not so heavy.'

'I dood! I dood!' piped the little fellow who couldn't say his 'k's' and 'g's'. 'I find lots o' 'tatoes!' and he scrambled after the others, dragging the lighter bucket after him.

'It's a good thing it's so dark,' said the big boy, as they

all got through the hedge on to the path, 'no one can see us here.'

The girl shivered a little: 'I feel like a real burglar in a detective story,' she said.

'I burgle-burgle,' chimed in the little one.

'Burglars don't usually carry detectives around in buckets!' said Mrs Pepperpot to herself. 'Just you wait, my fine friends!'

At last the children stopped at a door. They knocked and called: 'Open the door, Mother, and see what we've brought!'

The door opened and Mrs Pepperpot heard a woman's voice say: 'My! That's a fine bucketful; it'll keep us well fed for days. I'll heat the water in the pot straight away.'

'I ha' some too!' shouted the youngest, showing her the big potatoes in his bucket.

'Two buckets! That means you've taken one that doesn't belong to us. One of you'll have to take it back when you've eaten.'

'But, Mother!' said the boy.

'There's no "but" about it,' said his mother firmly. 'We may be so poor we have to help ourselves to a few potatoes now and then, but I hope to make it up to the owner of that field before too long. The bucket goes straight back!'

Mrs Pepperpot could hardly believe her ears; here was a family right on her door-step, so to speak, and she didn't know they were going hungry. They must be new to the neighbourhood, or surely someone would have helped them. Well, she would certainly let them have whatever potatoes they needed, no doubt about that. She had almost forgotten she was being a detective and a doll's size one at that, when the mother started lifting the potatoes out of the bucket to put them in the saucepan, which was now bubbling on the stove.

Poor Mrs Pepperpot! What should she do?

'A fine thing!' she said to herself, burrowing deeper and deeper into the bucket to hide herself. 'Here I am, being sorry for them because they're poor, when I ought to be sorry for myself, going to be boiled alive any minute now!'

At last all the potatoes were in the pot and only Mrs Pepperpot was left, but by now she was so covered in earth that the mother didn't notice her.

But the little boy did. He was peering into the bucket, and he put his small hand in and lifted Mrs Pepperpot out.

'That's torn it!' said Mrs Pepperpot and shut her eyes.

'What a funny li'l 'tato!' said the little boy. 'I teep it.' And he ran off with her into the scullery, where he hid behind the door. The rest of the family were too taken up with getting the meal ready to notice where he went.

Sitting on a box, the little boy held Mrs Pepperpot very carefully on his knee.

'You my 'tato?' he asked.

Mrs Pepperpot nodded: 'That's right. I'm your 'tato.'

The little boy's eyes grew round with amazement. 'You *talking* 'tato?' he asked.

'That's right,' said Mrs Pepperpot again. 'I'm a talking 'tato.'

'Tan I eat you?' he asked, looking at her very closely.

Mrs Pepperpot shivered a bit, but she spoke very calmly:

'I don't think I would, if I were you, sonny. I don't make very good eating.'

Just then his mother called him to eat his dinner. So he put Mrs Pepperpot down on the box and said: 'I ha' dinner now. You my talking 'tato—you stay here I—tum back soon play wi' you.'

'Well, sonny,' said Mrs Pepperpot, 'I may have to go, but I'll come back tomorrow and then I'll bring you a present. How's that?'

'You bring me 'nother talking 'tato!' he said and ran back to his mother who was putting a great heap of mashed potato on his plate.

Mrs Pepperpot wondered what she should do next. If she climbed back into the bucket and waited for a ride home in that, it might take hours before the boy went back to the field, and Mr Pepperpot would be fretting about her. Just then there was a little scratching noise behind the box and a mouse peeped out.

'Hullo,' said Mrs Pepperpot in mouse-language.

The mouse came out to look at her, and Mrs Pepperpot had never seen such a skinny creature.

'If you'll help me get out of here,' she said, 'I have a nice piece of bacon at home you can have.'

The mouse pricked up its ears. 'Bacon, did you say? We haven't seen bacon in this house for a very long time.'

'Why d'you stay here if there's so little to eat?' asked Mrs Pepperpot, as she got on the mouse's back.

'Well,' said the mouse, starting off through a hole in the wall, 'I've been with the family all my life, you know, so I don't like to leave them in the lurch. I mean, what would people say if they found out there wasn't enough food here to feed a mouse?'

When they got to the foot of the hill leading to her house, Mrs Pepperpot thanked the mouse and promised to put the piece of bacon behind the box in the scullery the next day. Then she very conveniently grew large and hurried on home.

Mr Pepperpot was standing at the front door, anxiously peering out into the dark. 'Where have you been all this time?' he asked.

'Looking for my bucket of potatoes,' said Mrs Pepperpot. 'Can't you see how grubby I am? Crawling on my hands and knees in the mud I was, but I couldn't find it anywhere.'

* * * * *

Did the boy bring back the bucket? Did Mrs Pepperpot have the children arrested? And what about the little boy's talking 'tato? Well, all that is part of another story.

Mrs Pepperpot and the brooch hunt

THE LAST TIME Mrs Pepperpot tried her hand at playing detective you may remember she nearly ended up as mashed potato. But she still has a secret longing to be one of those smart detectives you see on the films—the kind that solve everything as easy as winking.

Meanwhile, she has decided not to arrest those potato thieves. Instead, she goes to see the family almost every day and she knows all their names. There's Mrs Grey, the mother, who tries to keep the home together. It's very difficult for her, because her husband's been out of work for many months and now he's gone to the coast to see if he can get a job on a boat. Then there's Peter, who is ten and a sensible boy, and Betty, who is eight, and little Bobby, who is only three. He keeps asking about his talking potato, and, though the other children don't know what he's talking about, Mrs Pepperpot does, so she has bought him a clock-work frog to play with instead.

Each time she visits the Greys she brings some potatoes,

and she doesn't forget the hungry mouse, either; he gets a bit of bacon rind behind the door in the scullery. When she goes home the children often walk part of the way with her and talk about all sorts of things.

Once she happened to say that she had lost a little silver brooch—one she had been given as a christening present.

'I hate to lose it,' she told the children, 'because I've had it all my life and it's a pretty little thing.'

'Why don't you let us be detectives and help you find it?' Peter asked.

'Oh yes!' cried Betty, clapping her hands. 'That would be fun!'

'*I* want to be deti-deti too!' shouted Bobby, dancing up and down.

'Oh, it's hardly worth making too much fuss about,' said Mrs Pepperpot, though she secretly rather liked the idea.

'Come on, Mrs Pepperpot,' said Peter, putting on a grown-up detective sort of voice, 'tell us where you last remember seeing the lost item.'

Mrs Pepperpot smiled: 'Now, let me see; I think I wore it at Nelly North's when we had a club meeting there last month.'

Peter got out a piece of paper and pencil and noted this down.

'Right,' he said, 'when can we start investigations?'

'Well,' said Mrs Pepperpot, 'I'm busy all day tomorrow with the washing, but we could meet here about four o'clock, and by then I may have thought where else I might have left it.'

'And we can work out a plan of campaign,' said Peter importantly.

So the children promised to meet Mrs Pepperpot by a certain big fir-tree on the road between their house and hers at four o'clock the next day, and they were very excited about it, especially little Bobby, who kept talking about the deti-detis till his mother put him to bed.

Next day at four o'clock sharp they all met at the tree. Mrs Pepperpot had brought a torch, because it got dark so early.

'First we'll walk over the meadow to Nelly North's Farm,' she said. 'I have an idea it might be under her sofa. She's not a very tidy person, but I don't want to offend her by hinting she hasn't cleaned her room properly, so I want you, Peter, to take this torch and shine it under the sofa while I keep Nelly talking. You must do it secretly, mind, so that she doesn't notice.'

'What about Bobby and me?' asked Betty.

'You'll have to keep watch outside,' said Mrs Pepperpot.

So they started off across the meadow, walking in single file along a narrow path with Mrs Pepperpot in

front, shining the torch. Suddenly the torch flew up in the air and Mrs Pepperpot disappeared! At least, that's what the children thought, for, of course, *we* know that she had shrunk again! The torch was still alight when it landed, but Mrs Pepperpot had rolled into the long grass, and it was Bobby who found her and picked her up by one leg!

'Here's my talking 'tato!' he shouted, dangling poor Mrs Pepperpot upside down.

'Put it down, Bobby,' said Betty, 'it might bite!'

'No!' insisted Bobby, who had now set Mrs Pepperpot on his hand. 'It's my talking 'tato!'

Mrs Pepperpot had now got her breath back, so she said as quietly as she could: 'That's right, children, Bobby *has* seen me like this before.'

'Why, it's Mrs Pepperpot!' cried Peter and Betty together. 'However did you get so small?'

'That will take too long to explain,' said Mrs Pepperpot, 'but it happens to me from time to time, and last time Bobby found me in the bottom of the potato bucket, so that's why he thinks I'm a talking potato.'

'Let *me* hold you,' said Betty. 'I'll be very careful.'

'Yes, I think I would feel a bit safer,' said Mrs Pepperpot, as Bobby was jogging her up and down in his excitement, making her quite giddy.

'What about our search? Will we have to call it off?' asked Peter.

Mrs Pepperpot didn't like to disappoint them, and she'd already thought up a new plan, but first she made them promise never to tell anybody about her turning small.

'You must hold up your right hands, as they do in the films, and swear you will never speak of this to a living soul.'

Peter and Betty held up their right hands and repeated Mrs Pepperpot's words, but little Bobby had to be told he would get a hard smack if he ever said he'd seen a talking potato!

'Now,' said Mrs Pepperpot, 'instead of me going in to talk to Nelly North, I want Peter to knock at the door. When Nelly opens it he must say that he's collecting for—let's see—a home for worn-out car tyres. If he says it quickly she won't notice, and then when she's gone to the kitchen to look for a penny, you just switch on the torch and shine it under the sofa in the front room, and if you see a shining object, bring it with you. Betty and Bobby and I will be waiting behind that tree over there.'

By now they had reached the road in front of North Farm and Mrs Pepperpot pointed her tiny hand at a tree standing a little way from the house.

'Right oh!' said Peter and walked bravely over to the door, hiding the torch in his pocket.

The others waited in the dark till he came back. It didn't take long, but Peter was quite excited when he came towards them, and he was holding something in his hand.

'Let me see!' said Mrs Pepperpot, who was standing on Betty's hand. Peter put the object down beside her and shone the torch on it.

'Oh dear!' she said, 'I'm afraid you've picked up the wrong thing. This is a silver ring that was sent to Nelly from her uncle in America; she said she had lost it the day of the meeting.'

Peter's face had fallen. 'What do we do now'

'It's no good going back, you would find it too hard to explain,' said Mrs Pepperpot. 'Put it in your pocket while we go on to Sally South's house just along the road here. That's another place I think I may have dropped my brooch when I was there for the silver-wedding party.'

So they walked on to Sally South's house, Mrs Pepperpot riding in Betty's pocket and Bobby kept putting his fingers in to see if she was still there.

Sally didn't know Peter when she opened the door to him, and she was a bit deaf, so she didn't quite catch what he was collecting for, but he looked a nice boy, so she went off for a penny from her money-box. While she was out of the room Peter got the chance to shine his torch under the furniture and even behind the grandfather cloth. There he saw something glittering, so he fished it out and put it in his pocket. When Sally came back he thanked her very nicely for the penny and ran back to the others who were hiding outside.

'Did you find it?' whispered Betty.

'I think so,' said Peter, bringing the little thing out of his pocket.

But when she saw it Mrs Pepperpot shook her head; 'Sorry, Peter, I'm afraid that's not it either. It's a medallion Sally's husband gave her for a silver-wedding present. He was very cross when he found she had dropped it that day.'

Peter looked quite disheartened. 'This doesn't seem such a good idea, after all,' he said. 'Perhaps we'd better give it up.'

'Is that the way for Detective Sergeant Peter Grey to speak?' demanded Mrs Pepperpot, who was really enjoying the hunt, though it was true she wasn't doing the hard work! 'Let's try East Farm; Mr Pepperpot and I were there just after Christmas for the baby's christening. I was godmother, so I carried the baby, and I expect the brooch fell off when I was putting the baby in his cot.'

'Can I carry my talking 'tato now?' asked Bobby who had been very good and quiet for a long time.

'All right, but don't you drop me now,' said Mrs

Pepperpot, whose clothes and hair were getting quite messed up with all this passing from hand to hand.

When they got to East Farm only Mr East was at home, looking after the baby. He was a kindly man and never minded giving children the odd penny. So he put down his newspaper and went out to search for a coin in his jacket pocket. The baby was lying in a cot, playing with his toes. Peter remembered what Mrs Pepperpot had said about putting the baby in his cot, so when he saw a small silver bell in the cot beside the baby, he quickly picked it up and pocketed it. Mr East came in and gave him the penny, and Peter thanked him politely and ran out to the others.

'I hope I've got the right thing this time!' he cried, jingling the little bell as he pulled it out of his pocket.

'Oh, you silly boy!' exclaimed Mrs Pepperpot, 'how could you think that was my brooch? It belongs to the baby's rattle which I gave him myself for a christening present!'

Peter looked very sheepish; 'Well, you see, I don't really know what a brooch *is*!'

'Why didn't you say so before?' Mrs Pepperpot was beginning to get cross. 'A detective needs to know what he's looking for!'

'*I* know what a brooch is,' said Betty, 'it has a pin which fits into a clasp and you put it in your shawl.'

'That's right,' said Mrs Pepperpot who was trying hard to think where else they could search. 'I've got it. I'm sure I wore it for Paul West's confirmation. It was pouring with rain that day and I took my umbrella; I bet it dropped into the umbrella stand at West Farm. Come along, children, if it isn't there we'll go home, I promise you.'

So they turned about and trudged down a little lane till they got to West Farm. Peter knocked, as before, but this time there was no answer, so he tried the handle and the door opened. There, just inside, was the umbrella stand Mrs Pepperpot had told him about, so he quickly shone his torch right down to the bottom of it, and, Goodness Gracious! there he could see a small pin with what looked like the letter 'P' on it! Surely that must be it, thought Peter and made a dive for it. Then he ran out to the others, hoping no one had heard him.

This time they were hiding behind a shed and Peter made sure he was out of sight of the house before he opened his hand: 'There,' he said, 'I've got it!'

'Show me,' said Mrs Pepperpot, but then she almost cried: 'This isn't my brooch—it's a tie-pin!'

'But it had "P" on it, so I thought it must be Pepperpot!' stammered poor Peter.

'I wasn't *christened* Pepperpot, was I? I only married him! The "P" stands for Paul who was confirmed that day, Goodness, how careless everybody is with their belongings!'

There was nothing for it now; they would have go give up and go home. What bothered Mrs Pepperpot was how to return all those things to their rightful owners. For once she really hadn't been very clever.

The three children were tired and walking slowly along the road, Betty holding Mrs Pepperpot, when suddenly they heard running footsteps coming in their direction.

'They're after us!' squeaked Mrs Pepperpot. 'Run, children!'

In their fright the children nearly fell over each other and poor Mrs Pepperpot was thrown right over the ditch into the field.

The footsteps were coming nearer.

'Stop thief!' shouted someone. It was Nelly North. 'I can see them.'

'There's the boy!' shouted Sally South who was following her.

Mr East was plodding behind with fat Mrs West. 'Come on, boy,' he shouted, 'you might as well give up!'

The children were crying by now and little Bobby stumbled over a stone and fell.

At that moment a small, but commanding voice came through the air. 'Hands up or I shoot!' it shouted. It seemed to be coming from nowhere and everyone stood stock still. Then it spoke again: 'This is the secret police calling with a message for the following people: Mrs

North, Mrs South, Mr East and Mrs West. Stand by please! Can you hear me?'

They were all so surprised to hear their name called, that they very meekly answered, 'Yes'.

'Right,' went on the voice. 'You can all expect a surprise in your letter-boxes tomorrow morning. On one condition, that you immediately go home and leave the children alone!'

The children had stopped running too, and watched with amazement as, one by one, Nelly North, Sally South, Mr East and fat Mrs West all turned about and walked away without a single look behind them.

'Phew!' said a voice right beside the children. There stood Mrs Pepperpot, as large as life. She was holding a a dock-leaf in her hand and it was curled in the shape of a large cone.

'What's that for?' asked little Bobby who had picked

himself up and was *very* pleased to see his friend Mrs Pepperpot again.

'The secret police always carry loudspeakers!' she answered, smiling at the children. Then they all went home to her house and had nice hot cocoa and pancakes.

*   *   *   *   *

Next morning when Nelly North looked in her letter-box she found the silver ring she had lost, Sally South found her silver medallion, Mr East found the silver bell from the baby's rattle and Mrs West found her son's tie-pin. They certainly were surprised!

But the one who was most surprised was Mrs Pepperpot. When she opened her letter-box she found a little parcel in it, and inside was her brooch. There was also a note from Peter, which said:

Dear Mrs Pepperpot,

    After the clue you gave us last night, your detectives have been able to solve the mystery. We have put your potato-bucket back in its place in the potato-field. Thank you.   *Yours truly,*

Detective Sergeant P. Grey

'Of course!' said Mrs Pepperpot to herself, 'I was wearing the brooch on the night when the potato thieves came, and I must have dropped it in the bucket!'

Mrs Pepperpot has a Visitor from America

IT's not so often that there's a letter in the post for
Mrs Pepperpot. But one day when she opened her letter-
box she found a big letter with many foreign stamps on
it. It was from her sister who lives in St. Paul,
Minnesota, U.S.A., and this is what it said:

> Dear Sister,
>
> I am now on my way to the Old Country and would
> like to visit you. Can you come and meet me at Fornebu Airport?
> That will make me very, very happy.
>
> Your loving sister, Margret Anne

'Well, well!' said Mrs Pepperpot to herself, 'so my loving sister is coming back to Norway? It must be forty years since we last saw each other and there wasn't much loving sister about her then. As I remember it, I always got the short end of the stick. We'd go to the store and it would be little me to carry the basket while Miss Hoity Toity Margret Anne talked with the boys. And at school . . . I shall never forget the day she said I'd spilt ink over her copy-book and ruined it. As if I'd do a thing like that! Then there was the other time she fell in the brook and said I'd pushed her in. If we went blueberry picking she'd pinch my basket because it was full and she was too lazy to get her own. And then . . .'

But we won't go on listening to all this miserable stuff, because it's quite clear that Mrs Pepperpot was in a very bad mood that day. All the same, her sister would have to be met at the airport; there was no getting away from that!

'I'll go,' said Mrs Pepperpot, 'but if Margret Anne thinks I'm going to doll myself up for her sake, she's much mistaken! I'll put on some old clothes of our mother's and a shawl round my head, and I'll take my broom along. Then my fine sister may not even want to know me!'

The day came and Mrs Pepperpot took the bus to the airport. It was quite a long trip and the other passengers were a bit surprised to see her get on in her old-fashioned clothes and carrying a broom.

At the airport there was a great crowd of people, and they stared even more at the little old woman with her shawl and her broom. Some of them were talking in foreign languages, and everyone was carrying heavy suitcases and pushing this way and that. By the time the loudspeaker announced that the plane from New York was about to land, Mrs Pepperpot was so confused, she didn't know if she was standing on her head or her heels. As it happened, it didn't matter very much, because at that moment she SHRANK!

'Oh my goodness!' wailed Mrs Pepperpot, as she rolled along the slippery floor and very nearly got trodden on,

'What a time for this to happen!'

But almost at once she felt herself snatched up by a large lady's hand and popped into a glass show-case.

'Somebody must have been trying to steal one of the souvenirs,' said the large lady and locked the door of the show-case.

There stood Mrs Pepperpot, shawl, broom and all! She could see the people coming in from the plane, and among them, looking anxiously round, was a lady in a smart fawn hat and flowers on her coat and dress which matched the flowers on her outsize handbag. She wore spectacles with jewelled rims which sparkled most amazingly.

'That must be Margret Anne,' thought Mrs Pepperpot, and a moment later she was sure, because the lady walked past the show-case talking aloud to herself:

'Oh dear, where can my sister be? I'd better wait a bit.'

She came back and looked into the show-case.

'Maybe I should buy some Norwegian souvenirs for my friends in America. Oh, what a wonderful doll! She looks just like my mother with that shawl, and she used to have a broom just like that. But the face isn't like her—oh no it has such a bad-tempered expression!'

Mrs Pepperpot was fuming inside: 'Has it indeed! I wonder what your mother would say if she could see *you*, dressed up as you are, in your American finery!'

Margret Anne went on talking to herself: 'I really must buy that doll to show my sister; she'll think it very, very funny!'

Mrs Pepperpot didn't think it funny at all, but held herself as stiff as she could while the large lady picked her up and gave her to Margret Anne, who paid for her and put her in her outsize handbag. Before it was closed, Mrs Pepperpot had time to see what a lot of knick-knacks there were inside: powder compact, lipsticks, paper hankies, face-cream, notebooks, pens and pencils, cigarettes. . . . Once the lid was closed Mrs Pepperpot was almost suffocated with all the different smells and she badly wanted to sneeze. But she kept as still as a mouse while her sister called a taxi.

Margret Anne told the taxi-man to drive all the way to the valley where Mrs Pepperpot lived, which was many miles away.

'That'll cost her a pretty penny!' thought Mrs Pepperpot. 'But at least I'll get a free ride.'

The taxi drove on and on, and Mrs Pepperpot must have had a little snooze, because suddenly she woke up to hear her sister say: 'Driver! Stop at this shop, please! I haven't been here since I was a child, and I want to go in and buy a few things for my sister. When she was a little girl she was always so good about carrying the groceries home for me.'

'Well, I never!' said Mrs Pepperpot inside the handbag.

Margret Anne went up to the counter and bought some smoked fish, some goat-milk cheese and some strong Norwegian sausage.

'I haven't tasted these things for forty years,' she told the grocer, who was a young man and didn't remember Margret Anne. She put all the things in her handbag on top of poor Mrs Pepperpot.

'Pooh!' said Mrs Pepperpot. 'I'll die if I have to stay in this smelly bag much longer!'

Just as she was going out of the shop, Margret Anne asked the grocer if he had a small bottle of ink.

'Good gracious! What does she want that for?' thought Mrs Pepperpot, as the ink bottle was poked into a corner beside her.

Then she heard her sister ask the taxi-man to drive to the school-house.

'I want to look at the room where my sister and I learned our lessons. It's all so long ago, but I've often thought how unkind I was when I told the teacher my sister poured ink on my copy-book.'

'I see!' thought Mrs Pepperpot. 'The bottle of ink is a peace-offering. Better late than never!'

When she had looked inside the little old school-room, Margret Anne asked the driver to stop a short way out of the village where there was a bridge over the brook.

'You see, that's where I once fell in when I was a child and I told my mother that my sister pushed me.'

'I got a good hiding for that, my fine lady!' said Mrs Pepperpot inside the bag.

'I'd like to sit on the bridge for a moment and think about how wicked I was. D'you think my sister will have forgiven me?'

The taxi-man laughed: 'Why, ma'am,' he said, 'she'll

be so pleased to see you after all these years, she won't worry about your little tiffs when you were young!'

'Perhaps she's not so bad, after all,' thought Mrs Pepperpot.

Margret Anne was dangling her legs over the edge of the bridge and staring down into the water, when suddenly she saw a great fish swimming by. She got so excited, she dropped the handbag into the brook!

'Help, help!' cried Mrs Pepperpot, as the bag went whirling downstream. She was rolling round and round inside with the cheese and the fish and, worst of all, the ink! The cap had come off and she was covered in the

stuff. Luckily the bag hit a stone which forced the catch open and Mrs Pepperpot was thrown out.

Remembering a diving lesson a frog had given her once, she went in head first to clean off the ink, and then she swam to the bank, pulling the bag after her.

'Now if only I could get back to my proper size!' she said, and, for once, it actually happened as she wished.

She was not far from home, so she ran up the hill as fast as she could go and into her house.

When Margret Anne arrived a few minutes later in the taxi, there stood her sister to greet her at the door, wearing a nice clean frock and with her hair neatly combed.

'Aw, honey! It's good to see my little sister after all

these years!' cried Margret Anne, as she flung her arms round Mrs Pepperpot's neck.

'Little is right,' thought Mrs Pepperpot, but all she said was: 'You're very welcome, Margret Anne, I'm sure.' She could see the taxi-man was grinning as he turned the car down the hill.

'Come on in and make yourself at home!' she went on, and led her sister indoors where the table was laid with strawberry layer-cake and pancakes with blueberry jam.

Margret Anne walked round admiring everything and saying how wonderful it was to be home. Then she remembered the lost handbag.

'It just fell out of my hand,' she told Mrs Pepperpot, 'and the water was running so fast it disappeared before we could catch it, though the driver did his best. I had everything in it, except my money, but what I'm really sorry about, honey, was a little old doll, dressed in a long black skirt with a shawl over its head and carrying a broom. It looked so like our mother—you'd have died laughing!'

'Is this the handbag!' asked Mrs Pepperpot, shyly holding up a large wet object that was still dripping on the floor. 'I got out of it—I mean, I *found* it—just down below the hill. But the doll has gone, I'm afraid.'

'How sad!' said Margret Anne, 'and the bag is a wreck!'

To console her sister, Mrs Pepperpot brought out one of those plastic dolls, dressed in the latest American fashion and with a pair of jewelled spectacles on just like Margret Anne. How they both laughed! And as they were hungry after all their adventures, they sat down to eat the delicious pancakes and layer-cake.

'I haven't tasted anything so good for forty years,' declared Margret Anne. Then she looked at Mrs Pepperpot and said: 'It's funny, sister, but I always thought of you as such a small person.'

Mrs Pepperpot grinned: 'There are times when I feel pretty small myself!'

Gapy Gob gets a Letter from the King

It's time we had a story about ogres. D'you remember we met some before?

There was a he-ogre who was called Gapy Gob, because he was so fond of eating he always had his mouth open for more. Then there was a she-ogre, or ogress, whose name was Wily Winnie, because she was always up to some trick or other.

Gapy Gob had two of the nicest little servants: a girl who did the cooking and was called Katie Cook and a boy who chopped the wood, so he was called Charlie Chop. *They* weren't ogres at all, just ordinary children, but they had no home of their own, so they lived with Gapy Gob, and he was very, very fond of them. Wily Winnie also had a servant, a very cunning cat called Ribby Ratsoup.

Gapy Gob and the children lived on the sunny side of a small mountain in a cosy little house with a cow-shed. They had one brown cow, but she only spent the winter in the shed, all spring and summer she grazed on the

high mountain pasture and gave them wonderful milk. While Charlie Chop kept the yard stocked with dry logs to burn on the stove, Katie Cook looked after the garden and saw that they always had plenty of potatoes and other vegetables. If it hadn't been for one thing, they would all three have been as happy and contented as kings.

But on the dark side of the mountain, where the sun never shone, lived Wily Winnie in her dark, untidy mess of a house. Her cat, Ribby Ratsoup, was so lazy that she never swept the floor or made their beds, but if she saw her chance to steal a nice bit of meat or fish, she made a huge steaming bowl of stew (don't ask me what *else* she put in it) and they lived on it for days.

Now these two envied Gapy Gob his nice house and especially his well-stocked larder. For Katie was such a good cook and housewife that she always had a large ham hanging up in the larder and a great bowl of milk with thick cream on top standing on the shelf.

Wily Winnie would have given the last remaining tooth in her big ugly mouth to have a taste of that lovely ham, and Ribby Ratsoup's whiskers trembled when she thought of dipping into that layer of golden cream! But it was no use, Katie always locked the door of the larder very carefully and hung the key on a belt round her waist.

So the ogress and her cat sat in their dark little kitchen and schemed and schemed till one morning in May Ribby came up with an idea.

A little while later, when Charlie Chop was standing in Gapy's yard, chopping wood as usual, he heard a rustling in the wheatfield close by.

'Who's treading down our young wheat?' he asked

loudly. He was pretty sure he knew who it was.

Right enough, out of the corn stalked Ribby Ratsoup with her tail in the air.

'It's only little me,' she minced, and tried to slip past Charlie. But he blocked the cat's way with the axe and demanded sternly: 'What d'you want, you good-for-nothing sly-puss?'

'Tut, tut! Such language!' said Ribby, getting up on her hind legs and dusting herself down. 'I have business with your master which doesn't concern you. Is he at home?'

'Maybe he is and maybe he isn't,' said Charlie, 'but he has no business with *you*, so you can just skip off home!'

'What a very rude servant Gapy Gob keeps,' said Ribby with her nose in the air. 'I shall have to tell him about you. Anyway, I have a letter for him from the King.'

'Rubbish,' said Charlie. 'The King wouldn't send a scruffy cat like you with a letter to my master.'

'That's enough!' said Ribby. 'Actually the postman asked me to deliver the letter, as I was coming this way, and now will you please let me pass!'

So Charlie allowed the cat to go inside the house, where she found Katie at the stove, busy stirring a pot of porridge for Gapy Gob's breakfast.

'Good morning and good appetite!' said Ribby, trying to curtsey with her stiff back legs.

'Good appetite is right,' said Gapy Gob, who was sitting at the table, drumming with his wooden spoon. He was very hungry and didn't like to be kept waiting for his meals.

Katie said nothing, but Ribby walked round the table, purring in her cattiest way: 'Don't worry, Gapy Gob,' she said, 'you'll soon have the most scrumptious porridge. We all know what a good cook Katie is. Of course, in our house we do have breakfast rather earlier, my mistress is so very particular!'

'In this house we eat when the food is ready,' said

Katie crossly, 'and it's no later today than it usually is. Anyhow, what d'you want, Ribby? There are no herrings for you to run off with today, if that's what you're after!'

'What an idea!' said Ribby. 'You and Charlie must both have jumped out of bed the wrong side this morning!' Then she turned her back on Katie and gave Gapy Gob one of those smiles that reach from ear to ear.

'I've brought something for you,' she said.

'What is it?' asked Gapy Gob, who loved getting presents.

'The postman asked me to deliver this letter to you personally,' said Ribby, as she pulled a big envelope from her apron pocket. 'It's from the King.'

Gapy Gob's eyes grew as round as saucers. 'From the King?' he stammered. 'What does he want with me?'

'Let me see,' said Katie, trying to snatch the letter from Ribby.

But Ribby showed her claws and hissed: 'Keep your fingers to yourself, Miss Hoity Toity. The King's writing is so fine it can only be read by cat's eyes.'

'Read it to me, Ribby, there's a good cat,' said Gapy coaxingly, 'and you, Katie, just get on with the porridge.'

Ribby Ratsoup opened the envelope and pulled out a sheet of paper.' "To Mr Gapy Gob from His Majesty the King," ' she began importantly.

' "As it has come to our notice that Mr Gapy Gob has

been eating more ham and cream—as well as more porridge—than is good for him, we hereby decree that he must from now on live on butter toffees exclusively. . . ." '

'Exclu—whatever-it-is, what does that mean?' asked Gapy Gob.

'To anyone who has had schooling like myself,' said Ribby, twirling her whiskers and looking slyly at poor Katie at the stove, 'it is quite simple. It means that you can only eat butter toffees and *nothing* else at all!'

'Mm, I wouldn't mind that!' said Gapy Gob, who was already licking his chops.

'Can I go on?' asked Ribby.

'Oh yes, please do,' said Gapy.

' "Whatever ham and cream is now in Mr Gapy Gob's larder must be handed over to Madam Wily Winnie immediately. Signed H.M. King." '

Quick as a flash Katie took the letter from Ribby's hand. The writing was so small she couldn't read it and as for the signature, it looked more like a cat's cradle!

'It's all nonsense!' she told Gapy. But he wouldn't listen; he was sure the letter came from the King, and, besides, he liked the idea of eating butter toffees for a change.

'Did the King send any toffees for me?' he asked.

'No,' said Ribby, 'but, as it happens, I have some in my

apron pocket. Here you are!' And she poured a whole pile of toffees in coloured paper wrappings on to the table. 'I'll have to go home to my mistress now, but we'll be back this afternoon for the ham and the cream!'

'Mind you bring some more toffees!' said Gapy Gob, who was already munching three, 'I won't get far with this little handful!'

Ribby promised to bring lots more toffees, and bounded off into the wheatfield, ploughing a great path through the corn, while Charlie Chop tried to hit her with a log of wood.

Inside the house Katie was standing in front of Gapy Gob, her hands on her hips: she was very angry. 'Fancy you believing all that stuff!' she said.

But Gapy Gob was munching his eighth toffee and finding it very, very good. 'The King knows what's best for me,' he said, with his mouth full, 'and nothing you can say will make any difference. You can throw all that porridge out of the window—or eat it yourself, if you like. Just give me my plate and I'll eat the rest of the toffees with a spoon.'

Just then Charlie came in for his breakfast.

'What's Gapy Gob eating?' he asked his sister.

'Butter toffees that Ribby gave him,' she said, 'and he's not even bothering to take off the paper.'

'But you know toffee is bad for his teeth!' said Charlie. 'Anyway, what's wrong with porridge?'

'The King has forbidden me to eat porridge—or ham— or cream; I'm just to eat toffees and it's wonderful!' said Gapy Gob, grinning at them both between munches.

Well, the children gave up after that. They just ladled out some porridge into their own little wooden bowls and ate it up without another word.

By now Gapy Gob had eaten twenty-eight butter toffees and was just starting on his twenty-ninth when suddenly he threw down his spoon and gave a loud wail. 'Ouch!' he shouted, 'it hurts!'

Katie and Charlie took no notice, but just went on eating.

'Ouch!' he shouted again, holding his face in his

hands: 'Can't you see I'm in pain, children? Do something about it!'

'What can *we* do?' asked Katie. 'You'd better write a letter to the King.'

'Or send for Wily Winnie and that clever cat of hers!' said Charlie.

'Don't be like that!' said Gapy Gob, and he put his head on his arms on the table and started to cry. 'I tell you it hurts like anything!' he sobbed.

'Oh, very well,' said Katie to Charlie, 'I suppose we'll have to help him. You bring that scrubbing brush and we'll take him down to the waterfall.'

'What are you going to do with me?' asked poor Gapy Gob.

'Come along now, and don't ask questions,' said Katie, helping him to his feet and leading him outside. Then they took him down to a place where there was a little waterfall over some rocks.

'Now,' said Katie, 'you sit down and lean your head back under the waterfall. That's right!' she said, as Gapy Gob obediently held his head under the rushing water.

'Now open your mouth!' said Katie, and she beckoned to Charlie to start brushing Gapy's teeth. The scrubbing brush was just right, as Gapy's mouth was almost the size of a hippopotamus's.

Poor Gapy Gob! He was nearly choking with the water

pouring into his mouth, and the scrubbing brush tasted
of soap and disinfectant, but very soon it was over, and
all the sweet, sticky toffee had been washed away.

Katie had brought a towel to dry him with. While he
was sitting on the rock she could reach his head, and she
rubbed and rubbed till he was quite dry. But Gapy Gob
was still unhappy. 'It hasn't stopped hurting! Look, in
there, that tooth!' and he pointed inside his mouth.

Charlie climbed on the ogre's knee and peeped in; sure enough, one tooth had a big hole in it!

'No wonder it hurts!' he said. 'I'll soon fix that!' And he went over to a tree-stump and pulled off a big lump of resin (that's the gummy stuff that oozes out of trees). He rolled in into a nice ball in his fingers—just like the dentist does—and plugged it into Gapy's tooth.

'That's better,' said Gapy Gob, 'it's stopped hurting altogether!' Then they all went back to the house and the ogre thanked both his faithful servants.

'I never want to see another butter toffee in all my life,' he declared, 'and I don't care *what* the King says!'

'It's not the King you have to worry about,' said Katie. 'What about Wily Winnie and Ribby Ratsoup who are coming here this afternoon to fetch the ham and the bowl of cream?'

'Oh dear, oh dear, I'd forgotten about that!' wailed Gapy Gob. 'What shall I do?'

'Don't worry,' said Charlie, 'we'll find a way to fix those two minxes.'

So, in the afternoon, when the ogress and her servant, the cat, arrived, they were ready for them.

Wily Winnie and Ribby Ratsoup were a bit nervous. 'You knock!' said Wily to the cat.

'No, you do it!' said Ribby, and then the door opened

and they both fell into the kitchen in a heap.

'Hullo!' said Gapy Gob, and gave them both a pleasant smile.

Wily Winnie picked herself up. 'We've just come for . . .' and then she didn't know what more to say.

But Katie helped her out. 'Oh yes,' she said, 'we've packed up the ham in a paper parcel and put a cloth over the cream bowl, so that it won't upset when you carry it. Here it is, all ready for you on the table. We hope you will enjoy it as much as our master enjoyed the toffees. Did you bring him some more toffees?'

'Oh, no!' cried Gapy Gob. backing into a corner. 'No more toffees—ever!'

'Well . . . Thank you very much!' said the ogress. 'We'll be off home then. Come on, Ribby, you carry the cream.' And she took the large paper parcel from the table and walked out, followed by Ribby, carefully balancing the covered bowl between her paws.

As soon as they were out of sight of the house, Wily turned to Ribby. 'Let me have a taste of your cream,' she said, and put out her hand for the bowl.

'Oh no,' said Ribby, holding on to the bowl, 'not till you give me a slice of your ham!'

In the tussle that followed, the bowl fell on the ground and the contents started running down the road.

'Look what you've done!' shouted Ribby.

'How dare you answer me back!' shouted Wily Winnie, and she hit the cat over the head with the paper parcel. It gave a great crack, and out flew—not a ham, but an old broom with a broken handle!

'Of all the dirty tricks!' said the ogress, and stamped her foot so hard it made the ground tremble.

But Ribby was down on all fours, trying to save some of the cream by licking it up. She took one taste and then she spat it out, right into Wily Winnie's face!

'It's white paint!' she hissed. 'We've been double-crossed!'

Much later, when Gapy Gob and the children went for their evening walk to watch the sun go down, they could see Wily Winnie many miles away, running up and down the mountain, still chasing her cat with that old broom! And they laughed and they laughed and they laughed!

Mrs Pepperpot and the Budgerigar

NEAR Mrs Pepperpot's house stands a very pretty little cottage with a garden round it. There is also a handsome double gate decorated with trees and flowers and leaves, all made of wrought iron and painted shiny black. Entwined in the leaves on one side of the gate is the word 'Happy' and on the other the word 'Home'. So when the gate is shut it reads 'Happy Home'. As a matter of fact, the cottage belongs to a Mr and Mrs Happy. The wife's first name is Bella, but no one's ever heard the husband's first name, as he hardly ever speaks to anyone, but just sits under the sunshade in the garden and reads his newspaper. Mrs Pepperpot thinks 'Mr Glum' would have suited him better.

The Happys are only there in the summer holidays, but then Mrs Pepperpot sees quite a lot of Mrs Happy. She pops over to borrow a bit of rhubarb or a cup of flour, or to snip a few chives or some parsley. This goes on nearly every day, and they always have a little chat and then Mrs Happy says: 'You really must come and visit

me one of these days and meet my Pipkins—he is such a
darling bird!'

Pipkins is Mrs Happy's budgerigar, which she brings
with her from town, so that he too can have a nice
country holiday.

'He's getting so clever at talking,' said Mrs Happy one
day. 'I've taught him to say four whole words now. As
soon as I have a free day, Mrs Pepperpot, I'll invite you
over.'

Mrs Pepperpot had never seen a budgerigar and was
very curious to hear a bird talking, so she thanked Mrs
Happy and hoped she'd soon be asked.

But the days went by, and although Mrs Happy still
kept coming over for this and that which she'd forgotten

to buy at the store, she always seemed to be too busy to invite Mrs Pepperpot to her house.

Then one morning Mrs Pepperpot had been picking sugar-peas for her husband's supper and she found she had quite a lot over.

'I could take them over to Mrs Happy,' she said to herself. 'Then perhaps she would let me have a look at that budgery—thing-e-me-jig. I'd dearly like to hear a bird talk.'

So she put on her best apron and scarf, popped the peas in a paper bag and walked over to 'Happy Home'. She went through the wrought-iron gate, up the path and through the open front door. Inside the hall she knocked on one of the closed doors. No one answered, but she

could hear Mrs Happy talking to someone inside.

'Come on, darling,' she was saying, 'just to please me, say "Thank you, Mama!"'

'That's funny,' thought Mrs Pepperpot, 'I never knew Mrs Happy had any children.' She knocked again.

'Wait a minute, my love,' said Mrs Happy inside, 'there's someone at the door.' And she opened the door just a tiny crack.

'Oh, it's you, Mrs Pepperpot,' she said, slipping through the door and shutting it behind her. 'How kind of you to call.'

'I just brought you these peas from the garden,' said Mrs Pepperpot and handed her the bag.

'Thank you so much; I love sugar-peas!' said Mrs Happy. 'I wish I could ask you in, but just now I'm busy with my little boy . . .'

'You never told me you had a son,' said Mrs Pepperpot.

Mrs Happy laughed. 'Oh dear, no, I mean my Pipkins, my little budgie! He's all I have, you know, and just now I'm making him practise the words he can say, so that my friends can hear him when they come to tea this afternoon. They're coming all the way from town.'

'Well, I'll be going then,' said Mrs Pepperpot, who was a bit disappointed at not being asked in.

'Come round tomorrow morning,' said Mrs Happy, 'and have a cup of coffee and help me finish up the cakes.'

When she got home Mrs Pepperpot remembered that she hadn't time next morning, as that was her washing day.

'I'll slip over later and tell her I can't come,' she said to herself. So, about three o'clock, she walked over to the cottage and again she found the front door open, so she went into the hall and knocked on one of the inner doors. As there was no reply, she opened the door and found herself in the sitting-room. It was all ready for the tea-party, she could see, with a pretty white cloth on the table, the best china set out and a big vase of flowers. On a smaller table by the window stood a cage.

Mrs Pepperpot couldn't resist going over to have a look at the pretty blue bird which was swinging to and fro on its perch. She sat down on the table beside the cage and said: 'Hullo, Pipkins, are you going to talk to me?'

The bird just looked at her.

'I don't believe it *can* talk!' said Mrs Pepperpot, and as she said that she felt herself SHRINK!

'So you don't believe I can talk,' said the budgerigar, but now, of course, he was talking bird-language, which Mrs Pepperpot could understand when she grew small.

'Well,' said Mrs Pepperpot, 'I hadn't *heard* you talking till now.' She was standing on the table, wondering how

she was going to get away before Mrs Happy and her
guests came in.

'As a matter of fact,' said the bird, 'you've come just
at the right moment. I want you to help me.'

'Help *you*? How can I help you when I don't even know
how to help myself just now?' said Mrs Pepperpot,
walking all round the cage to see if there was anything
she could climb down by. But she was trapped!

'Well, I want to play a trick on Mrs Happy,' said the bird.

'A trick, Pipkins, what sort of a trick?' asked Mrs Pepperpot.

'Please don't call me by that stupid name. Pipkins, indeed; my real name is "Suchislife". Don't you think that sounds more superior?' The budgerigar was preening his feathers as he spoke, and looking down his beak at Mrs Pepperpot.

'Oh yes,' she said hurriedly, 'very superior!' Secretly she thought it sounded like something her husband usually said when he hadn't won the ski-race: 'Ah well, such is life!'

'What d'you want me to do?' she asked the bird.

'I'll explain,' said Suchislife. 'But we must be quick, as Mrs Happy has only gone down the hill to meet her guests. First, will you open the door of the cage, please?'

Mrs Pepperpot did as she was asked and unhinged the cage door.

'Now, just step inside,' went on the bird, and Mrs Pepperpot walked into the cage.

No sooner was she in than the budgerigar hopped out and, quick as lightning, fastened the door-hinge with his beak!

'Got you!' he chirped merrily and flapped his wings with excitement.

Mrs Pepperpot glared at him through the bars. 'You needn't think you can be funny with me!' she said, 'or I shall take back my offer to help!'

'Sorry, ma'am!' he said. 'When I get my freedom it sort of goes to my head, don't you know. But please don't be angry; just listen to my plan.' He had flown up on top of the cage, and took hold of the cover which was hooked on to it. 'I'm going to put the cover on,' he said, as he pulled it neatly down over the cage with his beak, making it quite dark for Mrs Pepperpot inside.

'Now,' said the bird, 'Mrs Happy won't notice that you're in there instead of me. She'll want me to do my party piece to impress her precious guests, so when you hear her say: "Come on, pet, say 'Thank you, Mama' and 'Pipkins Happy'," you just tell her what you think of her.'

'But you haven't told me why you don't like her,' objected Mrs Pepperpot.

'She's mean, and for all her talk about how clever I am, she neglects me. I often have to go without fresh water or she forgets to give me any grain. But you'll soon see what she's like.' And with that Suchislife flew out of the window and hid in a tree to watch what would happen.

Mrs Pepperpot had just settled herself comfortably on the budgerigar's swing when she heard the ladies come into the sitting-room.

'D'you think it can really talk?' she heard one of them say.

'Four words; think of that!' said the second lady.

'Wonderful, isn't it?' said the third lady.

Mrs Pepperpot didn't know what to do. She could hear Mrs Happy getting the tea ready in the kitchen, and now she heard the ladies coming nearer the cage.

'Shall we have a peep at it?' asked the first lady.

'D'you think we dare?' said the second.

'We could just lift the cover a little bit,' suggested the third.

But at the moment a little voice from inside the cage squeaked: 'Don't touch the cover!'

'How very strange,' said the first lady. 'It said four words exactly. Mrs Happy! Your budgie has just talked to us— we heard it clearly.'

Mrs Happy came in with the cakes; she was so taken up with getting the tea served, that she didn't ask *what* words the bird had said. She didn't even notice the cover was on.

'My Pipkins is so clever! Now do sit down all of you and make yourselves at home.' And they all sat down and started chattering the way ladies do, and Mrs Pepperpot stayed as quiet as if she had really been a budgerigar under the cover. But she listened to every word that was being said.

'I must tell you,' said Mrs Happy, laughing gaily, 'about the funny neighbour I have just down the road. She's a little old woman with long skirts and a shawl, and she wears her hair scraped back like something from Grandma's time. She's a scream! She will come tripping in here, knocking at the door . . .'

From the cage came an indignant squeak: 'You invited her yourself!'

For a moment Mrs Happy didn't know what to say, but then she laughed again: 'Isn't he funny? You'd almost think he was joining in the conversation, but, of course, he doesn't know what he's saying. I'll get him to say his name, but first I'll take the cover off so you can see him.' And she got up to do this.

'Don't touch the cover!' squeaked the voice from the cage.

'That's what it said before!' said one of the ladies.

'How very odd!' said Mrs Happy. 'Perhaps someone else has been teaching him to talk while I was out. Well, we won't bother with him just now. I was telling you about the funny old woman down the road; she has the quaintest little house . . .'

'That's not what you say when you go borrowing rhubarb and sugar and eggs and parsley and anything else you've forgotten to buy. The little old woman's good enough for that, Mrs Snobby Happy!'

All the ladies were aghast. Mrs Happy jumped up and ran to the table to snatch off the cover. But her foot slipped and she fell, knocking the whole cage out of the open window!

While the ladies screamed and picked up Mrs Happy, Suchislife flew down from the tree where he'd been hiding. He quickly unhinged the cage door and let Mrs Pepperpot out. Then he hopped in himself and Mrs Pepperpot shut the door behind him.

'Well done!' he said. 'I watched the whole performance and you certainly gave that old cat just the right medicine.'

Mrs Pepperpot was still shaking with anger. 'She won't be wanting to borrow from me again in a hurry! Of all the ungrateful, two-faced . . .' But Mrs Pepperpot didn't have time to finish her sentence because just then she grew to her normal size. She picked up the cage with Suchislife inside and knocked on the front door.

Inside there was so much noise going on that they

didn't hear Mrs Pepperpot's knock, so she walked in.

What a sight! Mrs Happy was lying on the sofa, moaning and holding her head, while two of her guests were mopping up the third who had had the whole pot of tea spilt over her! They didn't seem to see Mrs Pepperpot, so she put the cage on the table and said: 'I found this in the garden. I suppose it must be the bird you were telling me about, the one that talks so well?'

'Take it away, Mrs Pepperpot, take it away!' groaned Mrs Happy. 'I never want to see it again!'

'But I thought it was the cleverest bird alive,' said Mrs Pepperpot, who could hardly keep from smiling.

'It's far too clever for me,' said Mrs Happy, 'and I'd be pleased if you would accept it as a present—in return for all the nice things you've done for me this summer.'

'Don't mention it, Mrs Happy,' said Mrs Pepperpot,

'but I'd be glad to take Suchis life—I mean Pipkins—home, if you really don't want him any more.'

Then Mrs Pepperpot carried the cage out of the door, down the path and through the handsome wrought-iron gates, and the little blue bird just jumped and down inside, saying one word over and over again: 'Happy, happy, happy, happy!'

'I'm happy too,' said Mrs Pepperpot.

The New Year's Eve Adventure

It happened every New Year's Eve. Mrs Pepperpot would say to herself: 'This year I really will watch the fireworks and listen to the church bells ringing in the New Year.'

Mr Pepperpot said the same. They would dress up in their best clothes, and sit down to a meal of boiled bacon and dumplings, followed by Mrs Pepperpot's special little cakes with cloudberry jam and whipped cream. Afterwards they would each sit in their favourite chair and read the magazines they had got for Christmas.

The only sound was the ticking of the clock; tick, tock, tick, tock. . . .

After a while Mrs Pepperpot would begin to feel sleepy, so she got up and made some coffee. When they had drunk the coffee, Mr Pepperpot would walk to the window to see if there were any rockets going off.

So the hours went by and when the clock finally struck twelve and the rockets shot up in great arches through the sky and the bell-ringer started pulling the rope in the bell-tower, well . . . you've guessed it . . . Mr and Mrs Pepperpot would be fast asleep in their chairs and never hear a thing.

So this year they decided not to bother to stay up, but just go to bed at their usual hour. When they had eaten their supper and drunk their coffee they sat reading their magazines till they got sleepy. First Mr Pepperpot started stretching and yawning.

'I think I'll turn in,' he muttered.

'You do that,' said Mrs Pepperpot, who had been looking at the same page of her magazine for the last twenty minutes. 'I'll just let the cat out. Come on, Pussy,' she called, 'you're going out in the snow.'

She followed the cat on to the doorstep and looked up at the moon to see if there was a ring round it.

Just at that moment she SHRANK!

If you've met Mrs Pepperpot before, you will know that she has this unfortunate habit of turning small – just the size of a pepperpot – at the most inconvenient times.

'Goodness Gracious!' she cried as she rolled over in the snow.

'What a bit of luck!' said the cat, 'Now you can come along with me and see something no human has ever seen. Jump on my back!'

That's another thing that happens when Mrs Pepperpot turns small; she can understand animal language and they can understand her.

'Well, if it's really special . . .' said Mrs Pepperpot, climbing on to Pussy's back, 'but I must be back home when they ring the New Year in.'

The cat set off with Mrs Pepperpot on her back. It was

8

very dark and the wind was blowing snow in her face, but she could tell they were going up the side of the mountain. Through the trees she could hear the sound of heavy feet and crashing branches, and as the moon came out from behind the clouds, she could see it was a big bull moose with his family behind him. In the tree-tops she could hear the squirrel chattering and above her head came the whir-ring sound of grouse wings. There was an owl hooting and a fox barking, and she could see the darting shapes of hares as they zig-zagged across the snow or ran round in a ring. But they were all going the same way and at last they stop-ped in front of a huge rock-face.

'What are they all stopping for?' whispered Mrs Pepper-pot, putting her mouth very close to the cat's ear.

'They're listening; don't you hear it yourself?' answered the cat.

Mrs Pepperpot listened and after a moment she *did* hear something; it sounded like the faint rumble of a motor-bike, very far away.

'That's him all right, snoring!' said the cat.

'Will you please explain?' Mrs Pepperpot said. She was getting tired of all this mystery.

'Well,' said the cat, 'behind that rock is the winter lair of the king of the forest, the big brown bear. He's been sleeping in there for several months now, but on New Year's Eve he has to turn over on his other side.'

'What happens if he doesn't turn over?' asked Mrs Pepperpot.

'Oh, it's terrible!' said the cat, 'if he lies on the same side all the winter, you see, he wakes up in the Spring in a very bad mood, all stiff and sore. Then he takes it out on the rest of us and woe betide any animal that gets in his way!'

'Well,' said Mrs Pepperpot, 'how d'you get him to turn over?'

'We make all the noise we can, but it's getting more and more difficult each year, as the King is getting older and deafer. We had a real job rousing him last year,' said the cat.

None of the other animals had said anything up to now, they were all so busy getting their breath back. But now one of the hares, gleaming in his white winter coat, spoke up:

'What we need is a new sort of noise – much sharper

than all this yowling of foxes, and tooting of owls – a bit of dynamite would be good, like the men use when they're blasting holes in the rocks.'

Mrs Pepperpot snapped her fingers: 'That gives me an idea! I have just what we need at home. But I shall need some help,' Mrs Pepperpot was thinking hard as she spoke.

The bull moose was standing close by. He looked as big as a house from down there, but she cupped her hands and shouted up to him:

'Hi, Moose! Can you carry me back to my house? I want to fetch my box of tricks.'

The moose at once knelt down in the snow, so that Mrs Pepperpot could climb on to his head, where she settled herself between his antlers.

'Right, let's go!' she shouted.

In no time at all the moose had run down the mountain to the valley and then up the hill to Mrs Pepperpot's house.

'You'll have to be very quiet,' said Mrs Pepperpot as the moose knelt down to let her slide off his neck. 'We don't want to scare my husband.'

Luckily the door to the outhouse was open, and there were no dogs or cats or hens in there to raise the alarm. Mrs Pepperpot went straight over to a large carton covered in paper and carefully tied with string.

'In this box there are enough bangs to wake a cartload of bears,' she told the moose, who was standing quietly in the doorway.

Over the years Mrs Pepperpot had bought firecrackers

and rockets and roman candles and so on to let off on New Year's Eve, but as they were never used, she had quite a big collection.

Now the problem was how to get the box hitched onto the moose, so that he could drag it back up the mountain to the bear's lair. Mrs Pepperpot got him to kneel down again, then she fastened a rope first round the carton and then round the moose's antlers. Then she swung herself back into her 'saddle' on his nobbly forehead, and away they went down the hill, the carton lurching along like a crazy toboggan.

'I hope the fireworks don't blow up on the way,' thought Mrs Pepperpot, but she said nothing to the moose, who was carefully avoiding the trees as they climbed up the mountain. Luckily the snow was thick enough to make a smooth path for the box, which was not very heavy.

The birds and the animals were all waiting for them when they arrived.

'Come on, everybody!' shouted Mrs Pepperpot as she jumped down into the snow, 'help me get the string and the paper off.'

The owl and the grouse pecked away at the string, and the foxes used their sharp claws to tear off the paper. At last Mrs Pepperpot could open the box.

'There you are, children,' she said, 'every kind of banger and firecracker you can think of. If His Majesty King Bear doesn't wake up when this lot goes off, you can take it from me he's dead!'

'How will you light them?' asked the white-coated hare who had suggested dynamite.

'Good question!' said Mrs Pepperpot, 'but luckily I had a box of matches in my apron pocket when I turned small.'

But first she told all the birds and animals to stand well out of the way. All except her faithful friend, the squirrel, who had helped her many times before. Sitting on his back, she told him to climb a few feet up a tall pine tree near the box. From there she struck all the matches at once and threw them into the box.

'Now shin up to the top as fast as you can,' she shouted, as the first bangers started going off. The squirrel kept to the far side of the tree-trunk, and when he got to the top he took a flying leap to the next tree, where they landed safely and well out of reach of any flying missiles.

'Phew! That was a near thing!' gasped Mrs Pepperpot, who had been more frightened by the squirrel's aerobatics than the hissing and popping that was going on below.

Looking down from so high, it really was a spectacular show, as the whole box of fireworks went up in one colossal din and blaze. It lit up the snow, the trees, the sky and the animals and birds scattering in every direction.

As the last bangers fizzled out and the sky grew dark again, Mrs Pepperpot heard a very different sound, and so did all the animals and birds; it was like the creaking of a heavy door followed by a long, loud 'Yaaaaaawn!'

'Hooray!' shouted all the animals and the birds squawked excitedly; 'King Bear has turned! King Bear has turned!'

The squirrel carried Mrs Pepperpot down to the ground and she found herself surrounded by stamping feet and flapping wings; everyone wanted to thank her.

'Help, help!' she cried, 'you're smothering me!'

But the next moment she was back to her normal size, standing in the snow by the big rock face.

Every bird, every animal had vanished in the darkness

– except one. Mrs Pepperpot felt warm fur rubbing against her leg.

'Is that you, Pussy?' she said, picking up the purring cat. 'Well, you certainly gave me a New Year adventure this year!'

And as she trudged back home through the snow, the church bells began to ring out and beautiful rockets lit up the sky over the village.

Fate and Mrs Pepperpot

Mrs Pepperpot is fond of fortune-telling, but she only does it for herself, never for other people. When she has finished a cup of coffee, she likes to peer at the grounds at the bottom of the cup to see what fortune has in store for her.

This was what she was doing one cold morning in January. 'My goodness!' she exclaimed excitedly. 'I can see a long journey over water! I knew my luck would change. Now all I have to do is pack my bag and wait for it to happen.'

She was just about to go up to the attic for her old suitcase, when she remembered that she had dipped her biscuit in the coffee, so there were biscuit crumbs mixed with the grounds and that didn't count.

'Ah well,' she sighed, 'I suppose I couldn't really expect it. And what would Mr Pepperpot do if I went off by myself on a holiday in the middle of winter?'

She picked up the magazine that was lying on the table. It was open at the page headed 'The Stars and You'. She looked under Taurus, for her birthday was in May. It said: 'Prepare for a journey over water.'

This was astonishing!

'It *must* be fate!' said Mrs Pepperpot. 'This time there's no denying it. I will pack at once.'

Then she glanced at the date of the magazine; it was a year old!

'I might have known it,' she said disgustedly, as she threw the paper into the stove. 'Anyway, who wants to go trapesing off to the South of France or wherever. I'm all right here, aren't I? Got my husband and my house to look after and my cat....' She got up and started bustling about,

18

sweeping the floor, cleaning out the sink and peeling the potatoes for supper. But just as she was standing there, she suddenly felt a tingling in the sole of her right foot. She waited for a moment; yet, it was quite definitely tingling!

'That settles it,' she said firmly to herself, as she went up to the attic to fetch her suitcase.

Tingling under your right foot, you see, is another sign that you are going on a journey, and this time Mrs Pepperpot was quite sure there was no mistake.

She came down with the battered old suitcase. 'Long time since you've had an airing,' she said, looking at it ruefully. 'Never mind. Next thing is to wash all my clothes to be ready for the trip.'

But she found she had no wash-powder, so she put on her hat and coat and a warm muffler and set out for the shop.

The shop was full of customers. At the door stood a lady with a handful of brochures. She was advertising a new wash-powder.

'This product is not like any you have used before,' she was saying, 'it will take all the work out of washing-day.'

'Can't fool me with that sort of nonsense,' muttered Mrs Pepperpot. But the lady went on: 'In every packet you buy today there is a numbered coupon, and one of those has a lucky number. Whoever gets the lucky number will win a seven-day sunshine holiday for two at beautiful Las Palmas in the Canary Islands. Don't miss this chance, ladies and gentlemen, the lucky number will be drawn tonight and displayed in the shop-window at closing time.'

She hadn't finished speaking before everyone started grabbing the packets of wash-powder. Some bought as many as six!

'Take them all year to get through that lot,' muttered Mrs Pepperpot. She just bought one packet.

'That's all I need for *my* lucky number,' she said as she trudged home through the snow. She was just wondering whom she should invite to go with her on her sun-shine holiday, Mrs North, perhaps, or Mrs West, when whoops! her feet slid from under her and she SHRANK!

She had been walking on the path where the snow was soft and not too slippery, but now both she and the packet tumbled on to the glass-hard surface of the road, just where it sloped steeply down towards the stream.

'Oh me, oh my!' she moaned, as she started to slide after the packet. 'This is a journey all right, but not quite what I intended.'

Faster and faster they went, till wham! The packet struck a tree-stump just be the edge of the stream. Mrs Pepperpot landed on top of the packet and the force of it pushed them both into the icy water!

Off they went again, whirling and bobbing in the fast-flowing stream, Mrs Pepperpot clinging on as best she could.

'Skipper of my own yacht on a luxury cruise!' she joked, but she didn't feel very cheerful. 'Not much hope of rescue here, I'm afraid.'

'Caw, caw!' croaked a voice from above. 'Don't say that!'

And before she had time to see who was there, she had
been picked up by her skirt and set down again on the bank
of the stream.

Mrs Pepperpot blinked at her rescuer, a big black crow.

'Thanks, pal, that wasn't a minute too soon! But could
you please hurry after my packet and rescue that too?'

'Caw, caw! Right you are!' cried the crow, swooping

and darting after the swirling packet till he could get a hold on it with his beak.

With some difficulty he hauled it to the bank where Mrs Pepperpot stood ready to help pull it out of the water.

'I'm afraid your wash-powder will be a bit soggy by now,' said the crow, when they had got it safely on land.

'Never mind,' said Mrs Pepperpot, 'thanks to you, I can still believe in my lucky day.'

'Anything to oblige, Mrs P. Many's the nice piece of bacon rind I've had at your back door. Glad to get a chance to do you a good turn.'

There the conversation came to an end, because Mrs Pepperpot grew to her normal size and the crow flew off. But she waved to him as she hurried home with her wet packet under her arm.

Indoors she emptied the packet into a bowl, carefully taking out the coupon which she put to dry on a towel. She noted the number: 347

'That's good,' she said, 'it has a seven in it. Sure to be a winner.'

Then she set to with her washing and she worked so hard, she never noticed the time, till she heard Mr Pepperpot open the front door.

'Hallo, my love!' he shouted, 'you'll never guess my luck!'

Mrs Pepperpot stared at him; in one hand he held a packet of the same wash-powder she had bought, and in the other a coupon!

'Let me tell you!' went on Mr Pepperpot excitedly. 'I went to the shop this morning on my way to work to get some baccy, and there was this lady. . . .'

'I know,' said Mrs Pepperpot, 'I saw her too.'

'You did? Well, of course I bought a packet of her wash-powder – come in handy, I thought, and you never know – stand as good a chance as anyone else. . . .'

Mrs Pepperpot couldn't bear the suspense any longer: 'Come to the point, man!'

'All right, all right! I just went back to look at the number in the window and it's the same as mine! 693.'

Mrs Pepperpot turned her head away.

'Congratulations,' she said. 'I hope you have a very nice trip.'

'Well!' said her husband, 'you don't sound very en-thusiastic. Don't you want to go on a sunshine holiday to the Canary Islands?'

'But . . . but . . .' stammered Mrs Pepperpot. 'How was I to know you'd be taking *me*?'

'You silly old thing – who else?' laughed Mr Pepperpot and gave her a smacking kiss.

Mrs Pepperpot Helps Arne

Mr and Mrs Pepperpot *did* enjoy their holidays in the Canaries and Mrs Pepperpot never shrank the whole time they were there. They bathed in the sea and got brown lying in the sun and in the evenings they listened to the music in the restaurant and tried the strange food they were served.

But at the end of the seven days they were quite glad to go home to Norway with all its ice and snow. It was nice, too, to get back to their own little house on the hill, and to sit down to their favourite supper of fried herring and boiled potatoes, followed by pancakes and bilberry jam.

'They can keep their foreign la-di-da meals,' said Mr Pepperpot, 'my wife's cooking is good enough for me!'

'I'll remember that next time you grumble!' said Mrs Pepperpot.

So the wintry days went on and soon it was time for the school-children to have their half-term holiday. Most of them were keen skiers and this meant they could ski all day every day for a whole week!

Mrs Pepperpot could hear them shouting and laughing as they rushed down the slopes near her house.

But one day when she was baking bread in the kitchen,

she looked out of the window and saw a little boy making his way slowly and carefully down the road below. He looked very unsteady on his skis.

Mrs Pepperpot opened the window and called to him:

'Hi there! Come up here a minute.'

The little fellow took off his skis and climbed up the hill. Mrs Pepperpot met him in the door.

'D'you like fresh-baked bread with butter and honey on it?' she asked.

'Oh yes, please,' said the boy.

'Well, come on in and sit down. I'll have a cup of coffee at the same time.'

While he munched the bread and honey, Mrs Pepperpot asked him his name.

'Arne,' he said.

'Why weren't you up on the slope, ski-ing with the others, Arne?' she asked.

''Cos I'm not very good at it,' said Arne, looking at her sadly, 'and the others tease me and call me a cowardy custard. They say I'm afraid of the moose up there in the pine trees and a lot of other stuff. They don't like me!'

He wiped a hand over his eyes and gave a little sniff.

'Don't you worry, Arne,' said Mrs Pepperpot, 'I won't call you a coward,' and she put an arm round his shoulders.

'This is my first winter in the snow. Before that, I lived in France with my mum and dad.'

'No wonder you're new to ski-ing then!' said Mrs Pepperpot. 'D'you know, when I was a little girl I was very afraid to go down those steep slopes. But I found a way to get over it.'

Arne was looking at her eagerly now: 'What did you do?'

'You'll laugh when you hear,' said Mrs Pepperpot. 'I took my mother's old dough trough – the very same one I've been using today to make the bread. Look, it's got nice high sides to stop you falling out, and I took it up to the top of that slope and rode down in it. In fact, it was such fun I wouldn't mind doing it again.'

'Weren't you frightened after that?'

'Never again,' said Mrs Pepperpot. 'If you like, we could try it together, because I have another trough as well.'

Arne looked doubtful.

'I don't know – people might see us. . . .'

'Not if we get up very early in the morning and go up to the top before anyone else is about.'

So Arne agreed and next day, when the sun rose, he and Mrs Pepperpot set off, each with a dough trough under their arm. They walked right to the top of the higher slope, where the row of pine trees cast a shadow on the hard glistening snow.

'I hope no one saw us,' said Arne, who kept looking back over his shoulder.

'Of course not,' said Mrs Pepperpot, 'all those big boys will be snoring their heads off at this time of day.'

But Arne was still nervous: 'Have you ever seen a moose come out of those trees?'

'Bless you, yes, but he knows me, and he won't bother us, I promise you,' said Mrs Pepperpot.

'I think I'll go first!' said Arne, as he settled himself in the dough trough.

'Off you go, then!' said Mrs Pepperpot and gave him a good push to start him off.

Arne shot down the slope. The wooden trough churned up the snow; it blew in his eyes, so that he had to close them, and he couldn't see where he was going. But he didn't mind, because there were no obstacles in the way and he was holding onto the sides very tightly. In fact, he was really enjoying the ride. That is, till the trough stopped and he opened his eyes.

There, on either side of him, stood the whole crowd of boys from his class!

'Here comes the champion tobogganer!' shouted one, and they all roared with laughter.

'The very latest design!' jeered another.

'What did you do with the old woman? Isn't she coming down in her trough too? Or perhaps she's even more scared than you are. . . .'

And so they went on, while poor Arne wished he could bury himself in the snow and that Mrs Pepperpot would not appear.

From the top of the slope Mrs Pepperpot had seen the boys arrive. She was just wondering what to do, when she SHRANK!

For once she was not too sorry to be tiny. At least the

28

boys wouldn't see her. She would just sit in her trough and wait till they went away.

But at that moment the bull moose came ambling out of the pine trees. 'Hi, Moose!' shouted Mrs Pepperpot from the trough.

The big animal came over and blew hot air on Mrs Pepperpot through his huge nostrils: 'What's the trouble this time, Mrs Pepperpot?' he asked.

'Well,' she said, 'I've had an idea, and if you'll help me today, maybe I can do you a good turn another time.

'Ho, ho,' he chuckled, 'what could a little lady like you do for me?'

'You'll be surprised,' she answered, and then she told him her plan: he was to sit in the big trough and slide down the slope to where the group of boys were standing. The last part of the plan she whispered in his ear, and then she gave him a good push and away he went.

Well, that big bull moose had the greatest difficulty in keeping his balance in the wooden trough, but he managed not to fall off till it came to a standstill at the place where the boys stood – or rather *had* stood. For they had seen him coming and had scattered in every direction as fast as they could go.

All except poor Arne, who was standing there with his trough. His eyes were filled with tears, so he didn't see anything till the moose came to rest right next to him.

As the huge beast got to his feet, Arne was too frightened to move. But the moose took a step towards him and then did something which made all the boys stare: with his big thick tongue he licked Arne's face!

Arne was no longer frightened; he could tell the moose was friendly. He put his hand up to the big head and stroked his ears. Then the moose quietly ambled back to the slope and disappeared in the trees.

And Mrs Pepperpot? Well, she appeared on the scene, as large as life, just as those boys came edging up to shake Arne by the hand.

'He's a brave boy, isn't he?' she said, putting her arm round Arne's shoulder; 'who'd have thought such a little fellow could tame that old bull moose?'

Spring Cleaning

It was a beautiful day in March. The sun was doing its best to melt the last remaining snow-drifts and cast a glow over the tall pine trees on the mountain ridge. Everything suddenly looked sharper and clearer in outline. Even the wooden walls of Mrs Pepperpot's house seemed to shine like polished tin. But when she looked at her windows she didn't thank the sun; it showed up how very dirty they were.

'Oh dear,' she said to herself. 'I can see it's time for spring-cleaning again. Well, I might as well get down to it straight away, I suppose.'

She went into the kitchen to get out her bucket, her scrubbing brush and plenty of soap and scouring powder. Mrs Pepperpot was pretty thorough when she got going – in fact, she enjoyed spring-cleaning.

She was just about to start on the windows when she heard a slow buzzing sound over by the stove. A big black fly had come out of the corner where it had been sleeping.

'Oho!' she said, 'So the sun's woken you up too, has it? Well, you needn't think I'm letting you lay eggs all over my house, making millions of flies to blacken my windows

32

in the summer. I'll fix you!' and she rushed at the fly with a fly-swatter.

But the fly got away, because at that moment Mrs Pepperpot SHRANK!

'You wait!' she shrilled in her tiny voice, as she rolled along the floor, 'I'll get you!'

'Don't worry,' said a voice from the corner.

Mrs Pepperpot turned round; it was a large spider hanging by its thread from a web it had spun between the grandfather clock and the wall.

'Don't worry,' said the spider, 'I'll deal with that pest.'

'You gave me quite a fright!' said Mrs Pepperpot, 'I don't mean to be rude, but I've never seen you so close to before, and I didn't know you were so hairy and ugly. . . .'

'I could return the compliment,' said the spider, 'but on the whole you look a bit better when you're small than when you're tramping round the kitchen in your great big shoes. Anyway, did you hear me offer to catch that fat fly for you?'

'Yes, I did,' answered Mrs Pepperpot, 'but I certainly wouldn't let you roll that poor creature up in your horrible web to be eaten for breakfast. No, indeed. If I had seen that contraption of yours before I shrank, I would have whisked it away with my broom!'

'Leave it to me!' said another little voice right behind her. This time it was a mouse.

'It's you, is it? And what d'you think a little scrap like you can do?' asked Mrs Pepperpot scornfully.

'Who's talking?' squeaked the mouse cheekily, 'you're not exactly outsize yourself at the moment. At least *I* can run up the clock – dickory, dickory dock!' he laughed. 'And then I can snip that web with my sharp teeth as easy as winking!'

'I'm sure you can,' said Mrs Pepperpot, 'but don't you see? That web is the spider's livelihood. Without those threads she couldn't catch her food and she would die.'

'Well, in that case,' said the mouse, 'I suppose you're supplying me with *my* livelihood when you leave the cover off the cheese dish in the larder, hee, hee!'

'You little thief!' shouted Mrs Pepperpot, shaking her tiny fist at the mouse. 'You push it off yourself, you and your wretched family. But I'll set a trap for you this very evening!'

'Did I hear a mouse?' asked another voice from the door. It was the cat. 'Where is it? I'm just ready for my dinner.'

'No, no!' shrieked Mrs Pepperpot, waving her arms at the cat, while the mouse was trying to hide behind her skirt. 'You leave the mouse alone, you great brute, you. He hasn't done you any harm, has he?'

'Woof! Woof! Who's a brute round here?' The head of a strange dog was peering round the door. When he caught sight of the cat he darted after her, knocking Mrs Pepperpot over as he ran round the table.

The cat managed to get out of the door with the dog close behind her when, luckily, at that moment Mrs Pepperpot grew to her normal size! She lost no time in throwing a stick at the dog while Pussy jumped on to the shed roof. The dog went on barking till Mrs Pepperpot gave him a bone. Then he trotted off down the hill.

'Dear me, what a to-do!' thought Mrs Pepperpot, 'But

it makes you wonder; every little creature is hunted by a bigger creature who in turn is hunted by a bigger one. Where does it all end?'

'Right here!' said a deep voice behind her.

Mrs Pepperpot nearly jumped out of her skin, but when she turned round it was her husband standing there.

'Oh,' she said, 'I thought you were an ogre come to gobble me up!'

'Well!' said Mr Pepperpot, 'Is that all the thanks I get for coming home early to help with the spring-cleaning?'

'You darling man!' said Mrs Pepperpot, giving him a great big kiss.

Easter Chicks

Every year when it gets near Easter time and the shop windows are full of fluffy cotton wool Easter chicks, Mrs Pepperpot sends a message to the children round about that she would like them to do her shopping for her. The children are only too pleased, because Mrs Pepperpot always gives them sweets, and sometimes even money to spend on themselves. So there is often quite a queue outside her door. But as soon as Easter is over and those yellow chicks disappear from the window displays, Mrs Pepperpot starts to do her shopping herself again.

Now why does the little old woman behave in this peculiar way? I'll tell you.

One Easter, many years ago, Mrs Pepperpot got it into her head that she wanted to rear chickens. She could have bought day-old chicks from a hatchery, but no:

'Chickens need a mother!' she declared.

So she went to a neighbour and borrowed a broody hen. Not all hens want to rear chicks; some spend their time preening their feathers, looking for food and laying their eggs wherever a box is handy. But a broody hen starts to collect her eggs in one nest and gets all hot and bothered if anyone tries to take them away.

The neighbour put the whole nest with ten eggs in a carton and the broody hen on top, and Mrs Pepperpot carried it home very carefully. She had already prepared a corner of her sitting-room with a little curtain across to keep out the draught, and the hen settled down very nicely.

Mr Pepperpot was not pleased: 'Proper place for a hen is in the out-house,' he said. But every time he went near the broody hen to take her out, she pecked and squawked so much, he had to give it up.

Every day Mrs Pepperpot lifted the curtain and peeped in to see if the hen was all right. She brought her water and some grain, but the hen was not very interested in eating or drinking. She just sat there, keeping the eggs warm.

The day came when the hatching should begin.

Mrs Pepperpot walked round the house, singing. She was so excited, she couldn't keep still, and every so often she went over to the corner and crouched down to listen.

'Those little chicks should be pecking their way out of their shells any minute now,' she told herself.

And then she heard an unmistakable sound: 'Cheep, cheep!' it said, very faintly.

Immediately the mother hen started clucking and fussing. Soon there were more cheeps, until at last the mother hen strutted out from behind the curtain, followed by nine little golden chicks.

Mrs Pepperpot clapped her hands with joy as she watched them following their mother. Then she knelt down to see what had happened to the tenth egg.

It was still lying in the nest, quite smooth and whole among all the broken shells.

'Oh, you poor little thing,' said Mrs Pepperpot, 'Perhaps you need some help with that hard shell. . . .' But as she stretched out her hand to pick it up, she SHRANK!

She not only found herself lying in the nest by the egg, but there was a great shadow towering over her – Mother Hen!

'Don't peck me!' she cried, because the hen looked very fierce, 'I was only trying to help your last chick out of the egg.'

The hen opened her beak and squawked at her. It sounded something like: '*Fi fi, finicula!*'

'Now listen!' said Mrs Pepperpot, trying to dodge Mother Hen's flapping wings, 'I'm Mrs Pepperpot – you know – the old woman who shrinks, and I understand animal and bird language – but I don't know what you're talking about.'

The hen just went on squawking and gabbling her strange nonsense: '*Fi fi finicula, ratagusa balla tella!*'

'Will you listen a minute!' Mrs Pepperpot was losing patience; 'I'm not trying to hurt your chicks. You just take them for a nice walk round the room and leave me to sit here till I grow big again. Now, run along!'

The hen took no notice. She charged straight at Mrs

Pepperpot and with her strong wings buffeted her right out of the nest on to the mat where all the baby chicks were darting about and cheeping their heads off.

'What a din!' said Mrs Pepperpot, scrambling to her feet and trying to keep out of the way.

Mother Hen now turned her attention to her family. Clucking in a commanding tone, she chivvied them into line and made them follow behind her as she walked slowly across the room.

Mrs Pepperpot stood watching the wonderful way the chicks obeyed her, when suddenly Mother Hen turned round and saw her there.

'*Seguira linia malachita*' she squawked and rushed at her, pecking at Mrs Pepperpot's hair.

'Ouch!' shouted Mrs Pepperpot, 'What d'you think you're doing? I'm not one of your children!'

The only reply she got was more gibberish and more angry pecks. So, to avoid being pecked to pieces, she fell into line and followed Mother Hen till they came to the spot where Mrs Pepperpot had strewn some fine oatmeal for the baby chicks to eat.

Mother Hen stopped and clucked to the chicks to gather round. Then she showed them how to pick up the meal and soon they all had their heads down, their beaks sounding like tiny drums on the floor. Mrs Pepperpot had to laugh as she watched them, but not for long, because Mother Hen was after her again:

'*Mangiamello, mangiamello!*' and more pecks rained on the little old woman's head.

'Stop! Stop!' she yelled. 'I don't know what you're saying, but I'll have some oatmeal, if that's what you want.'

She picked some up in her hand and pretended to put it in her mouth.

'*Uccella stupida,*' scolded the hen, flapping her with a wing.

'Oh very well, you silly old fuss-pot!' said Mrs Pepperpot, and she got down on all fours and pretended to peck at the oatmeal with her nose.

When the baby chicks had had enough, Mother Hen led them over to a pan of water which Mrs Pepperpot had put

42

there for them. Mother Hen showed them how to drink, dipping their beaks and then putting their heads well back.

'Drink like a hen? That's one thing you're not going to get me to do, madam!' declared Mrs Pepperpot.

'*Bere, bere!*' squawked the hen swooping on her so hard that she fell right into the pan of water.

The next moment she was back to her normal size and standing there with her wet clothes dripping on to the sitting-room floor.

'You're worse than my teacher at school!' said Mrs Pepperpot, rubbing her sore head.

The hen was now behaving very strangely, fluttering to and fro and calling anxiously.

'What's the matter?' said Mrs Pepperpot, 'looking for your lost chick?' and she went over to the nest and picked up the tenth egg. She broke the shell, but there was no chick inside.

'I'm afraid you'll have to do with nine,' she said, 'as I'm not following a hen around who doesn't even speak my language. Whoever heard of a bird that can't understand Mrs Pepperpot when she shrinks?'

'*Mi scusi!*' clucked the hen.

And suddenly Mrs Pepperpot understood what had happened. The hen was an Italian Leghorn and she was talking hen Italian!

The mystery was solved, and you would think Mrs Pepperpot would be satisfied. But she never got over the shock of having to be a baby chick and doing what she was told by Mother Hen.

So that's why she won't even look at those fluffy yellow Easter chicks in the shop window.

The Cuckoo

In May, when the first green veil of leaves cover the birch trees and the wagtail starts to follow the plough, that is the time for the cuckoo to arrive.

Mrs Pepperpot was just locking her door to go to the shop when she heard it:

'Cuckoo!'

'Cuckoo!' answered Mrs Pepperpot, but she didn't say it very loudly, in case the cuckoo might get annoyed. For Mrs Pepperpot is a little afraid of the cuckoo. It can bring good luck, but it can also bring you bad luck. It depends from which direction you hear it calling.

Mrs Pepperpot looked all around her, but couldn't see where the bird was sitting.

'Cuckoo!'

There it was again, and this time she was sure she heard it from the west.

' "Cuckoo from the west, all for the best!" ' she chanted, and went on her way down the hill, quite content. But soon she stopped, and a frightened look came over her face. What if her husband had heard the same bird? He would have heard it from the north, for he was working on the road down in the valley.

'Oh dear!' she said, ' "Cuckoo from the north, sorrow bring forth!" '

At that moment she SHRANK! and found herself sitting on the ground under a high pine tree. Up above she could hear the angry noise of her friend, the squirrel.

She called to him: 'Hi, squirrel! Could you come down here, please!'

'Chuck! Chuck!' he scolded, running down the tree trunk head first. 'What's up with Mrs Pepperpot this time? You look very woe-begone.'

'Well, its my husband, you see,' said Mrs Pepperpot, 'I'm afraid he'll have heard the cuckoo from the north, and that means bad luck for him.'

'Chuck! Just the sort of thing an old woman like you would worry about! What d'you want *me* to do about it?'

'I thought you might take me up to the top of the tree, so that I could talk to the cuckoo, and perhaps get him to call from the east. "Cuckoo from the East, harbingers a feast," you see.'

'Rubbish,' said the squirrel. 'But hurry up now. I've got better things to do than carry superstitious old women around!'

'So I notice!' said Mrs Pepperpot. 'There's egg-yolk round your nose.'

The squirrel's tail switched angrily. 'It's none of your business what I have for breakfast! Are you ready?' and he scuttled up to the top of the tall pine tree with Mrs Pepperpot.

Once up there, Mrs Pepperpot clung to a small branch. It made her giddy to look down.

'Bye, bye!' said the squirrel. 'I hope the cuckoo doesn't keep you waiting too long!'

'You're not going to leave me up here all alone, are you?' said poor Mrs Pepperpot.

'You silly woman! The cuckoo won't come near you if I'm here. I'll fetch you later.' And with that he was off.

Mrs Pepperpot's arms were quite stiff with holding on before the cuckoo finally alighted in the tree. He was a little surprised to find her there.

'Did you fall out of an aeroplane?' he asked.

'No, Mr Cuckoo,' said Mrs Pepperpot politely, 'I came up here to speak to you.'

'I'm a little busy just now . . .' said the cuckoo, opening his beak to call again.

'Stop, please!' cried Mrs Pepperpot.

The cuckoo shut his beak and looked at her in astonishment.

'Mr Cuckoo, will you do me a big favour?' she pleaded. 'Will you fly over to the east side of the valley and call from there?'

'Why should I?' said the cuckoo, 'I'm calling to my wife and she's on this side of the valley.'

'It'll bring good luck to my husband if you do. He's working down there on the road.'

The cuckoo looked flattered: 'Oh well, if you put it that way, of course I'll oblige.' And he flew off straight away.

A little while later Mrs Pepperpot heard him:

'Cuckoo!' he called and it sounded such a happy note, she was sure it would cheer her husband up.

Then she remembered she hadn't done her shopping yet, and Mr Pepperpot would be expecting a feast when he got home!

'Oh dear! Now what shall I do?' she wailed.

At that moment the squirrel reappeared.

'You moaning again?' he said. 'I'll have to get that cuckoo to sing to you from the south; "Cuckoo from the south will button up your mouth!"' he chuckled.

'That's enough of your cheek!' said Mrs Pepperpot, 'kindly get me down to earth at once!'

It was not a minute too soon. As her feet touched the ground she grew large again. She waved goodbye to the squirrel, picked up her basket and hurried to the shop.

When she came back she had bought her husband's favourite sausages and two pounds of macaroni, and for pudding she set to work making pancakes with bilberry jam. Then she laid the table with her good china and put a lighted candle in the middle.

'Hullo, hullo!' said Mr Pepperpot when he came in, 'Whose birthday?'

'Didn't you hear the cuckoo?' she asked anxiously.

'What cuckoo?' Mr Pepperpot looked puzzled.

'You mean to say you didn't hear it either from the north

or from the east?'

'Good lord, no,' said Mr Pepperpot. 'Much too busy with that mechanical digger; blasts your ear-drums, it does, all day!'

Just then they *both* heard the cuckoo, and this time it was right over their heads on the roof!

'That's the best luck of all!' cried Mrs Pepperpot, giving her husband a big kiss. 'Now we really can enjoy our feast!'

Midsummer Romance

———

In Norway at Midsummer the sun hardly sets at all, and at night the sky is almost as bright as during the day. So how do people get to sleep? If they're young and gay they don't bother; they stay up and dance round a bonfire on Midsummer Eve or go for long romantic walks in the woods till they can't keep their eyes open any longer, light or no light.

But Mrs Pepperpot's dancing days are over; this Midsummer Eve she decided to take a walk through the wood to visit Miss Flora Bundy, a spinster lady who lived by herself in a little cottage. Miss Flora was shy and timid and had hardly any friends to visit her, so Mrs Pepperpot thought she would cheer her up with some home-made cakes and a bottle of home-made wine.

'I feel like Little Red Riding Hood,' she thought, as she walked through the shadowy wood with her basket on her arm. 'I hope I don't meet that old wolf on the way.'

But she arrived at the cottage quite safely and knocked on the door. There was no answer. After she had knocked three times she tried the door and found it unlocked, so she went in.

'Are you there, Miss Flora?' she called.

Still silence. So she put her basket down in the hall and walked through the little sitting-room to the bedroom.

'No wolf in the bed, anyway!' she said, looking down at it. But what was that? Arranged across the pillow was a row of wild flowers – each of a different kind. Tears came into Mrs Pepperpot's eyes:

'Who would have believed it?' she said. 'Miss Flora collecting wild flowers to put under her pillow on Midsummer's Eve so that she will dream about the man she will marry. How very romantic!'

Then she looked again. There were only eight flowers; to make the dream come true, there should be nine different wild flowers.

'Of course!' she said. 'She's out looking for the ninth one.'

And, sure enough, when she looked through the window, there was Miss Flora walking up the path very slowly, her eyes fixed on the ground.

Mrs Pepperpot was just wondering how to explain her being in Miss Flora's bedroom, when she SHRANK!

Quick as lightning, she grabbed the edge of the sheet and climbed up, hand over hand, till she reached the pillow. Then she slipped in under it and lay still as a mouse.

Miss Flora came in and sat down on the chair by the window. As lonely people often do, she talked aloud to herself:

'It looks as if I won't find that ninth flower again this

year. Ah well, perhaps it's all for the best! It would be dreadful if I dreamed about anyone else but the dear postman!'

'The postman, eh?' muttered Mrs Pepperpot under the pillow, 'If anything, he's more shy than Miss Flora!'

'I'll just count the flowers once more,' said Miss Flora, when she had changed into her nightdress and was ready to get into bed.

Slowly she began to count: 'cornflower one, buttercup two, cowslip three, bluebell four, dandelion five, wild rose six, honeysuckle seven, poppy eight, cornflower nine.'

Did you notice? Miss Flora counted the cornflower twice. But *she* didn't notice that Mrs Pepperpot had put out her tiny hand from underneath the pillow and popped the cornflower from the beginning of the row to the other end!

Miss Flora clapped her hands and snatched up the flowers:

'There *are* nine. Hooray! Now I will go to sleep and dream about the man I love.' And she tucked the little posy under the pillow – right next to where Mrs Pepperpot was lying!

When Miss Flora had gone to sleep, Mrs Pepperpot eased herself from under the pillow and slid gently down the side of the bed on to the writing-table by the window.

As I told you, it was not really dark at all, so she quickly found a piece of paper and a pen. Being so small, she had some difficulty in holding the pen and writing the words large enough. But she managed it at last. Then she found a pink envelope and put the note inside. She wrote some more words across the front. Then she stood in the open window and gave a little whistle.

The sound was heard by a swallow in her nest under the eaves.

'I know who that is,' said the swallow, swooping down on to the window-sill. 'At your service, Mrs Pepperpot!'

'Thank you, Swallow,' said the little old woman, holding out the envelope. 'Will you please take this to the postman's house? But make sure he sees it, even if you have to wake him up with a peck on his nose!'

'No sooner said than done,' said the swallow and was gone.

Mrs Pepperpot sat on the window-sill, swinging her little legs and enjoying the warm night air. It wasn't long before the bird was back.

'Did you deliver the letter?' asked Mrs Pepperpot.

'Yes,' laughed the swallow. 'You should have seen the postman jump out of bed when I pecked his nose; he must have thought a wasp stung him!'

'But did he read what it said on the envelope?'

'He did. And I left him pulling on his trousers as he rushed out to get his bicycle. He should be on his way.'

'Good, good. My plot is working very well!' said Mrs Pepperpot, and thanked the swallow for her help.

The she sat down again to watch how things turned out.

But a postman on a bicycle takes much longer than a swallow on the wing to get from the village to the cottage in the wood, and Mrs Pepperpot was almost out of patience when he arrived, puffing a little from pedalling so hard. He was a tall, thin man who usually wore a sad expression on his face. This was because he was lonely and had no one to care for him at home.

Now, as he stood in front of the little cottage, Mrs Pepperpot could see he was smiling.

'At last!' he said, 'For years I've waited for this chance to visit dear Miss Flora. And now perhaps I can bring her good news this Midsummer morning.'

So Miss Flora had never had a letter delivered before? thought Mrs Pepperpot: 'The poor lady! Won't she be surprised?'

The postman went up to the door and gave first a timid knock, then a louder one. He was just about to knock for the third time, when the door opened, and there stood Miss Flora in a pretty flowered dressing gown.

'Oh!' she gasped. 'Is it really you, Postman?'

'I've brought you this letter,' he said, holding out the pink envelope.

'For me?' Mis Flora looked very surprised. 'Who can have written to me?' And she opened the letter then and there.

The postman waited while she read it: 'I hope it brings good news?'

'How strange,' she said. 'Just one line: "Congratulations and best wishes from the queen of the flowers".'

Peeping from behind a flower-pot on the window-sill, Mrs Pepperpot now saw the postman kneel on one knee in the dewy grass and heard him say:

'Dearest Miss Flora, to me *you* are the queen of the flowers!'

And what did Miss Flora do? She kissed her dear postman and they went indoors, hand in hand.

At the same moment, Mrs Pepperpot fell off the window-sill and grew to her normal size.

'Well,' she said to herself, as she walked home. 'That was a good Midsummer night's work. I hope they find the cakes and wine for their celebration.'

Mrs Pepperpot and the Pedlar

In August Mrs Pepperpot's garden was full of bright dahlias and asters and marigolds. They made her feel so cheerful, she decided to put on her new blue and yellow striped skirt with a clean white blouse, fastened at the neck with a red brooch.

From the oven came the delicious smell of a ginger cake she was baking, and she was just about to put on the coffee-pot, when a shadow passed across the window.

Before he had time to knock on the door, Mrs Pepperpot saw who it was. She rushed to the cupboard and pulled out an old black shawl and threw it round her shoulders. It hung well down over her striped skirt and when she had mussed up her hair and looked really miserable, she went to the door and opened it.

'Come in,' she said in a funny old granny voice, and in walked the person she least wanted to see that day, Mr Trick. A travelling salesman he called himself, but he was more like an old-fashioned pedlar, he had so many different things in his suitcase. He had the knack of calling just when Mrs Pepperpot had managed to save up a little money (which she kept in a cracked blue cup), and by the time he left she had always somehow spent every penny.

'Hullo, hullo, hullo!' he greeted her loudly. 'Are we doing a little business today?'

'How can a poor old woman like me do business?' she asked in that squeaky voice. 'Where would I get the money from?'

'Got it all safely stashed in the bank, I suppose,' laughed Mr Trick. 'Not like me, never make enough to put in the bank. All I get from some people are kisses and promises.'

Mrs Pepperpot had to laugh at his cheek, and soon there she was, rummaging through his open suitcase and pick-

ing out useless things like cotton ribbon and a coffee strainer, though she had two already. Meanwhile Mr Trick went on talking about banks:

'No, I don't believe in them; make it a point of honour never to have a bank book.'

'*I* make it a point of honour never to burn a cake,' said Mrs Pepperpot. 'So I'd better go and see if it's done.'

'Allow me, Mrs Pepperpot,' said Mr Trick, 'I'm an expert on baking. I will inspect your cake while you go on inspecting my goods.' And he went out into the kitchen.

Mrs Pepperpot went on rummaging, and at the back of the suitcase she found a secret pocket. There was a book in it, and when she pulled it out she saw it was a bank book with Mr Trick's name inside!

'No bank book, indeed! I'll teach you a lesson, Mr Smart Alec Trick.' And she hid the book behind the curtain. But when she turned back to the suitcase, she SHRANK and tumbled in among the hankies, socks and other fancy goods.

When Mr Trick came back he was surprised not to find her and called out her name a couple of times. But then he closed the suitcase and seemed in a hurry to leave. He strapped it on the back of his moped, and soon poor Mrs Pepperpot was having a very bumpy ride along the main road to the next town. There Mr Trick took the suitcase with him into the biggest bank and opened it on the counter.

Luckily he was talking to the cashier when Mrs Pepper-

pot sneaked out of the case and hid behind some forms on
the counter. Because now he started looking for that bank
book and had everything out of the case in his frantic
search.

'What can I have done with it?' he wailed. 'I want to pay
in some more money, and I'm sure I put the bank book in
my case when I left home.'

The cashier told him he could just sign a piece of paper
to show how much he was paying in, and Mr Trick pulled
out lots and lots of notes from his inner pocket. Last of all
he counted out some small coins; they came to exactly the
amount that Mrs Pepperpot had saved in the cracked blue
cup at home!

'Well!' said Mrs Pepperpot to herself. 'You not only tell

lies, but steal a poor woman's savings! If I was my right size I'd call the police.'

But she was still tiny, so what could she do? She puzzled for a moment, then she hit on an idea. Pulling out one of the forms from its holder, she dipped her finger in the ink-stand and wrote as large as she could:

'Your bank book has been found at Mrs Pepperpot's. Please fetch it at once.'

She pushed the piece of paper along the counter, so that Mr Trick would see it when he stopped chatting to the cashier.

'What an extraordinary thing!" said Mr Trick when he read it. 'Someone must have telephoned.'

While he and the cashier were trying to work this out, Mrs Pepperpot slipped back in the suitcase and was relieved when it was picked up and strapped onto the moped again. Off they went on the bumpy road back to Mrs Pepperpot's house. When they got there Mr Trick rushed straight to the door. As he knocked, there was the most terrific bang! He looked back and there stood Mrs Pepperpot, as large as life, beside his moped with the contents of his suitcase strewn all over the hillside!

'D'you keep bombs in your case?' she asked innocently, as she came forward to open the door.

'Certainly not!' said Mr Trick, who looked very uncomfortable. 'I had a message about a book I had left. . . .'

'A *bank* book, Mr Trick,' said Mrs Pepperpot, 'with your name clearly on the inside.'

'Well, yes . . .' he answered, 'of course, it was my little joke about not using banks. . . .'

'Your joke, too, I suppose, to take a poor old woman's savings from a cracked blue cup?' And she went over and turned the cup upside down. It was empty.

'I can explain – honestly I can!' Mr Trick was talking very fast now; 'I took the cake out of the oven and put it on the table. Then I saw the money and was bringing it in for you to pay me for the goods you chose and then you'd disappeared!'

'A likely story! I ought to call the police and show you up for the menace you are to poor old women like me. Now give me my money and be off before I change my mind.'

With a trembling hand, Mr Trick counted out the money he had stolen and was just about to slink off, when Mrs Pepperpot called him back.

'You've forgotten something,' she said and handed him his bank book.

The Moose Hunt

There's one week in the year that Mrs Pepperpot hates: that's the first week in October when people with guns are allowed to shoot the moose. All the rest of the year the big animals roam in the forest as they like and nobody hurts them.

Mrs Pepperpot had her special friend, the big bull moose, and in the summer she was always running down to the stream at the edge of the forest with cabbage leaves or lettuce for him. In winter during the snow she put down great armfuls of hay. So neither the big bull moose nor his friends and relations ran away when they saw her coming.

But as the time came near for the shooting to begin, Mrs Pepperpot got more and more agitated. How could she warn the moose not to come out in the open, but to stay hidden deep in the forest?

Several days before the hunt she stopped taking green stuff down to the place where she usually fed them. Instead she took a dustbin lid and a wooden ladle and stood there, banging away and shouting as loud as she could to frighten the animals away.

Then came the night before the hunt and Mrs Pepperpot was walking up and down in her sitting-room, wringing her hands.

Mr Pepperpot took no notice; he was very proud of the fact that he had been asked to take part in the hunt with two local big-wigs, Mr Rich, the landowner, and Mr Packer, the chain-store grocer. They would be coming to fetch him early in the morning, and Mr Pepperpot was busy getting his green felt hat and jacket ready.

'How can you be so heartless and cruel?' asked Mrs Pepperpot tearfully.

'Nonsense, wife,' he answered. 'The hunt only goes on for ten days and only a few moose get shot. After all, we can't have those great elephants tramping down all the young trees, can we? Besides, it's good sport.' And he took down his gun to give it a clean.

'They're not elephants; they're very graceful,' said Mrs Pepperpot, 'and I don't want you to kill them.'

'Well, you can't stop me,' said her husband firmly.

'We'll see about that!' she muttered and walked out into the night.

She walked quickly down the hill, but just as she had crossed the stream and gone through the gate, she SHRANK!

'For once I'm not sorry to be small!' she said, picking herself up and looking round. 'At least the animals can understand what I say now – if I can *find* any animals.'

She started calling: 'Any moose about? Mooooose! Can you hear me?'

66

But it was so dark and her voice was so small and thin that no moose either saw or heard her.

But one creature did; her faithful friend, the squirrel. He happened to be sitting in the tree above her.

'What are you yelling for?' he asked and scuttled down the tree.

'Oh squirrel, thank goodness you've come,' said Mrs Pepperpot. 'You must help me warn the moose. They musn't come out in the open, for tomorrow the men will be there with their guns and will shoot them.'

'Right,' said the squirrel, 'I'll get my bush telegraph into action and send messages to as many as I can.'

'Thank you!' said Mrs Pepperpot, 'I knew you would help. But there's more to be done; I have a plan to foil those evil huntsmen. Bend down and I'll whisper it to you.'

The two of them whispered together for a long time before Mrs Pepperpot grew large again and the squirrel scuttled away to carry out the plan.

Mrs Pepperpot went home; now she could sleep with a quiet mind. In the morning her husband thought she must have come to her senses at last, for there she was on the doorstep with him, ready to greet the smart hunters with their picnic baskets and expensive guns and dogs.

Mrs Pepperpot was a little surprised to see Mrs Rich there as well, all dressed up in check trousers and a big feather in her hat. But she smiled at her too, and wished them all a good day's hunting as they left.

67

Then Mrs Pepperpot went shopping. On her way down she met Nora North, who said:

'Fancy seeing you out today. I thought you'd be sitting at home crying your eyes out for the poor moose.'

Mrs Pepperpot put on a solemn face and answered: 'Yes, it's a sad day for me and all animal lovers. But there we are, I can't change the law, so what's the good of moping?'

In the shop Mrs Pepperpot went to the counter selling toilet goods and First Aid things. She bought a good length of bandage, some splints and plenty of soothing ointment and witchhazel. The sales lady asked if Mr Pepperpot had had an accident.

'Oh, no,' said Mrs Pepperpot, 'but it's just as well to be prepared.' Then she went home again and waited.

Bang! A distant shot rang out.

'Oh dear!' said Mrs Pepperpot, covering her ears with her hands, 'I hope that was a miss.'

She went outside and stared anxiously in the direction of the forest. Wasn't that someone coming out of the gate? It *was*, followed by a sad-looking dog.

Mrs Pepperpot waited while the person slowly climbed the hill. When he got nearer she could see it was Mr Packer, but he was limping and supporting himself on a stick!

'Why, whatever happened to you, Mr Packer?' she cried.

'Oh, it was terrible!' moaned Mr Packer. 'My dog here had just got a good scent and I was ready with my gun as soon as a moose came in sight, when a whole flock of grouse came whirring out of the undergrowth and flew right at me! They knocked my hat and my glasses off and I ran into a fallen tree, giving myself the most awful bump. I'm sure my leg is broken!'

'Poor Mr Packer!' said Mrs Pepperpot, helping him indoors. 'Let's have a look at your leg.'

It turned out not to be broken, but Mrs Pepperpot put the splints on all the same and bandaged it so tightly, the poor man could hardly move.

Next to arrive was Mr Rich. You never saw such a sight! Not just his hat was green now; he was covered in grassy green slush from head to foot.

His dog had picked up a good scent which led them along the edge of a small bog in a glade. When suddenly a squirrel leaped clean out of the top of a tree on to Mr Rich's head, causing him to lose his balance and topple into the bog.

'I might have been drowned!' he wailed, squelching through the front door into the kitchen. There, curiously enough, Mrs Pepperpot had a big tub of hot water waiting, complete with a towel and dry underwear for just such an emergency. But Mr Rich was too wet and miserable to ask any questions.

'I hope nothing has happened to Mrs Rich and my husband,' said Mrs Pepperpot, looking quite concerned. They didn't have long to wait before the two of them came up the hill, holding hands and groping their way, as if they were blind. Which they were, almost. For they had walked into a swarm of bees and their faces were quite swollen with stings.

'Oh, you poor, poor things!' cried Mrs Pepperpot, 'how lucky I have some witchhazel!' And she set to work dabbing their faces and making hot cups of coffee for everyone.

'Blest if I even heard those bees coming!' grumbled Mr Pepperpot, when the rest of the party had gone home.

'God's creatures work in mysterious way,' smiled Mrs Pepperpot, 'and I don't mean only the human kind!'

Mr Pepperpot and the Weather

Mrs Pepperpot never listens to weather reports.

'If the sun shines I'm glad; if it rains I stay indoors,' she says.

But Mr Pepperpot listens to every single weather report both on TV and radio. He nods wisely when they talk about depressions over Dogger Bank or when the man on TV pushes arrows around to show where the troughs of high pressure are moving to.

'Just as I thought,' said Mr Pepperpot.

Not only that; he also remembered all the old country sayings about the weather, and all the traditional signs and portents. It wouldn't matter so much, thought Mrs Pepperpot, if he didn't always look for signs of *bad* weather. If Mr Pepperpot saw a holly tree full of red berries, he was sure the winter would be hard. If he heard thunder in September that meant storms at sea.

'More likely to be rats in the attic that you heard!' muttered Mrs Pepperpot.

Or he would say that it was foggy and that a foggy autumn brings a frosty Christmas.

'Try cleaning your spectacles!' said Mrs Pepperpot, 'You might get a clearer view.'

She was getting sick of all this moaning about the weather, and she decided to provide Mr Pepperpot with a *good* omen for a change.

If the fruit trees bloom in October, she'd heard him say, it meant the winter would be mild.

There was only one fruit tree in Mrs Pepperpot's garden, an old apple tree right outside the sitting-room window.

'Beggars can't be choosers,' she said, and she sat down to make apple-blossom out of pink and white crepe paper. It took her all day, but at last she had a whole basketful of pretty pink and white flowers, which she hid in the outhouse.

Evening came and so did Mr Pepperpot. When she had given him his supper, Mrs Pepperpot fetched the basket of blossoms and hung it on as high a branch as she could reach. Then she started to climb up the tree herself.

But, of course, the inevitable happened; she SHRANK!

Luckily, she fell into the basket which swung on the branch, but didn't break it.

'Phew!' said Mrs Pepperpot, 'this is going to be hard work. If it had been daytime, I could have got the squirrel or the crow to help me; now I shall have to manage myself.'

Indoors Mr Pepperpot settled down in his armchair to watch TV. He had the radio on at the same time, in case he should miss any of the weather forecasts. So, while the TV was showing a film about girls in bikinis swimming in the

warm South Seas under a blazing sun, the radio was telling
Mr Pepperpot that a hailstorm was on its way to his area.

It was all very confusing, and Mr Pepperpot looked out
of the window instead, just to see what the weather was
really like.

What he saw made him blink; he couldn't believe his
eyes! Out there in the garden the old apple tree was
covered in pink and white blossom. Not only that, but
more and more flowers kept appearing and they even
seemed to be moving – creeping along the branches!

Finally there was just one flower moving; it was climbing up the trunk of the tree, right to the topmost branch, which seemed to bend towards the flower, then bounce back with the flower attached like a cheeky little flag at the top.

Mr Pepperpot was stunned. It was a miracle! But just as he turned to call Mrs Pepperpot to come and look, there was a sound of breaking branches and twigs, ending in a dull thud, like a sack of flour hitting the ground.

Mrs Pepperpot came through the door, holding her hand on her hip and limping a little.

'Where have you been?' asked Mr Pepperpot.

'Out,' said Mrs Pepperpot.

'What were you doing?' he asked.

'Coming in,' she answered.

'D'you know what?' said Mr Pepperpot, 'The old apple tree is in flower. Just come and see!'

They both looked out. But all was dark; there was not a sign of a pink and white blossom! They had all fallen off when Mrs Pepperpot fell out of the tree.

'You must have dreamed it,' said Mrs Pepperpot.

'But I saw it as clear as I see you now!' he declared. 'And it made me feel so happy to think we were going to have a mild winter.'

'You go right on thinking that, my dear,' said Mrs Pepperpot, 'stick to the good omens and leave the rest.'

And she went out into the garden and gathered up the paper flowers in her apron.

Mrs Pepperpot in Hospital

Mrs Pepperpot was in hospital.

Why? Well, you remember she fell out of that old apple tree when she was trying to make it blossom with paper flowers? After that her hip went on hurting for some time, so she went to the doctor, and he said she would have to go to hospital for X-rays, and stay overnight.

So there she was, in a nice clean hospital bed, lying next to a little girl called Rose who was going to have her tonsils out.

Rose was very unhappy. She was nearly seven years old, so it wouldn't do to cry, but she stuffed the sheet into her mouth and her little shoulders shook as she lay there with her back to Mrs Pepperpot.

'Can I do anything for you, pet?' she asked.

'Yes, please,' said the little girl stifling a sob. 'Could you tuck in my bedclothes?'

As Mrs Pepperpot went over to Rose's bed to tuck her up more comfortably, she SHRANK!

Rose was most surprised, because she thought the little old woman had disappeared. But Mrs Pepperpot called to her from the floor.

'I'm down here,' she shouted in her small voice.

'Goodness!' said Rose, looking over the edge of the bed. 'You must be Mrs Pepperpot!'

'Right first time!' said Mrs Pepperpot. 'And now it's your turn to help me.'

'What d'you want me to do?' Rose asked brightly, her tears quite forgotten.

'Pick me up in your hand and put me on your pillow,' said Mrs Pepperpot.

So Rose lifted her up.

'Fancy us two being in the same hospital,' she said.

'And in the same bed,' said Mrs Pepperpot, trying to make herself comfortable, but she kept slipping off the pillow.

'Haven't you got a box I could lie in?' she asked.

Rose brought out an empty chocolate box from her locker and made it up with a hankie for a sheet and her face-cloth as a coverlet.

'Now we can pretend you are my little doll,' she said. 'That was why I was sad, because I hadn't brought my doll from home. But it doesn't matter when I have you to play with.'

First they played hide and seek, with Rose shutting her eyes while Mrs Pepperpot found clever places to hide all over the bed. Then they tried 'I spy' till Rose got tired and wanted to go to sleep.

She looked sad again, and when Mrs Pepperpot asked her what was the matter, she said:

'Mummy always sings to me before I go to sleep.'

'Oh,' said Mrs Pepperpot, 'that's easy! Just wait till you hear *my* song.'

This is what she sang:

> 'The Rose is white, the Rose is red,
> The Rose is now a sleepy-head.
> Soon she'll be as right as rain
> And play ring-a-roses with me again.'

But then she couldn't remember any more, so she tried to think of something else with roses:

'If Moses supposes his toeses are roses, then Moses supposes erroniousleee . . .' she began, but stopped when she saw Rose's eyes were closing.

The little girl was not quite asleep. She turned her head a bit and murmured:

'I wish my pussy was here to lick my ear – he always does that before I go to sleep at home. . . .'

Mrs Pepperpot looked around, but there was not much chance of finding even the smallest kitten in a hospital ward. So she thought of another idea. She took off her woolly night-cap and dipped it in the water-glass on the table, and then she gently rubbed Rose's ear with it till she was fast asleep.

The door opened. It was the night sister coming in.

She came over to Rose's bed, but Mrs Pepperpot had popped into the chocolate box and covered herself with the face-cloth and was lying as still as any doll.

'That's one child who doesn't miss her mother,' said the night-sister, smiling down at Rose. 'She's sleeping like an angel – and so is her dolly.'

But when she turned round and found Mrs Pepperpot's bed empty, she rushed out of the ward shouting for the doctor. In a moment she was back, followed by two doctors and two nurses, all looking for Mrs Pepperpot, who by

now, of course, had grown to her normal size and was lying in her own bed, as good as gold.

'Hullo,' said the chief doctor, 'the X-rays show your hip has mended, so you can go home tomorrow.'

'Thank you, doctor,' said Mrs Pepperpot. 'But what about little Rose?'

'Oh,' said the doctor, 'she'll be as right as rain!' and he walked out, followed by the rest of his staff.

'And play ring-a-roses with me again,' added Mrs Pepperpot, smiling at the sleeping Rose.

Mrs Pepperpot's Christmas

One morning Mrs Pepperpot woke up and found she had shrunk. She climbed to the top of the bed-post and swung her legs while she wondered what to do.

'What a nuisance!' she said. 'Just when I wanted to go to the Christmas Market with Mr Pepperpot!'

She wanted to buy a sheaf of corn for the birds' Christmas dinner, and she wanted to get them a little bird-house where she could feed them every day. The other thing she wanted was a wreath of mistletoe to hang over the door, so that she could wish Mr Pepperpot a 'Happy Christmas' with a kiss. But Mr Pepperpot thought this was a silly idea.

'Quiet unnecessary!' he said.

But Mrs Pepperpot was very clever at getting her own way; so even though she was now no bigger than a mouse, she soon worked out a plan. She heard her husband put his knapsack down on the floor in the kitchen and she slid down the bed-post, scuttled over the doorstep and climbed into one of the knapsack pockets.

Mr Pepperpot put the knapsack on his back and set off through the snow on his kick-sledge, while Mrs Pepperpot peeped out from the pocket.

'Look at all those nice cottages!' she said to herself.

'I'll bet every one of them has a sheaf of corn and a little house for the birds. And they'll have mistletoe over the door as well, no doubt. But you wait till I get home; I'll show them!'

At the market there were crowds of people, both big and small; everyone shopping, and there was plenty to choose from! At one stall stood a farmer selling beautiful golden sheaves of corn. As her husband walked past the stall Mrs Pepperpot climbed out from the knapsack pocket and disappeared inside the biggest sheaf of all.

'Hullo, Mr Pepperpot,' said the farmer, 'how about some corn for the birds this Christmas?'

'Too dear!' answered Mr Pepperpot gruffly.

'Oh no, it's not!' squeaked the little voice of Mrs Pepperpot.

'If you don't buy this sheaf or corn I'll tell everyone you're married to the woman who shrinks!'

Now Mr Pepperpot above all hates people to know about his wife turning small, so when he saw her waving to him from the biggest sheaf he said to the farmer: 'I've changed my mind; I'll have that one, please!'

But the farmer told him he would have to wait in the queue.

Only a little girl saw Mrs Pepperpot slip out of the corn and dash into a bird-house on Mr Andersen's stall. He was a carpenter and made all his bird-houses look just like real little houses with doors and windows for the birds to fly in and out. Of course Mrs Pepperpot chose the prettiest house; it even had curtains in the windows and from behind these she watched her husband buy the very best sheaf of corn and stuff it in his knapsack.

He thought his wife was safe inside and was just about

to get on his kick-sledge and head for home, when he heard a little voice calling from the next stall.

'Hullo, Husband!' squeaked Mrs Pepperpot, 'Haven't you forgotten something? You were going to buy me a bird-house!'

Mr Pepperpot hurried over to the stall. He pointed to the house with the curtains and said: 'I want to buy that one, please!'

Mr Andersen was busy with his customers. 'You'll have to take your turn,' he said.

So once more poor Mr Pepperpot had to stand patiently in a queue. He hoped that no one else would buy the house with his wife inside.

But she wasn't inside; she had run out of the back door, and now she was on her way to the next stall. Here there was a pretty young lady selling holly and mistletoe. Mrs Pepperpot had to climb up the post to reach the nicest wreath, and there she stayed hidden.

Soon Mr Pepperpot came by, carrying both the sheaf of corn and the little bird-house.

The young lady gave him a dazzling smile and said: 'Oh, Mr Pepperpot, wouldn't you like to buy a wreath of mistletoe for your wife?'

'No thanks,' said Mr Pepperpot, 'I'm in a hurry.'

'Swing high! Swing low! I'm in the mistletoe!' sang Mrs Pepperpot from her lofty perch.

When Mr Pepperpot caught sight of her his mouth fell open: 'Oh dear!' he groaned, 'This is too bad!'

With a shaking hand he paid the young lady the right money and lifted the wreath down himself, taking care that Mrs Pepperpot didn't slip out of his fingers. This time there would be no escape; he would take his wife straight home, whether she liked it or not. But just as he was leaving, the young lady said: 'Oh, Sir, you're our one hundredth customer, so you get a free balloon!' and she handed him a red balloon.

Before anyone could say 'Jack Robinson' Mrs Pepperpot had grabbed the string and, while Mr Pepperpot was struggling with his purse, gloves and parcels, his tiny wife was soaring up into the sky. Up she went over the market-place, and soon she was fluttering over the trees of the forest, followed by a crowd of crows and magpies and small birds of every sort.

'Here I come!' she shouted in bird-language. For, when Mrs Pepperpot was small she could talk with animals and birds.

A big crow cawed: 'Are you going to the moon with that balloon?' 'Not quite, I hope!' said Mrs Pepperpot, and she told them the whole story. The birds all squawked with glee when they heard about the corn and the bird-house she had got for thcm.

'But first you must help me,' said Mrs Pepperpot. 'I want you all to hang on to this balloon string and guide me back to land on my own doorstep.'

So the birds clung to the string with their beaks and claws and, as they flew down to Mrs Pepperpot's house,

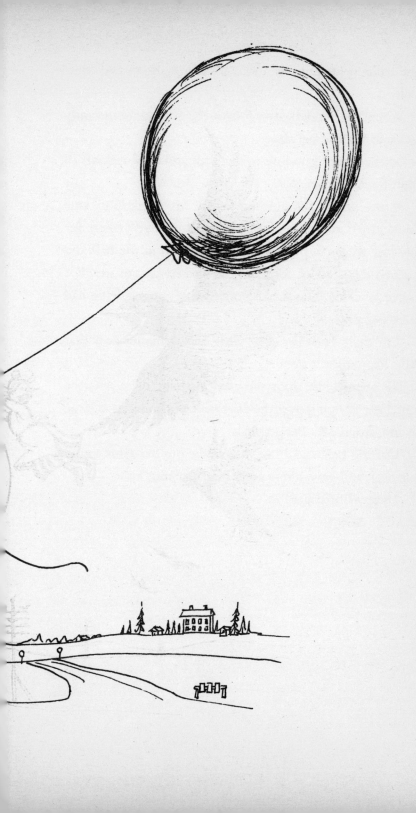

the balloon looked like a kite with fancy bows tied to its tail.

When Mrs Pepperpot set foot on the ground she instantly grew to her normal size.

So she waved goodbye to the birds and went indoors to wait for Mr Pepperpot.

It was late in the evening before Mr Pepperpot came home, tired and miserable after searching everywhere for his lost wife. He put his knapsack down in the hall and carried the sheaf of corn and the bird-house outside. But when he came in again he noticed that the mistletoe had disappeared.

'Oh well,' he said sadly, 'what does it matter now that Mrs Pepperpot is gone?'

He opened the door into the kitchen; there was the mistletoe hanging over the doorway and, under it, as large as life, stood Mrs Pepperpot!

'Darling husband!' she said, as she put her arms round his neck and gave him a great big smacking kiss:

'Happy Christmas!'